# HYSTERICAL LOVE

*a novel*

---

## LORRAINE DEVON WILKE

HYSTERICAL LOVE
by Lorraine Devon Wilke

Copyright © 2015
Lorraine Devon Wilke
All rights reserved.

ISBN: 1506176941
ISBN-13: 978-1506176949
LCCN: 2015900574

No part of this book may be reproduced in any written, electronic, recording, or photocopying form without written permission of the author, Lorraine Devon Wilke. Please do not participate in or encourage piracy of copyrighted materials in violation of the author's rights. Purchase only authorized editions.

This is a work of fiction. All names, characters, businesses, organizations, places, events, and incidents are either products of the author's imagination or used fictitiously. Where real-life public names or places appear, the situations, dialogue, and incidents concerning those people and places are entirely fictional and not intended to depict actual events or to change the entirely fictional nature of the work. In all other respects, any resemblance to actual persons, living or dead, or any resemblance to events or locales, are entirely coincidental.

Cover design by Grace Amandes
Cover photograph by Lorraine Devon Wilke

www.lorrainedevonwilke.com

As always, for Pete and Dillon
*My heart and soul*

# ONE

I AM FLUMMOXED by relationships.

That is not a glib statement; it's the frank admission of a man who can't seem to get it right, even under what would seem to be the very best of circumstances. Relationships bewilder me. They knock me to my knees, and leave me baffled as to why something as essential as love is so damn fraught with confusion. At least for me. Which is disappointing. I don't think I'm an anomaly, but I did think I'd have it figured out by now.

It's not that I don't fully appreciate the value of a good relationship. I do. I'm the guy who wasn't a player in school, high school *or* college. I always had a girlfriend and was always loyal and faithful to that girlfriend. Not because I'm so good, but because I'm not good at chaos. I hate the complication of it, the balancing of opposing forces (i.e., more than one girlfriend), and I'm a horrible liar, all requisites of a successful player.

And, truth be told, I *like* being in a relationship: the comfort, the dependability, the shared meals and regular sex. These are all good things for a man who wants to avoid complication. So why, you may ask, am I flummoxed?

Because, despite my affinity for the state of being, relationships tend to explode on my watch. I'm not sure how or why, but it's typically things like her deciding I'm not motivated enough, or me deciding she's not fun enough (I had one who "hated the outdoors"...what do you do with that?), or both of us deciding the other is unexciting enough that moving on would be more exciting than staying put. But it's always messy, it's always painful, and it usually involves weeping, tossed closets, and new sets of keys. So as I've attempted to evolve in life, I've tried my best to choose better and do it right. *More* right. At least as right as I can.

Which I thought I'd done over these last three years. Thought I'd gotten it really right on both the choosing and the doing. But as I sit on the edge of a strange bed in a strange bedroom and reflect on the very strange night that has just ensued, it's clear I miscalculated. Misjudged. Regardless of good intentions, I once again set the whole damn thing on fire. Or she did. I'm still not sure.

Even more disheartening, this relationship had gone much further than any previous. It lasted longer, had less drama, and we'd actually embarked upon those iconic discussions of the future, that gaping, wide-open, impossible to imagine place I'd been assured was both warm and welcoming. I thought, I think we both thought, we were out of the danger corridor, that weird zone after the early hot years where relationships wander to get battered by irritation and boredom. We were past that, we'd transcended, we were golden.

We were fucked. By love-smugness. It gets you every time.

In retrospect, I should have caught it. That smugness should have been fair warning. But while I was off reveling in our relationship excellence, our learned skills at the craft of compromise, our sense that we exemplified the very best of love in a modern world, I missed the fact that it had all been going too well. And we know what happens when *that* happens. You dare acknowledge the joy and happiness you've managed to gather around you like soft little bunnies of optimism and, somehow, despite amazingly good behavior on everyone's parts, and often against the nature of all parties involved, someone in the room pulls the pin. I just didn't figure it would be her (or was it me?), or on the night we finally set a date for our wedding.

Now, there's a word with some weighty baggage...*wedding*. Just saying it stirs a reflexive response that settles somewhere near the pit of my stomach, though not for the reasons you might expect. Not the cliché of commitment phobia or the panic that I'd wake up one morning and realize I had no idea why she was in my bed and what particular point there was to marrying her. No, I can honestly say I'm wild about this woman who would strap on a white gown to publicly declare she'd love me forever. The problem?

Thirty-three. That's the problem. I am now thirty-three. And I have a theory about that number:

Something bizarre happens to a man at thirty-three, some particular strain of dread and confusion. Not the whininess of, say, twenty-four, or the doom and gloom of forty, but something completely endemic to thirty plus three years. I don't know why that is. Maybe because Belushi, Alexander the Great, a few rock stars, even Jesus Christ himself succumbed at the age. But thirty-three is a mile-marker for those of us with plans to make it through.

My mother calls it "tweeniedom," a land, according to her, that's populated by overgrown teens who, kicking and screaming, are about to be forced into their deeply dreaded adulthoods. I'd say that's a bit harsh, even a little unfair, because, I'm telling you, this thing is *real*. And it's strange. You hit the year and it rolls over you like no year of life you've lived so far. My friend, Bob, who has a propensity for titling things, calls it Fate Turmoil Syndrome. He's also referred to it as Advancing Age Agitation. I think it's the Kingdom of Hell, where one minute everything is right in your world, the next...hissing madness in the blink of an unwary eye.

Let me set the stage for my particular conflagration so you get the whole picture:

First of all, I'm Dan McDowell, the thirty-three-year-old male in question: a softball aficionado (currently in off-season), a reader of the classics, a decent best friend type, and a working photographer. Which means I make an actual living at my craft, even if it is predominately grade school pictures, corporate yearbooks, family portraits, and the occasional wedding. In the artier industries you don't snub your nose at these sorts of things.

I live in Los Angeles—Toluca Lake, to be more specific, the gentrified but modest suburb attached to the hip of hipper LA where you can rent a decent house without bartering away your first-born. I'm that rare breed of native actually born in the city, though people tell me that's not so rare anymore, not since mommy blogs made it clear you really *can* raise children in Hollywood. I have one older sister, Lucy: thirty-five, never married and currently single, who owns a small, very successful restaurant in the Larchmont District. We get along, if scrappily. And I have two marginally eccentric parents: my father is a retired high school American Lit teacher; my mother, the good wife who lovingly endures him—I mean, adores him. They live not too far and far too close, but as a nuclear group, we manage okay. That's the family of origin.

Then there's Jane, my fiancée. At least until recently. Like earlier tonight.

We've been together for three years, happily ensconced in a small but classic bungalow in a complex of equally small, classic bungalows on a street where the most vivid feature is the daily presence of an ice cream truck owned by a sweet guy named Tomas. Beyond sheer nostalgia, that truck is beloved for its toffee ice cream bars (that might just be me) and the fact that local parents can regularly indulge their kids without having to brave LA traffic, always a boon. The rest of our neighborhood, while tasteful and well-maintained, is generally less colorful than Tomas's truck, though Jane and I have contributed a decorative Color-Me-Mine door plaque that reads "Dan & Jane Live Here" in vibrant hues. Jane's idea. A nice touch that always makes me feel located.

Jane is Jane Bennett, a lovely, moderately insecure, generally delightful twenty-eight-year-old I've known and loved these past three years. She's a UCLA graduate, originally from a small farm town in Montana, an accountant working at a business real estate company in a job she seems to like well enough. And she's a looker, as they say, though in that real-girl way that makes you feel lucky but not too intimidated: long dark hair, great eyes, athletic body (thankfully this one *does* love the outdoors!), and a killer smile. She tells me I'm hot—says she particularly loves that I'm tall, blond, and generally well-dressed—but I suspect I fall somewhere on the same looks spectrum as she does. Just two average/hot people who found each other and fell in love. Which we did back when I was shooting portraits for her company's website and she was the one who made sure I got paid. We've been together ever since and were moving toward the inevitable "till death" portion of our trajectory when...yep, hissing madness.

You know those experiences that are so unexpected, so out-of-the-blue, that you can't quite piece them together afterward when you're trying to reconstruct the debris field? Your memories of the event are hazy and out-of-sequence; you can only recall them in weird, disassociated flashes, like those drug trip montages in bad B-movies? That's how the scene that cracked the core of Jane's and my relationship played out. And since everyone in this hometown of mine is a screenwriter, and I've had occasion to read a few in my time, I can think of no better way to relay the incident than in movie scene format:

BEDROOM - NIGHT

Spent and sweaty, we're in a postcoital spoon on the bed. Our madly discarded clothes are everywhere (testament, I think, to our continuing sexual chemistry), and there's an iPad and a large desk calendar that have been kicked to the foot of the bed in the rumpus of wild lovemaking. The mood is all glowy, sweetness, and light. Conversation commences:

                    JANE
        (whispering in my ear with a smile)
So, we're really doing this?

                    ME
          (smiling and acquiescent)
I believe we are.

                    JANE
I do think July will be perfect. We can count on the weather; everyone'll be relaxed, no crazy family stuff. Right?

                    ME
Absolutely. If Dad gets twitchy it'll be warm enough to just hose him down.

This was funny enough that we both laughed…then there was a slight pause. I pulled her to me and we did that soulful stare we're known to do in our goopier moments.

                    JANE
Are you sure, Danny? *Sure* sure?

                    ME
I love you, Janie. Really, truly, and till the end of time. So, yes…*sure* sure.

From there we lunged into a trademark kiss: deep, passionate, and long enough that a break for air was required. I'm not sure how it struck her, but I was pretty impressed.

                    ME (cont.)
Damn, woman, how is it that you are still as hot as the day we first met?

She slides out of bed with a playful grin.

                    JANE
I have my ways.

                    ME
Yes…yes, you do. And I love those ways. As I love you. You and your lovely ways.

She turns to me, suddenly more serious.

                    JANE
Dan, can we honestly and truly say, without a shred of doubt, that we're comfortable with the idea of being the *only* ones we'll ever be with for the rest of our days on this earth?

Odd tone shift. Terrifying topic. I sit up.

                    ME
That's an interesting question at this particular moment, but, yes, that's the plan. Why? Are *you* not comfortable with the idea?

                    JANE
No, not at all. I mean, yes, I am. But I'm also realistic. And we *have* only been with each other since the day we met and that's already been three years.

She's smiling, playful…all good fun, right?

      JANE (cont.)
Three long years of *just me*.

She's still smiling, but my eyes avert for a split second. *A split second.* And, dammit, her radar pings.

      JANE (cont.)
What was that?

      ME
What?

      JANE
That look. What was that?

      ME
What look? There was no look. I was just thinking, yeah, wow, I cannot believe it's already been three years! I mean, it's been such a great—

      JANE
I *am* the only person you've been with since we met, right?

And once again, like an idiot sticking a fork in his eye, I take another unfortunate beat that lasts a titch too long.

      ME
Um…technically. I mean, yes, of course, I—

The temperature drop is like the girl's room in *The Exorcist*. Which is also the sound of Jane's voice from that point on.

JANE

TECHNICALLY?!

As I recall, my thought processes then seized up, switching from clumsy to pure adrenaline-rush-protective-mode, thrashing madly to find a balance between the good, honest guy I am and the moron who just opened a door he now could not easily shut.

ME

No—I mean, yes! Yes, you are—you have been the only person…except for this weird little bit right after you and I first got together. You know, that gray area right after Marci and I ended it and you and I hooked up? It was just that weird closure period that happens after a relationship ends, where she showed up a couple of times, all sad and freaked out, and it—

My babbling was cut short by the projectile hit of a well-aimed pillow, but I unwisely continued, now folding a little indignation into the mix.

ME (cont.)

What? We weren't even living together yet!

JANE

WE WERE DATING! We'd slept together! We had a commitment! There was no "gray area"! No gray area at all!

I'll concede to some of that: we *were* dating, we *had* slept together, but, if memory serves, we hadn't yet done the "this is exclusive" thing. I figured that was worth pointing out.

ME

We did *not* have a commitment at that point! Yes, we were dating, but it was the beginning stage where things were still undefined. She and I were winding down and there was a little overlap. What's the big deal?

I'll wrap the script right there, mostly because I'm not sure how to articulate the cacophony that followed. Clamor? Pandemonium? Frenzy? Suffice it to say it involved a lot of screaming and yelling, most of which I blanked out, except for the parts that focused on the annihilation of my previously esteemed character…and the fact that Jane was hurt, really hurt.

Because, apparently, it *was* a big deal. A trust issue, she repeatedly asserted, an issue of many tentacles for Jane. In her defense—in case I'm making her sound like a hysterical female, which she typically is not—I should mention that the only other time she got this close to the altar was with a dickhead who waited for the rehearsal dinner to tell her he'd been married twice before. So while I understood her retroactive horror at my unmentioned sexual overlap, the degree of rage made clear I was paying some fee for dickhead's oversight as well.

But whatever the catalyst, the mitigating issues, or the underlying intent of either party involved, the endgame involved the contents of my closet being flung around the living room, and a calendar ripped to shreds by my now-declared *former* fiancée, who was acting like a lunatic and demanding that I move out. Immediately. Which I did. I could've argued the point—actually I *did* argue the point—but by then my computer, my camera bag, and several pairs of expensive slacks were out on the lawn, and one never knows when those damn sprinklers will pop on. And, frankly, if there's one thing I've learned from a life of serial monogamy, it's that there's wisdom in retreating to fight another day.

# TWO

NOT THAT I wanted to fight another day, believe me. I am not a fighter. I just want it to be all better, all of it. Back to normal, no wounds, no bleeding; let's move on, can we, please?

But given her refusal to communicate either by phone, text, or email, it was clear Jane was less aligned with that general philosophy. So I decided to be patient: take my hits, give her time to settle down, then gently bring matters back to a place of logic and forgiveness. I had no doubt we would get there. We had a wedding to plan.

Besides, moving out was not that herculean of a task. It involved me dragging my duffle about thirty feet to the bungalow across the way, the home of the aforementioned Bob—Bob Fiedler, my longtime friend and colleague, and Jane's and my neighbor. Bob and I met as freshmen at Otis College of Art and Design in Los Angeles and have been solid friends ever since. There's an easy simpatico between us. We understand each other. We have history. We trolled the streets and online portals together looking for paid photography work after graduation. We shared places on-and-off throughout the years, and he's the person who got Jane and me into this complex when a spot opened up, so he's responsible for the proximity of our habitation. He also got me the gig at Jane's company, so he's marginally responsible for my now-shattered engagement. I'd say he owes me a day or two of bunking privileges.

And not to sound too sitcomy in an attempt to be culturally relevant, but he's a gay man. I'm straight, he's gay, and we've boldly gone where people go pretty much every day of the week in this 21st century, modern men proving that male friendships can healthily exist between polar orientations. Plus—and I don't know if it's *because* he's gay, probably not—there's something to be said for a male friend who has the sensitivity to be a good listener *and* throws a killer curveball (we're in the same softball league). He's also an amazing cook (shines at neighborhood potlucks), and there's no one who kicks my ass more when I get pissy about work, my parents, my life, women, whatever. Bottom line, he's a good guy, proven, once again, when—sometime after one in the morning, post-debacle and me too wiped out for words—he opened his home and second bedroom for "whatever the duration of your exile," promising a hot meal and a sympathetic ear after work the following day.

Good to his word, we were now in his kitchen: his signature meatloaf in the oven, him at the stove searing Brussels sprouts, while I ran down the whole sorry mess. He confessed he'd gotten the gist when Jane was at a particularly high-pitched portion of the melee— that's how close our places were—and, of course, there *were* the slacks on the lawn. He got right to his analysis:

"Couldn't you have just said, 'absolutely, sweetie, you're the only one I've been with the whole damn time' and left it at that? Was there any point in bringing up the 'overlap,' as you put it, from three fucking years ago?" Bob was a big believer in the convenience of fiction. I've already mentioned I'm not a good liar.

"The point was honesty, Bob. I realize that's an earnest concept with you."

"An earnest concept? What does that even mean?"

"It means you're handy with the occasional twisting of truth."

"Which is often kinder than truth itself. Like, say, last night."

"Maybe so. And had she not leapt like a cheetah the second I blinked, I might have re-thought the strategy. But, then again, what's the point of committing to marriage if you don't have a basic foundation of honesty?"

"That sounds real pretty, Dan, make a meme. But you weren't feeling so honest back when old Marci was showing up all crazy-ex-girlfriend while you were busy sweet-thinging your Jane, were you?"

"That's cold."

"Face it, it wasn't necessary information then, it wasn't now, and it's going to haunt your ass until death do you part."

"Assuming we even get to that point. But hey, no worries, we'll figure it out. It can't be that big a deal no matter what she says. I'm thinking maybe a day or two, a week at the most. Is that cool with you?"

"It's fine, whatever you need."

"And don't let me cramp your style; just give me the signal when to get scarce and I'm gone."

"I'll make this easy for you, bro. If I've got champagne open and a hot guy dancing to Bruno Mars, there's your cue. Can you handle that?"

"Absolutely, no problem."

"You sure? Because I can remember a few times when it kind of was."

Which was slightly unfair, if largely true. It wasn't that I couldn't handle that Bob was gay—I'm a political progressive who believes we are who we are, as we come into this life, and no part of that is any more right or wrong than anything or anyone else. But Bob has never been shy about flaunting his sexual activities and, yes, there were a few times when we were rooming together that those activities found their way into our various communal spaces. I can't say I analyzed my reactions all that closely, but I suppose I *was* a bit uncomfortable on occasion. He asked me back then if it would have mattered if he'd been feeling up a girl on the kitchen floor instead of a guy and I honestly couldn't say. But it wasn't about judgment or disapproval; it was about sexual squeamishness, the unfamiliar paradigm. I couldn't explain it any better than that. So, true: we *did* have some tense moments on the topic, but we were good enough friends to get past it.

And I figured—since he was doing me the favor this go-around—I'd be an ass to expect him to change anything on my behalf. "Listen, it's your pad, your life, I'm the one who's barging in here. So, please, just do your thing and I'll adjust accordingly."

"I appreciate that, buddy. And I'll try to rein it in while you're here. It'll be good practice; I have to go see the folks soon." Bob's parents were still pretending he'd be marrying a woman one of these days.

With all salient issues worked out, we sat down to an excellent meal, toasted our roommate status once again, while I, with great effort to avoid thinking about the woman across the way, promised Bob it wouldn't be long.

# THREE

IT WAS LONG.

By the end of the second week, and with little headway on either productive conversation or even the opportunity for productive conversation, it became clear my forgotten peccadillo of years previous had scraped a scab for Jane much deeper than I'd understood. Which made me feel bad, genuinely regretful, that the woman I loved was so hurt by a thoughtless act (or two) I hadn't chosen to share with her out of fear of, well...hurting her. Ironic.

Mostly, I missed her. Sleeping with her, touching her, making love to her, even watching TV with her. Everything felt out of synch, suspended and discomforting. I kept having to readjust my habits at Bob's, remind myself of new routines, try not to put my fist through a wall after the fourth or tenth or twentieth time she didn't respond to a call or text or email. I didn't understand the conviction and resolve of her standoff, but mostly I just missed her.

In my best moments, usually in the earlier parts of the day, I was stoked with optimism, convinced that *today* I'd be able to affect a change of some kind. I was anxious to make it up to her, start the healing, get us back on track. I rehearsed all sorts of grand speeches in which I expressed my sincere remorse, declaring restorative affirmations of loyalty and devotion, but those mental first-, second-, and third-drafts kept piling up as days passed and non-responsiveness was her only response.

Which, by day sixteen, stirred another layer of reaction in me. Anger. Defensiveness. Indignation. Real resentment, frankly, that everything good about me, about our relationship, our desire to build a life together, could be so easily dismissed, so quickly discarded, over what I felt was largely forgivable behavior of long enough ago that some proportionality was warranted. I mean, *come on*! I could understand if it was last week—or even months into our relationship. But *it was right at the very beginning…and three years ago*! Don't I get a break for my fidelity since? Or even, let's just say it, for exhibiting a remnant of sensitivity toward a grieving ex? (I do realize that's a stretch.)

These were the sorts of circuitous, rambling, largely unhelpful conversations I was having with myself while alone in the second bedroom of Bob's house, watching my own from the south-facing window like a stalker with a broken heart. The only information I could glean from conversations with others, meaning my sister Lucy, who'd spoken to Jane at least once since I'd been kicked out, was that my fiancée viewed my behavior as a harbinger of bigger trust issues to come and was, therefore, in no rush to welcome me home. Since Lucy had allowed herself to get pulled into the fracas by virtue of her interaction with my stonewalling girlfriend, I decided it was time for some one-on-one with one of the gender. Plus, Lucy is the most uncluttered female I know, and I needed some uncluttered *anything* right now.

Waiting in the office area of her trendy and quite extraordinary restaurant, I looked around at this shiny thing my sister created and was, as I always am, honestly mystified. How did she do this? Lucy had been a crappy waitress with no real plans for her life when she literally fell into this opportunity after meeting a restaurant investor at a rock club. Rumor has it that he was married and she'd had an affair with him, but whatever the impetus, he'd seen her potential, something the rest of us had not. And from there, this weird, argumentative, and seemingly unambitious woman became the owner and creator of a smartly designed bistro foodies gushed over, courtesy of a chef the critics anointed a culinary star.

I had to admit: it made me jealous. I'd always been the artistic one in the family; how did this burst of creative imagination suddenly emerge from the lazy sibling? While Lucy was going to community college and being ambivalent about her direction in life, something which drove our father insane, I'd actually gone to a prestigious school for a craft I was passionate about, followed by over a decade of working my ass off toward commensurate success in that field. But other than a few "street photography" exhibits of minimal importance, I had little to show for this ambition beyond a decent paycheck and the admiration of grade school parents across the basin. Yet here she was: regularly covered by the *LA Times* and getting "feelers" from the Food Network. Still, and despite my envy, I couldn't help but be proud of her. And right now I needed some of that hardcore logic she seemed to having flowing from her fingertips.

"Maybe you're not soul mates," she stated matter-of-factly, her crazy red hair jammed under the brim of a flour-dusted Clippers cap. I was now in the kitchen, slumped across one end of the large stainless steel worktable, watching with bored fascination as she pounded the life out of a slab of bread dough. This pronouncement was dazzling in its disappointment. "That's it? That's all you've got? Lame-ass hippie bullshit about soul mates? I thought that went out with est and macramé."

"It's making a comeback."

"Really?" My sarcasm was unsubtle.

"Just think about it."

"I thought you loved Jane."

"I do love Jane. I think Jane's probably the best girl you've ever been with. I'm just being the devil's advocate."

"How about being *my* advocate for a change? I'm not getting much of that these days."

"Bob isn't the cuddly sort?" She looked up with that lopsided grin of hers.

"He's very cuddly, just not with me."

"Listen, I don't really know, do I? I think you're both great people, but there have been times when I've wondered if you really were each other's best bets."

I'd never before heard Lucy express doubt about my relationship with Jane. "Why would you think we weren't each other's best bets? And what a weird fucking way to put it."

"Dan, you asked, I'm sharing my thoughts. You can tell me to fuck off if you don't want to hear them."

"I just might." But I *did* want to hear them; her thoughts were why I was here. "Okay, whatever. Lay it out."

"It's no big thing. All I'm saying is, you're very different people, with different backgrounds, different influences, and different ideas about how to solve problems. That's not always a deal breaker, but when you look at what's been going on with you guys, I don't know, that might be something to consider. My opinion, for what it's worth."

"And yet somehow we've managed to successfully solve all sorts of problems over these last three years, differences or not."

"Yeah, well, maybe not so much this time around, right? What did you say it was so far, sixteen days? That's pretty extreme, Dan, to go three years of living together, then when you hit your first big obstacle, bam, you're out for over two weeks and counting. That seems crazy to me. I'm suggesting it might be a compatibility issue."

I sighed deeply. She had a point; I just wasn't ready to admit it. "I don't actually think we're *that* incompatible. Things are usually pretty seamless with us. This was a particularly unique bump in the road."

"Really? Seems like pretty standard bad boyfriend, boundary issue crap to me; the typical 'when did we get exclusive?' debate. The stuff most people holler about for a minute or two, then get over."

"Well, who's to say we won't get over it?" I decided to let the "bad boyfriend" remark go.

"Said the man on day sixteen. Look, I have no doubt you're compatible enough with day-to-day stuff; obviously you wouldn't have three years going if you weren't. But my experience tells me it's when the more challenging issues come up that you notice disparities you hadn't paid much attention to before. Believe me, I know, I've been there. Down that same fucking road."

She had. Many times.

"And, come on, Dan, you guys are *so* different. You can't tell me you don't see that!"

"I don't! I've always thought of Jane and me as substantially similar people. How is it you think we're *so* different?"

"Okay, how about your basic, human imprinting, family-of-origin stuff? Like, you're a creative, raised by a man who was obsessed with words and literature, who practically browbeat you into an appreciation for the arts, who told us higher culture was the only dividing line between man and beast. She was raised on a pig farm and became a bookkeeper."

"An accountant."

"An accountant, whatever, who just might not be as attuned to the same worldview as you. I'm suggesting that's possibly why this moderately fucked-up thing you did three years ago has turned into such a clusterfuck. Soul mate deficit."

"Okay, even if you're right, what does that ultimately mean in the real world? What do I do with that?"

"I don't know; maybe you—"

"And how does her being hypersensitive right now translate into her not being my soul mate, or me not being hers, or whatever the fuck you're saying?"

"I think sixteen days is a little more than hypersensitive."

"So do I! Which is why I wanted your perspective on how to get past it. But all you seem to be saying is that without this magical assignation from the gods we're doomed, so what's the fucking point?" I was flailing now.

"Jesus, Dan, calm down, it's just a theory."

"But you're making it sound so hopeless! That's not helping, just so you know."

Her office phone rang. "I have to get this. Don't slit your wrists, I'll be right back."

She dashed into the office while I sat on the table picking at broken bread crusts and thinking this was not remotely the conversation I thought I'd be having. I figured Lucy would give me her usual pep talk about "understanding a women's perspective," assuring me that Jane was just going through a crisis and I needed to do whatever was required to win back her trust, that sort of thing. I did not expect magical thinking, certainly not from her. We humans truly are evolving creatures.

When she returned I jumped right back in, albeit a little less hysterically. "Be straight with me, Lucy. Do you honestly believe this bullshit about soul mates, or is this something your new age bartender shared over closing-time cocktails?"

"Don't be condescending."

"I'm serious. Do you really believe this stuff?"

"Why do you think I'm still alone?"

"Because you're neurotic and hard to please?" She threw a ball of dough at me, which I caught and popped in my mouth.

"Scoff away, little brother, but I've been through enough crappy relationships to realize something indefinable is at play when it *does* work. Maybe some kind of Divine Intervention, I don't know. It's all a mystery to me. But at this point of my life, I want whatever happens to be authentic. And I think holding out for a soul mate might be worth the wait. It's certainly better than wasting my time on someone in-between."

"Assuming the soul mate theory has merit."

"Assuming."

I hopped off the table, swallowing hard to get the dough down, perplexed that my usually grounded sister sounded like a full-fledged member of the goddess community. "Did Jane say something to you about this? About our differences, about the possibility of us not being soul mates?"

"All Jane said was you're a cheating asshole who she can't trust anymore. The rest is all me. And, hey, if it doesn't resonate, forget it."

And that was basically all I got, beyond a brioche to die for and further confusion. I left wondering if she'd joined a cult.

Suffice it to say, it *didn't* resonate with me. I don't typically believe in the sort of fluffy romanticism that holds to the idea of souls reuniting, or fate-directed connections, or any school of thought that perpetuates the myth that why we fall in love, or who we fall in love with, is other-determined. It always seemed pretty simple to me: chemistry. You meet someone and you either have chemistry or you don't. If you don't, you walk away or you spend enough time together to see if chemistry gets stirred up. If it does, you're good to go; if it doesn't, you move on. I don't know how it happens or why, but it's either there or it isn't.

Soul mate theory. Divine Intervention. Give me a fucking break.

# FOUR

SO NOW, INSTEAD of planning my own wedding, I was bouncing from the inanity of my sister's conversation to what would likely be further weirdness at my parents' home, where I was headed to discuss the photography needs of their fortieth anniversary, an event they'd chosen to celebrate in style because my dad insists the odds of him being around for their fiftieth aren't good. Always an optimistic guy.

My parents live in Encino, a classier version of the many suburban enclaves tucked neatly into the San Fernando Valley north of the city, in a house we moved to when I was in middle school. It was a place I loved as a kid—what with a swimming pool and big cabaña for all manner of teenage boy fun—but when I come here now I'm amazed at how detached I feel. As if somehow in the ensuing years it went from being "the family home" to "this place my parents live."

Of course, there's nothing much the same about it since Lucy and I moved out. My dad turned my bedroom into his workout space and Lucy's has basically become the junk room; or, as my mom likes to call it, "the treasure chest." I'll let you picture the chaos going on in there.

Since their involvement in this story is substantial, let me more formally introduce them:

My mother is Esther McDowell: sixty-nine, used to be a knockout, still pretty but now in the classic matron mode, a look achieved with floral tunics and black "loose pants," as she refers to them. This sartorial statement is topped by her ever-present "champagne blond" wig, some version of which she's worn since her hair grayed in her early forties. Lucy and I spent years trying to talk her out of this eccentricity, embarrassed that our mom looked like an older, chubbier Dolly Parton without the famous rack, but she's remained adamant. She is a jolly sort, though; seems to be smiling most of the time, even when her irascible husband is wearing on her one last nerve, which, I can only imagine, is most of the time.

Then there's him. Big Jim McDowell. Think Clint Eastwood after the good-looking *Dirty Harry* years and more into the *Gran Torino* era. Formerly tall and handsome, he's now squinty (legally blind in one eye, though that's been since childhood) and slightly humped. He's seventy-three in that intimidating old-guy way, yet with the lethargy of someone who rarely leaves the room. Which is odd, since he's still a hearty tennis player who loves to kick my ass as often as he can coerce me onto the courts (which is weekly). He was originally an English teacher, switched to American Literature when he discovered he wasn't fond of teaching "idiot teens" how to write a decent paper. Convincing them to read good books couldn't have been much easier, but at least *he* enjoyed the materials. He taught at one of the better local high schools, thankfully not one Lucy and I attended, and was reportedly well respected by both colleagues and students, more than one claiming he'd inspired them as writers or teachers themselves. He was an avid reader of the most erudite of literature, a passion that led him, as Lucy pointed out, to endow us with an appreciation of the arts, but now he says he's done "paying homage to the literary arrogance of self-important authors," stacking his bedstand with James Patterson and Dan Brown. I've heard my mother mention how dashing and courtly he was in their early years, but the only remnant of that seems to be his habit of opening doors for women. And though never particularly playful or perky, he was always a good guy with a good heart who used to have *some* color, *some* personality. Since his retirement? Pallid all around. Pallid mixed with streaks of biting superiority and cynicism, a combination that makes him one very tough character. At least for me.

And I was here now with the two of them—Jim and Esther— seated on the plastic chaise lounge in their "sunroom" (basically a large back porch with walls and windows), eating my second BLT while Esther hovered in anticipation of any and all of our needs. Jim was parked in the massage recliner with the TV table in front of him, bouncing from one sporting event to another, acting as if I wasn't there and we had nothing to talk about.

I, however, had other demands on my daily schedule so I launched into a preliminary discussion of what, exactly, they wanted from me in terms of their event. "So, Mom, I'm thinking I'll shoot mostly in color, get lots of candid shots, maybe do some black and white portraits of you and Dad at some point—"

"Why are we making such a damn big thing about these pictures?" Jim growled without a break in his channel surfing. "Just tell anyone there with a camera to take some shots, end of story."

Esther would have none of that. "I want to memorialize this memorable event, and I see no point in leaving that to 'anyone with a camera' when we have the best photographer in town right here in the family!"

She smiled at me and I couldn't help but wonder how my father managed to be such a dick in the presence of sweetness and light. She sat down on the chaise, way too close, as she so often does, almost on my lap, and I was reminded that she could also drive a person crazy. "Um, Mom...personal space." She said "oops" and slid over. It was a routine; always happened.

Jim seemed intent, for some reason, on maintaining a pissy

attitude about the party planning. "Look, I don't care what you do, son. If your mother wants you here shoving that big camera of yours all over the place, making everyone feel like they have to smile like monkeys and suck in their guts, so be it. Just leave me out of it."

"Oh, no you don't, Jim McDowell!" Esther had her own kind of fierce when pushed too hard. "I want some fun pictures we can enjoy for years to come *and* I want nice ones of us together, so you're going to have to stop being a crab long enough to let Danny get that done."

At this point she was picking up Jim's plate and swiping the tray table with a napkin, blocking his view of the TV long enough that he snapped. "Esther, for God's sake, either sit down or go in the kitchen or take your son outside to discuss this party, but get out of my goddamn way!"

I felt a familiar rush of responsive annoyance and tried to compensate with a little sweet talk to my mother. "Great sandwich, Mom. You always were Queen of the BLTs!"

"Oh, thank you, honey! I know they're your favorite and I wouldn't want you to starve to death, living all alone with that bachelor friend of yours!"

"My 'bachelor friend,' as you put it, is named Bob, as you well know, since you've both met him several times, and, interestingly enough, he happens to be one of the best cooks around."

"Hah! Why doesn't that surprise me?" Jim snorted with a predictable dash of homophobia.

"Jim! For heaven's sake!" Esther admonished, shooting me a nervous smile while doing her own version of the Jim McDowell compensation dance. "I know he's a very nice man, honey; we're just worried about what all this means. What does all this mean?"

We were finally getting to it. The elephant in the sunroom. They loved Jane, they'd no doubt talked to Lucy, and odds were good Lucy told them all about Jane. Specifically about Jane kicking my ass out to live next door with "that bachelor friend."

Jim didn't disappoint. "Your sister tells us you've been out of the house for over two weeks. What the hell is going on over there? I hope you didn't do something stupid. You've got yourself a great girl with that one, buddy."

"I'm aware of that, Dad, and, no, I haven't done anything stupid. Frankly, it's a personal matter I'd rather not get into."

"We understand, honey, but what's it about?" Apparently "personal matter" had different meaning to my mother.

I knew I wasn't going to be able to brush this off without throwing at least a bone or two. I did an inward scan, looking for something logical enough to shift the onus from me and maybe even a little onto Jane, just enough to make me look less bad by comparison, always a goal when it came to my father. A cliché popped to mind and I decided to go with it; clichés usually worked with these two. "I think she's got a kind of cold feet thing going." Yeah, I actually said that. And I'm not proud.

The old man bit. "Cold feet? I'd think she'd be pretty clear at this point what the hell she was getting herself into. And what's she waiting for anyway? She's almost thirty, for God's sake!" Jim measured most things by the parameters of age; no doubt a good reason for my many issues with being thirty-three.

Esther chimed in. "Would you like me to speak to her, honey, sort of woman-to-woman? She and I have always gotten along so well and it might be nice for her to talk to someone who's had a bit more experience."

Before my brain could process the possibilities of that suggestion, Jim rolled his eyes. "Oh, yeah, that oughta do it. Dr. Ruth here." Esther looked immediately crushed; I leapt to parry.

"Thanks, Mom, that's sweet, but we'll get it worked out—"

"You better, son," Jim cut me off. "You're already thirty-three and if you keep frittering your life away you'll end up with nothing to hang your hat on."

What'd I tell you? There were so many clichés in that sentence I lost count. "Well, Dad, I actually *am* aware of the passage of time, and very focused on not frittering my life away, so I think the decision about who I marry is important enough to be really sure." I had no idea where I was going with this. I was plenty sure about Jane. Plenty.

"Oh, suddenly you're not sure. Three years of experimentation weren't enough to figure it out. You got what you wanted with no commitments but now you're not sure. Which is exactly why—"

Esther mercifully butt in with a sincere frown on her face. "This is the first time I've ever heard you say you weren't sure about Jane. You always said she was the one for you. I hope this isn't another one of your tweeniedom episodes, honey. Those do happen to you from time to time. Have you met someone else? Someone from your work maybe? Do we know her?"

The conversation had reached a level of absurdity so quickly it was mind-boggling. And now that I'd cast doubt on the certainty of both Jane *and* my marriage, I had to get us off the topic while buying myself more time, since I still had no idea when I might be sleeping in my bed again. "Mom, no, come on; we're getting way off track here. I haven't met anyone else, and, you're right; I did think she was the one—I *still* think she's the one. I think it's more that—well, once we locked onto the date it struck us both that, as sure as we've been and as much as we love each other, we needed to step it back a bit, get some added clarity. I personally want to give at least *some* thought to the question of whether or not she's my…soul mate." I felt queasy even saying it. Jim looked a little green himself. Esther was frowning again.

"Well, Danny, shouldn't you have figured that out *before* you set the date?" Oh, the sweet logic of Esther.

"That would have been ideal. But hey, it's just a theory…" I offered feebly.

Jim practically exploded at this point. "Goddammit, what is it with you kids? You make everything so damn convoluted! This theory, that theory—you want a theory? You're dealt a hand and you play it. End of story." He was always one for ending the story.

Esther's lips tightened ever so slightly. "Not everyone's story." She spoke so quietly I could barely hear her, but I was too focused on my own response anyway.

"Are you serious, Dad? That's your theory? 'You're dealt a hand'? That's all there is to picking a life partner?"

"Jesus, just like your mother. Everything's a goddamn debate." He turned back to the television, head shaking as if we were too dense to grasp the finer points of his analysis. Esther, however, wasn't letting anything go.

"I debate? I don't debate. Do I debate, Danny?"

"Well, actually, Mom—" With that, she exited for the kitchen. I felt like a traitor.

Jim jumped back in. "Let's cut to the chase, son. Forget soul mate, forget life partner, forget all that gibberish. You got a wife and you got a husband, that's it. Simple stuff that only idiots make complicated. And isn't it funny that even with all your damn theories and ideas, your Google and your social media, you kids aren't any better off than we were. Take a look at your sister!" I felt some relief that we were off me for a moment but had no idea where this was headed.

He climbed out of his chair and lumbered over to the bookshelf to ferret around for a cigar. (My mother regularly hid them.) I couldn't help but notice, as I often do, how damn tall he still was. Taller than me. And every inch the "big man" as he continued his diatribe:

"Is she any better off because she's been all the hell all over the world, had eighty-seven different boyfriends, knows everything there is to know about everything, blah, blah, blah? I still don't see her settling down, don't see her dealing with commitment, let alone starting a family! 'What's the rush?' she says to me."

I was struck by a relevant thought. "Interesting thesis, Dad, particularly when you factor in that you were older than Lucy before you got started on all that family stuff yourself."

He didn't appreciate the rebuttal. "Always the big know-it-all, aren't you? I'm talking about *women*, son. *Women* have different timetables when it comes to these things."

My dad, coaching me on women and their timetables. "Yeah, I got that, Dad, I'm not an idiot. All I'm saying is, I think anyone—man or woman—who starts and runs a very successful business by their mid-thirties is pretty much good-to-go in the commitment department."

He gave me a look I've known my whole life, a menacing squint intended to convey just how little he appreciated my thoughtful counterpoints. "Apples and oranges, buddy, apples and orange," he growled. "A wise person knows that no matter what you do in business, if you lollygag too long before you settle into something on the personal front, life passes you by. Then the whining starts about how you can't have kids because you waited too long and we're all supposed to feel sorry for you and the whole damn thing is ludicrous. Time to wake up, kiddo! Life is not sitting around waiting for you to figure it out; get off your duff, quit nit-picking, and take your place at the table!"

A literal Jim-litany of bombast and bullshit. With so many points ripe for response, I could have offered a dissertation, but the strongest urge was to get the hell out of there. "I hear ya, Dad—"

"Nah, you don't hear me. You don't pay one damn bit of attention. But like you say, it's your life." He was back in the recliner, remote in hand, cigar smoke wafting around his ears.

Esther came in from the kitchen with a plate of cookies, waving her hand in a futile attempt to disperse the billows. "Oh, for goodness sake, Jim, that is smothering everyone! You put that thing out unless you plan to go outside!"

I was stunned when my dad actually tapped the ash into a nearby plate and put the still-glowing cigar out on command. I presumed his making no comment, or even looking at my mother while engaged in this activity, was meant to suggest it was all his idea. So oddly passive aggressive. But whatever the ritual I'd just witnessed, it was a rare thing. Esther, however, barely blinked, as if she'd always known she had this power. I was impressed.

I was also more than ready to get going but she, apparently, had a few remaining points to make. "Danny, sweetheart, let me say this: whatever your father thinks, I trust that you'll give this matter a lot of thought and figure it out before too much more time passes. Jane is such a good woman. And while I do think your soul mate idea is very romantic—"

"Actually, Mom, it's Lucy's idea—"

"Okay, well, I'm simply saying you can waste a lot of time looking for your soul mate out there somewhere, but sometimes the person right in front of you is exactly who you're supposed to be with." She smiled coyly at Jim, who had no reaction other than to lob another retort:

"*Or* you can decide someone is your soul mate and it turns out the feelings aren't mutual. What do you do then? Cry like a baby? No, you accept what comes your way and make the best of it. You better figure out soon which way that falls for you."

Esther gave Jim a look I couldn't read. I felt like there was some code in whatever it was he was rambling on about, but I had no idea what it might be. She, surprisingly, seemed to, sighing so deeply even he noticed.

"What? I'm talking to our son," he barked.

Esther ignored him, looking directly at me. "Your father thinks I don't know what he's really saying."

What *was* he really saying? I was completely baffled, but she just stormed off to the kitchen as Jim clicked over to another sporting event.

There was no doubt their usual bickering had taken a sharper edge. Given the unsettled nature of my own personal life, the rancor of theirs felt more abrasive than usual. I pushed to wrap things up as quickly as I could. By the time we'd batted around every known possibility related to the matter of parties and pictures, it was decided I'd arrange for a photo booth and call it a day. I could not have been more thrilled with the decision.

\* \* \* \* \* \*

As I walked to the car, a dish of Esther's lasagna in hand (with reiteration that she didn't want me starving to death with my "bachelor friend...*Bob*"), my father followed slowly behind as if I were five and might not make it there on my own. I got the feeling he sometimes felt true regret after his more sour family exchanges and looked to find ways to soften things up before we said our goodbyes. If atonement was the goal, however, the glibness he typically employed didn't cut it.

"Real sorry to see you go, kid; you got a way of lighting up the room," he cackled.

"Yeah, that's me." I loaded the lasagna onto the passenger seat of my old Audi, walked around him, got in and started the engine.

He leaned in the driver's window, peering around as if he'd never seen the inside of a car. "What is this thing, a '78, '79? It's a bucket, that's for sure! Now, if you spent the money to get the damn antique plates, at least then it would look like a choice."

"I'll get right on that, Dad. And when I do decide to get a new car you'll be the first to know."

"I'm not holding my breath. We still on for next week?"

Tennis. Dreaded tennis. I have no idea why I put myself through it, week after week. Some attempt to keep family ties intact. "Yeah, I guess."

"Good!" He slapped my shoulder. "Tuesday. Four-thirty. Court Three. Don't be late. I've got a new racket and I'm lookin' to wipe your ass."

"Not if I kick yours first," I retorted weakly.

"Yeah. In your dreams, little boy." For a weird second I thought he was going to kiss my cheek and, startled, I leaned the other way. But he just gave me another quick slap, turned and headed back to the house.

As I drove off, watching him in my rear view mirror, I decided there could be no one on this earth who was more of a walking contradiction.

# FIVE

ZOEY SARAFIAN, MY twenty-four-year-old assistant at Joaquin's Photography Studio up on Ventura Boulevard, had me out in the lobby of the studio—pamphlets and promo sheets spread everywhere—as she explained the many varieties of photo booths available for hire. Earlier in the week I'd mentioned my parents' event as a potential job for her, and now her chattering and pamphlet flapping filled every square inch of visual and aural space. I had to appreciate the enthusiasm with which she approached the task, but Zoey's general state of frenzy often triggered a breaker switch in my head and I'd have to tune her out. Like now. With the photo booths. And the chatter.

    As I sat there pretending to listen, I suddenly caught sight of an exceptionally attractive woman making her way past the studio, her eyes turned toward me as she glanced inside…or more likely at her reflection in the window. I watched, fascinated, gazing at the angular planes of her face, the lines of her body as she briskly strode by, and, in my admiration, found myself wondering if I truly *could* say I was capable of being with only one woman for the rest of my living days.

It's a big ask. But marriage does ask that of us, wives ask that of us, and certainly it's a worthy question, one I'd pondered since the moment, years ago, when I realized that a stable personal life requires the choice. In most circumstances. The ones that don't, well, probably not my thing. So I willingly play the monogamy card. It's not a bad trade-off when you're madly in love and hotter than hell for the woman with whom you'd make that commitment. When you've been barred from the house for three weeks and counting, there's a certain perspective shift. I assumed it was as temporary as my banishment.

Truth be told, there was part of me that wanted to marry Jane so I *could* contain my life, give it boundaries in which I could completely be myself and yet freely explore every possibility as a man, a husband, a friend, and a sexual partner. Boundaries always made sense to me. I needed boundaries. I was that kid who walked into Toys "R" Us and went into spasms of panic at the endless shelves of cars and trucks, overwhelmed by the sheer volume of available choices. My mother would have to handpick three possibilities, then invite me to choose one of the bunch. There was relief in that, the paring down of options, the only way my little psyche could handle the "paradox of choice."

With women? The world of available, countless, lovely women? Like the gorgeous blonde walking past the window? Yes, boundaries made sense there too. Choosing one out of the many made sense. And loving Jane, wanting Jane, feeling safe with Jane, made the boundaries of marrying *her* make sense. I could do it. I could. And I still wanted to. I wanted the comfort of Jane-boundaries.

By now the beautiful woman was gone and Zoey had moved on to the benefits of silly photo props, waving oversized sunglasses with glee as I concluded yet another conversation with only myself.

# SIX

BEFORE I LEFT the studio I checked my messages and, no, not a peep from the elusive Jane. Which was, as always, a painful event, but one with noticeably less visceral punch now that we were almost into week four. I had either become inured to my fate or was just unwilling to believe this was really happening. But the need to sort out the next rent payment was upon us and that would hopefully compel some connection.

There *was* a chirpy message from my mother, thanking me again for coming out to the house the previous week, checking in again about the photo booth, and apologizing, yet again, for the snit-fest I'd witnessed between her and my dad. I decided the only way to cease her obsessive checking and apologizing was to call…again.

"Mom, you don't need to keep apologizing for Dad. I'm his son; if anyone knows how cranky he gets it's me, so don't worry about it."

"I just don't want you to think badly of him…or of us. I know it's not fun being around bickering people, even if they are your parents."

Even *if?* "I don't think badly of you. I can't say I always enjoy the way he treats you, though. Personally, I think he's an ass a lot of the time and I don't know why you put up with it."

"I know he can be difficult. But we forgive him because he's a good man and he loves us all."

"Hey, if that mantra works for you, fair enough. I just want to be sure you don't put up with more than you need to."

"Oh, honey, I put up with much more good than I do bad, so I'm fine. He's more bark than bite, you know that!"

"Sometimes even the bark gets old."

"I know. I'll talk to him about it, see if he can try to be a little more pleasant when we're all spending time together. It's so seldom we do, I hate wasting any of it on arguments and crabbiness. Maybe you could come over more often. He might behave better that way."

I had to laugh at her transparency. "I'm sorry I haven't been around much, Mom; it's been busy lately. I'll plan to stop by next week."

"I'm not trying to make you feel guilty, sweetheart, but certainly I'd like to see you more often! Oh, and when you do come, can you be sure to bring my baking dish back with you? It's my favorite one and I'm making another lasagna for my book club this weekend."

She was a trip, Esther. Smarter than she let on half the time, and someone who honestly made the ideal of unconditional love a true mission statement. It was her politics with my father that eluded me.

I thought about them on my way home and came to the conclusion that they were *both* responsible for perpetuating the roles they played with each other. Two strong people dodging and feinting all day long just to avoid getting to it, whatever *it* was. That sharpness between them was a symptom; I didn't really know the cause. If you asked me if I thought my parents loved each other, I'd say "yes" in the most automatic of responses; deeper thought, however, might suggest a different answer. Their relationship seemed more about tolerating each other than anything else. I'm not sure what love's got to do with any of that.

Expert that I am.

When I pulled in the driveway of my temporary residence, I couldn't help but notice Jane's car wasn't in its usual spot and no lights were on inside. Which meant she was out. Which was very unusual for her on a Thursday night. She was all about the Thursday primetime lineup—me hitting the ice cream truck for a full-night supply, the two of us cozying up with popcorn and the plaid comforter. Apparently there were now better things to pull her attention on said night, which tightened what was becoming a permanent knot in my stomach.

And, frankly, bugged the crap out of me. I found it unconscionable that she hadn't offered much in response to my last, rather vulnerable, email in which I said something like, "Okay, this has now gone on long enough. What are we doing and can I please come home so we can discuss it?" The best I got was a text saying, "I need more time," a repeated put-off that was wearing very thin.

Bob was nowhere to be found so I threw myself on the comfortable bed of my comfortable guest room, a big plate of Esther's lasagna by my side, and briefly wallowed in some serious self-pity. Not good; it sparked the slightest edge of panic, and there was no point going down that road. So I called Lucy. We hadn't spoken since our last conversation at the restaurant, and I could think of nothing better to do right now than bitch about how her soul mate theory had further demolished my state of well-being, particularly with the parents.

"Why did you tell *them* that, of all people?" Lucy yelped. "They have about as much romantic imagination as bridge trolls!"

"I know, it was stupid. But they caught me off guard with the Jane thing and I clutched. Thanks for making sure they had all the details on that, by the way."

"They ask questions, I tell them the truth. Something you might want to try from time to time."

"I'm a very honest person in most situations."

"That's true. Except this one with Marci." Lucy's grin was palpable, even over the phone.

"Yes. Except that one," I retorted dryly. "You didn't say anything about that to them, did you?"

"No! Even I'm not that cruel. Can you imagine Dad's response to that?"

"To what, specifically?"

"The post-breakup Marci shags."

"Ah, the shags. Yes. He'd have a field day with that. The 'coarseness of your character' and all." I'd gotten that speech a few times in my life.

"Plus, he thought Marci was a slut, so how fun to have proven him right on that count! He'd have so enjoyed it!"

"He thought she was a slut? She wasn't a slut. She just had problems letting go."

"Oh, I'd say you both had problems letting go."

"Can we not talk about Marci right now?"

"You brought her up!" Lucy laughed.

"No, I think you did. In fact, there's been more discussion about her in the last few weeks than I had the entire time we were together. By the way, Mom actually found your soul mate theory quite touching."

"Thanks for pinning that on me, asshole. Now I'll never hear the end of it."

"You're welcome. You can use it to conveniently justify why you're a barren old maid despite pushing menopause. Dad's pretty concerned about your arid womb."

"Ew, too weird and disgusting—Dad thinking about my female parts."

"That is weird and disgusting. But it's *all* weird with them, isn't it? All the bullshit they get into. I felt like their sniping was off the charts the other day."

"They always snipe, what was so different?"

"I don't know; I'd just never seen her get *that* tense with him before. I felt like the whole soul mate thing unearthed some ancient resentments heretofore unknown. I mean, what was all that 'your father thinks I don't notice what he's really saying' bullshit, or the stuff about the 'hand you're dealt,' or whatever all that mess was? I have no idea."

There was a pause on Lucy's end. "Huh. I always wondered if it was true."

"If what was true?"

"I don't know if it makes any sense to share this information with you at this late date."

"Which, of course, now means you must."

"There was a woman," she said cryptically. Lucy loved saying things cryptically.

"A woman? As in, *another* woman?"

"Not like that...it was before Dad met Mom."

"What are you talking about?"

"Okay, here's the thing: I was sworn to secrecy by Mom. Which has been a bit of a burden, to be honest, because I've wanted to talk to you about it a million times, it's all so strange!"

"What's so strange? Just tell me, for God's sake!"

"Actually, it's a pretty intriguing story. I found out about it back when we were packing up for the move to Encino. Remember how Mom and Dad did all that culling and tossing of their accumulated crap? I don't know if you remember, you were only twelve at the time and not paying much attention to what we adults were doing—"

"You were fourteen."

"But I was a mature fourteen. Anyway, my assignment was to help them clear out the attic and storage space and there were shitloads of boxes and huge bags of garbage to deal with, remember that?"

"I have some vague memory." I really didn't.

"Well, according to Mom, one day she goes out to the garbage area with a few trash bags, and she sees this accordion file in a box of old papers and stuff. She'd never seen it before so she gets curious, opens it up to see what was inside."

This *was* intriguing. I sat up.

Lucy continued: "There were mostly old magazines in there, nothing too interesting. But she notices Dad's name on this one typewritten piece and, of course, wants to read it. So she sneaks the whole file back inside and looks through it all."

Lucy then took a long enough pause that I hollered, "What? What was it?"

"Oh, sorry, I had to fix this little flower thing."

"Little flower thing?" I was confused.

"I'm surrounded by about fifty-six small vases; I'm doing the arrangements for our catered gig tomorrow."

"You're catering now?"

"Yeah, pretty much every weekend."

"That's great."

"That's exhausting. Anyway, back to the story—"

"Wait, hold on a sec, okay?" This was going to take long enough that I needed some libation after downing my lasagna…which I'd done at some point during the conversation. I set the phone down and raced to the kitchen for a beer. Standing there taking a few sips, I couldn't help but push the window curtains aside to see if the lights were on yet at Jane's. Nothing. Still dark. What was up with that? Could she be dating already? Were we actually *there*? I shook my head, dismissing the idea, took another slug of beer and headed back to the bedroom. I picked up the phone. "Okay, I'm here. Carry on."

"So, anyway, Mom said Dad told her that, a few years before they met, he'd decided to try for a college-level teaching position and figured it would do his bona fides some good if he was published. Apparently he didn't think he had a novel in him, so he submitted essays and short stories to various literary journals and actually got a few published."

"And that's what was in the file?"

"Yes. But he never got the college gig and, according to Mom, shelved the idea of creative writing after that."

"Doesn't surprise me. Can't picture Dad thinking creatively for long enough to sustain a writing career. But I'm still not connecting the dots."

"Well, this is where it gets interesting. Mom said he'd shared the published stories with her right after they first met, so finding the magazines in the file was no big surprise. Though she did think it was terrible he didn't want to save them for us as family heirlooms."

"Yes, who needs blue-chip stocks? But let's get back to the mysterious typewritten thing."

"It was a manuscript, something she'd never seen before, tucked in with all the magazines. It still had the rejection lettter from the memoir journal stapled to it, with Dad's letter to them underneath."

"What did it say?"

"Which, the rejection letter or Dad's?"

"Dad's. I'm familiar with the verbiage of rejection."

"Well, Dad's said something about how this was a true story about love and heartbreak, something he'd personally experienced and thought their readers would find relatable."

"That could not sound less like Dad."

"He *was* only twenty-three at the time."

"How do you know that?"

"The date on the story. Anyway, when Mom read the manuscript, she said she found it incredibly emotional, basically a heartbreak treatise about 'the one that got away.'"

"Mom used the word 'treatise'?"

"No, idiot," Lucy laughed. "*I'm* the child of an American Lit teacher!"

"And you read it too?"

"Yes."

"Thoughts?"

"I don't remember the details, but it *was* very impassioned. It was about this girl Dad met right after college, when he and a few of his friends spent the summer in San Francisco before they all started their jobs and stuff."

"He wrote a story about a love affair he had? For intended public consumption? How utterly human and so not *him*."

"Exactly. And, understandably, Mom was a little hurt by it, mostly because he hadn't shared it with her, but also because he'd never told her about this woman. Which she thought was strange, since it did sound like it was a pretty important relationship to him…or at least one that had some impact on his attitudes about love. Anyway, she ended up giving me the file and telling me to save it for posterity. Which I have."

"Did she ever confront Dad about it?"

"Not that I know of. That would be *so* not her style."

"Yes, better to get all passive aggressive like she did the other day. So what's the skinny on this other woman?"

"Barbara from Oakland. That's about all I remember. One minute it sounded like she was just a typical summer romance, the next he'd wax on about soul mates and destiny to the point that you'd have to believe it meant *something*. Who knows? But once in a while when Mom and I are alone and she's feeling grumpy about Dad, she'll allude to his 'girlfriend' in a pretty snarky way. Obviously it got to her, built a nice little foundation for her basic insecurities."

"How weird is all that?"

"I know. Mom made me promise to never tell Dad she dragged that file out of the garbage, and especially not that she gave it to me, so I never have. But, personally, I think it's pretty hard to believe he and this woman were really soul mates, considering how it all played out."

"Unless they *were*—or at least he thought they were—and the theory let him down. Which could explain why he gave up on it."

"Yeah, maybe."

"I can't believe I didn't know any of this."

"I didn't think you'd be that interested."

"I probably wouldn't have been prior to my own marital implosion; now I'm completely intrigued. Do you suppose there's a genetic component to being crappy with relationships?"

"Maybe. Look at me! Anyway, I shoved the file in with a bunch of my old shit out in the garage and there it lies. You can read it any time you want. You might find it illuminating."

"The shadow father. Did you have the pages DNA tested?"

Before she could respond, I was jarred from conversation by the sound of Bob's stereo springing to life with some shatteringly loud hip-hop. Apparently he was now home. And, given the scent of vanilla candles wafting through my door, would also be entertaining. Dammit.

"Hey, Luce, it looks like Hannibal's got a kill coming in for the evening. I better run or I'll be forced to listen to the screams."

"Feel free to camp here tonight, but I'm going to be at the restaurant until late."

"Please take me with you. I need a purpose in life."

She laughed. "You could come over here and clean up after I'm done with these flowers. That'd be purposeful."

"Aagh…" I rolled on the bed like a whiny toddler. "I want to do something fun! Something with people who actually like me and think I'm cool."

"Then you don't want to spend the evening with me," she teased. "Listen, I gotta go. Later."

"Oh yeah, me too, lots of important stuff going on. So, you said you were busy?"

She'd hung up. As I moaned loudly into my pillow, Bob stuck his head in the door. I leapt up as if late for school.

"Relax, he's not here yet," he grinned, making sure I noticed he was carrying a champagne bucket and two glasses.

"So…big night then. Guess I'll take off."

"That'd be the plan."

"Cool. Lucy invited me over anyway."

"Perfect."

"So, about coming home later…"

"Not if you wish to remain blind to the alternative lifestyle. There may be nude dancing in the living room." He chuckled as if he was joking. I was pretty sure he wasn't.

I got up and pulled on my jacket. "Okay then, dance away and

I'll see you tomorrow." But he was already gone, Kanye was a'thumpin', and I was left to slink out the door with absolutely nowhere to go.

## SEVEN

I STOOD OUTSIDE on the lawn like a poor lost child and looked over at my old house. The door plaque was conspicuously missing, leaving behind an oval of unbleached paint and the pathetic little nail where it had once hung. I'd felt a stab of grief when I first noticed its absence weeks earlier, grief followed by real annoyance that Jane actually felt it necessary to take down the damn door plaque just to make a point. I figured I was supposed to interpret this as "Dan and Jane Live Here *no more*," but that missing plaque was the closest I'd gotten to any kind of communication about the status of our relationship.

A light was now on in the kitchen. Clearly she'd returned from wherever she'd been earlier; wherever that might have been I could not even guess. And there I was, standing between my two homes—lights on, people present, and nobody in either who wanted me inside. I'd be forgiven for feeling sorry for myself.

Then I got to wondering what she was doing. Bet she was in there washing dishes or singing along to old Aretha. Not a half-bad voice, I have to say. She loves "Chain of Fools." Can really wail that puppy. In fact, just a few short weeks ago (which now feel like a year ago), we were sitting together on the couch inside that house watching the *Muscle Shoals* documentary, her commenting how, "Aretha recorded right there in that studio," while I bopped along to Wilson Pickett…what a night that was! We talked about how fun it would be to go visit the place, even researched B&Bs in the area. Now I'll probably never get to Alabama.

Maybe she's making a pie. She likes to bake when she's stressed out. Or maybe she's not that stressed out. Maybe it's just me. *She seems to be taking all this in stride, the disruption and wedding postponement…possible cancellation.* Which is weird to me, since she's not typically an emotionally stunted person.

Pie does sound good right now. Have I mentioned that Lucy taught her how to bake pie? Now she makes what is, hands down, the best pie ever made. Particularly her apple. I love her pies, so comforting and homey—

"Why are you lurking out here?" Suddenly there she was, Jane in the flesh, standing on the porch with a dishtowel in her hands and a frown on her face.

"Are you baking pie?" I asked. The non sequitur threw her.

"No. Why would I be baking pie?"

"I always loved your pies."

"Dan…what do you want?"

"Could you stand having dinner with me?"

# EIGHT

IT SEEMED LIKE a good idea at the time, particularly since spontaneity is a trait she once told me she admired in a man. But now that we were seated at the table of one of our favorite neighborhood restaurants, picking at our food and gazing around the room as if it were beyond fascinating, doubt set in. Given that this was the first time we'd been in each other's presence in almost four weeks, after three years of barely a night apart (there *were* those couple of nights when... well, you know), I would have expected a tad more emotion. Maybe some basic social interaction. When even eye contact was not forthcoming after a full and very awkward fifteen minutes, I finally jumped in.

"Jane."

She looked up. No warmth in the least, but no hate-beams either. It was something.

"Is this still a hiatus or has it become an actual, undeclared breakup? Because I think it merits some conversation either way."

She took a bite of her salad, chewing slowly, no immediate comment, which compelled me to continue.

"I couldn't help but notice you took down the door plaque. I presume that was a message? Since we haven't talked about it—actually, haven't talked about anything—it's a little hard to know what, exactly, the message is. Which seems relevant, since I'm still fielding calls from the caterer."

Jane shifted in her seat like a recalcitrant teen wanting nothing more than to flee the table. I found it astonishing that we'd descended to this place of distance in such a short period of time. Finally she spoke. "I'm sorry about the door plaque. It came down that first night. It felt weird to put it back up under the circumstances."

"Which exact circumstances?"

She looked more miserable than I'd ever seen her. I did not understand what was going on, a point I was about to make when the waitress approached with our meals and we paused to get that activity accomplished. After she left, extending a pleasant and futile, "enjoy your dinner," Jane gazed down at her baked chicken in silence, while I remained intent on conversational headway.

"Jane, talk to me. I think it's only fair that I get some idea of what we're doing, what you're thinking at this point. We can't ignore each other forever. There are some things we'll have to take care of depending on how this goes and I'd like to get that sorted out."

"I thought you just wanted to share a meal. I really don't want to get into all this right now. I understand why you'd want to, Dan, but I'm sorry, I'm not ready."

"And why is that? Don't you think almost four weeks is long enough?"

"It probably should be, but for some reason it's not."

It struck me then that perhaps I hadn't apologized sincerely enough for my past transgression(s). There'd been some belligerent *"Okay, I'm sorry!"* comments made the night of the blowout, but nothing since. More authentic contrition might be warranted...and maybe even the missing piece. It was worth a try.

"Jane, I hope you know how truly sorry I am that I hurt you, I mean that. Back when the thing happened it really did seem like one of those transitional confusions; that really *is* all it was to me. But when I got past that point, and we were further along in our relationship, I felt so protective of what we were building together I didn't want to risk screwing it up over something that was so utterly meaningless. To me. I understand it's a different perspective for you."

I'm not sure what I expected as a result of this touching speech, but I hoped it would be along the lines of her throwing herself into my arms and, with kisses all over my face, sobbing, "I'm sorry too, Danny! We love each other, we're not perfect people, so let's just forgive and forget and start over!"

What I got was a minor nod and the rather anemic: "I believe you. Thanks. And I know I'm probably making too big a deal out of this Marci thing, but I can't really explain it. I don't understand it myself. I did get back into therapy this week."

Beyond my disappointment at her tepid response, I was surprised about the therapy. Jane once told me that her year of counseling during college was a total waste of time and money, and that "yoga and a good vitamin regimen trumped Freud any day."

"I guess that's good…right?" I wanted to be supportive without sounding relieved. "How's it going?"

"I've only had one session."

"How did that go?"

She suddenly looked up with a truly pained expression and said, "Everything's changed. In one split second everything I felt and believed just…changed. I don't know why it was so dramatic, but it was, and now I don't feel secure enough about what's happening to even think about a wedding."

Her frankness was appreciated, but I was severely shaken by the sentiment. "What changed? What happened? We had a fight, it sucked, but I'm still me, you're still you, what changed? I mean, really think about it, Janie. One minute we're happy, we're in love, we're talking about our wedding, then all of a sudden I'm cornered into telling you I—"

"*Cornered?*"

Christ, we were already parsing words. "Well, come on, it was a bit of a set-up, don't you think? Your question?" I wasn't sure this was the best tack to take at the moment, but it's what I was honestly feeling. And honesty *was* the mission statement these days.

Her face darkened further, however, indication that my current candor might not be getting us any closer to reconciliation. "A 'set-up'? So, me getting all flirty and asking a silly question about being the only one you'd be with for the rest of your life was a set-up in your eyes? That sounds like a guilty man talking to me!"

Actually, it did to me too. Not that I was about to concede the point. "Jesus, Jane, you've turned this into the crime of the century! Seriously. Think about what it was, not what you're blowing it up to be. It's probably worth a few angry words, but I'm thinking your reaction might have more to do with previous dickhead and his two secret marriages than it does with me." This was my first chance to make that particular point out loud. It seemed relevant.

"Maybe it does! Something about lying, dishonest men. So maybe it has to do with both you assholes!"

And *now* we've got false equivalency. All I could manage was, "Wow."

She looked up, surprised, I think, at my lack of volley. "Sorry, that was mean. I presume *you* were never married before." There was the slightest smirk on her face.

"Thank the stars for that one indisputable truth."

But there was to be no more humor. She slumped in her chair as if the weariness of battle had finally claimed her. "Dan…I don't know. I don't know how to explain it. There's just something about knowing you lied to me."

"I didn't lie, I—"

"Left something out, I know."

"Yes, I left something out. Something that was so insignificant to me that it didn't seem worth hurting you over. So I left it out, something that happened three years ago. I probably shouldn't have, but I did. And because of that, the entire foundation of our relationship has crumbled. Does that make any sense to you?"

"No. But doesn't that say something right there?"

"What does it say?"

And then she was crying. As frustrated and put-upon as I was, I felt a jab right to the center of my heart. Real regret that this incredible woman I loved was so badly hurt by something I'd done. I wanted to get us past this moment, past this chapter, get us home and into each other's arms. Which is why what she said next startled me.

"It says we're not ready for marriage."

I looked at her, incredulous at the continuing out-of-proportion nature of her reaction. So much so that I was now pushed beyond regret, beyond pleading and sorrow, to a point of unmitigated anger. "Then, dear God, let's kill it and end the suffering, okay? This is fucking stupid at this point."

"Maybe that is the best thing to do..." She was once again staring at her chicken.

"Great. Clean and simple. I'll call off the caterers, you can let the hall know we won't be needing them, we'll each handle our own families. Come on, this'll be fun."

"Don't be flip, Dan."

"Oh, I'm not being flip!" My voice had taken on a sort of high-pitched shrill. "I'm relieved to stop dancing around all this cagey bullshit. We're finally making big kid decisions, yippee!"

"Please don't start another fight! This is torture for me." She was still crying, but I wasn't feeling as charitable.

"Yeah? Well, it's been a little hard for me too, Jane, in case you haven't noticed. Which, of course, you haven't because my welfare couldn't be further from your mind. But *you* kicked *me* out. I'm the one who's been living out of a suitcase with the most popular man in Toluca Lake, a few feet from my home, wondering if I'll ever be sleeping in my own bed again."

"This is not really about your comfort."

"Oh no, you do *not* get to do that! You do not get to make this about me and my comfort. We both know that's not what's going on here. Now, coming home might be nice, considering I do pay half the rent and—"

"DAN, shut up! Just shut up!"

That shut me up.

"I'm *hurt*, you hurt me, don't you get that? This shouldn't be so hard to understand! You had sex with another woman after you starting having sex with me, after I thought we were being exclusive with each other. It doesn't matter that it was your ex-girlfriend, it doesn't matter how long ago it was or whether it was one or two times; it matters that somehow you thought that was okay…doing it and then not telling me about it. How am I supposed to trust what we have now? How do I go ahead and plan a wedding when I'm worried we'll be divorced in two years after you remember something else you might have 'left out'?"

I felt like we were going round and round and getting nowhere. "Believe me, that's all of it, you now know my every offense since the day we met. There's nothing else to 'leave out,' and I will keep saying that until you believe me."

Tears were dripping onto her plate. She looked so utterly despondent. I reached out for her hand.

"Janie, come on. Let's please get past this. I'm all-in, still ready to go. And, hey, if two years ends up being all we can manage, so be it. That doesn't sound too bad at this point, right?" Serious mistake. I actually chortled in a misguided attempt to lighten things up. Did *not* work.

She shook off my hand. "I can't believe you think anything about this is funny."

I'm an idiot. "I don't, Jane. Really, I don't. It's awkward, and I don't know how to make it better. That makes me stupid, I guess."

"You *are* stupid," she said simply. It seemed we had once again hit an official Jane tipping point; she got up and charged out of the restaurant.

I had now been abandoned by the third person of the night and it wasn't even nine o'clock. This was a day that seriously needed to end. I headed off to Lucy's and my other second bedroom.

# NINE

TUESDAY. FOUR-THIRTY. Court Three. Our set day, set time, set court. Every week. And still I have no idea why I go through this ritual with my father. I hate tennis. Did I say that already? I think I did. It's something I say often.

See, I'm a lousy tennis player; he's a great tennis player, and he finds sadistic glee in kicking my ass on a regular basis. The gloating seems specifically attached to his being a superior player despite his one-eye blindness, but there is nothing about the activity that is fun for me. I've suggested softball, my sport of choice, but he'll have none of that—probably as lousy with a bat as I am with a racket. But since I'm not a masochist, I can only assume my concession to his sport has to be that it's the one shot we've got at any kind of ongoing relationship. I may have surges of true annoyance with the guy, but he is, after all, my father. And somewhere in all the noise and shouting the relationship remains important to me.

I've also mentioned his being a contradiction and that's completely true...and whatever the difference between contradiction and paradox, he's probably both. I've always found it difficult to picture him as a teacher, a good teacher at that, or a writer, a lover of books. His impatience is legendary, he's dismissive of sentiment, and he seems impressed by almost nothing, all of which combine to make his previous self impossible to reconcile with who he is now. Something must have changed on a cellular level to take him from those earlier traits to the cantankerous, one-trick pony he's become. You want a conversation with my dad? Talk sports. He'll stand in a room full of intelligent people discussing intelligent things without saying a word until some goon starts yammering about ball scores; then he lights up like a lantern. In fact, nothing interests him more these days, not art, films, politics; forget literature. The man has shed that skin like a damp coat and what's emerged is a far less interesting human being, at least to my point of view.

But he loves beating his kid at tennis. So I play tennis with him. We give where we can.

On this particular day I'd come directly from a job, a corporate gig shooting women in pantsuits and men in navy blazers who chattered nonstop in that weird business school jargon that makes my teeth grind: "adoptive processes," "aggressive mediocrity," "burning platforms," and so on. My simple statements like, "Please stand near the window," sounded witless by comparison. I was grateful Zoey was there to assist—and offer hilarious commentary—but it was the inclusion of a very hefty tip from the CEO, who said he liked my style, that saved the day. I wasn't sure what he meant by my "style," since I didn't feel I'd infused any into the proceedings, but Zoey said later I'd caught some nice light. Either way, I was happy to take the cash and run.

The timing of the day got me to the court early, however, and it was hotter than usual. I was now sweating like a dockworker, wishing Jim would get as much pleasure from a forfeiture as a game, but no such luck. He showed up spry and bouncy, ready to rumble. We played and played…and played. And after enough on-court slaughter to bloody both my knees and pull a muscle in my right shoulder, we finally called it—for Jim, of course—and headed to the sidelines for

Gatorade and gloating.

"Now *that's* a workout," he said triumphantly, arms raised like Rocky at the top of the stairs.

"You happy?" I wanted to be sure I'd fulfilled my filial imperative.

"Hell, yeah. Kicked your ass. Even with one good eye." That last line was so predictable I said it right along with him. Which he didn't appreciate. "Hey kiddo, when you can beat me with two good eyes, let me know."

I shook my head with a smirk. "That's all it takes to make this worth your while, Dad, kicking my ass? You really are a cheap date."

"Don't start whining like a girl. That's why I never play with your sister…she whines."

"Bullshit. You never play with my sister because she *wins*."

He turned to me with that sneer I know so well, then bellowed with a hard laugh. "That's good! 'Cause she wins.' Good one, Danny. You're a funny guy. A lousy tennis player but a funny guy."

"Glad I amuse you." There was an edge to that. He noticed.

"Hey, I'm out here playing tennis with you. Isn't that the point?"

Interesting that he'd put it that way; maybe we both felt duty-bound. Kind of touching, in a bent sort of way. "Sure, Dad…that's the point." I cleared a spot for him on the bench.

We sat in silence slugging back our sports drinks when he gave me a sideways glance and asked, "You back with Jane yet?"

"Nope. You still fighting with Mom?"

He looked genuinely surprised. "When were we fighting?"

"That wasn't fighting the last time I was over there? The whole soul mate thing?"

"Nah, that's just what we do. It's our routine. Your mother is a good old gal but sometimes she's a pain in the ass. I've got my way of dealing with her."

"I noticed. Very romantic."

"Yeah, little boy, grow up and try it sometime."

"You *do* make it look good, Dad."

"Always the smartass, aren't you?" He stood up and started pulling his things together. "I gotta go. She's got me running errands today and the list is long." He shot me a wry look. "Maybe you single boys do have a point!" He winked. I didn't wink back; seemed disloyal to my mother. "Good game, son. You ain't never gonna win, but I like a guy who never stops trying."

With another back-smack and grin, he was off. I appreciated his nod to my tenacity. It might not improve my game but if it scored points with Big Jim, it was worth something.

## TEN

WE WERE NOW days past the epic restaurant fail, but with Jane continuing to distance herself, and no further clarity on the officialness of the breakup, I decided it was time for a strategy change. If she wanted a true sabbatical, I'd give her one. No more calls, texts, or emails. Nothing. I'd drop off my half of the rent in a nod to sustaining integrity, then I'd give it another month. If nothing new happened within that time, I'd make a few executive decisions: officially call off the wedding, take my name off the lease, find a new place to live, and move on with my life. At least then I'd have some control over my day-to-day existence. Which I did not have at the moment.

That could be attributed, at least partially, to the fact that my day-to-day existence had once again planted me at Lucy's house. I love Bob, but *everyone* loves Bob. He says he's taking advantage of the "bull market" (interesting choice of phrase), and I can't say I blame him, but the situation hasn't done much for my growing sense of displacement. Thank God Lucy was in a celibate phase, with a guest bedroom that was always available, one I took full advantage of on a more regular basis than, probably, either of us appreciated.

As I was getting settled into the room, she pushed through the door with the notorious accordion file and set it on the bed. "This is it. It's not that much, a few magazines and the Barbara manuscript." She shuffled through the file and pulled out the yellowed pages. "Here you go."

"Ah, the star attraction." I took it from her eagerly.

"Enjoy the step into the twilight zone."

"Now you're just trying to scare me."

"You should be scared. You won't recognize the man." She grinned. "Okay, I'm heading in; sleep well. I'm leaving early so call me tomorrow night and let me know what you think."

"Will do." Before she closed the door I called out. "Hey, Luce…"

She popped her head back in.

"Thanks for the room. I know it's been a lot lately, but I'm hoping either Jane's therapy works or Bob hits a dry spell."

"It's okay, Mr. Sensitive," she laughed. "I'll start charging when it gets too crazy. Happy reading!"

She shut the door behind her. I crawled into bed and pulled the blanket up around me; sat back with the manuscript, feeling as though I really *was* about to enter the twilight zone.

Whatever my dad may be, he's the guy I know. Right in line with most men of his generation: outspoken about anything that has to do with anyone else but keeps his own stuff pretty close to the vest. Lots of foibles and flaws, but still a good guy. Just not *my* kind of guy.

And I had a powerful curiosity to know what made him tick back before he became the kind of guy he is now. That, and who, exactly, this Barbara was.

# ELEVEN

## *THE WOMAN BETWEEN THE LINES*
*By James McDowell*
*October 15, 1966*

*It was the summer of 1965, a sunny day at Ocean Beach in San Francisco, a place filled with beach bathers, Sunday walkers, kite flyers, and happy families with little children. Four of my best buddies and I were in the area for the summer, there to celebrate our college graduations and have a little fun before we settled into whatever was next. For some of us that was a job, for others it was the looming reality of the draft and the Vietnam War (with one-eye blindness, I was out of that grim equation). Both options came with membership into a club we couldn't avoid but wanted to put off for as long as we could: taking care of business, otherwise known as "responsible adulthood."*

*My senior class roommate hailed from San Francisco, and he convinced us that the city by the Bay was the place to be that summer. We couldn't argue, certainly not with everything going on in the world, so we took the road trip up the coast and spent a good part of that summer* at his folks' place in the Marina District, most often finding our way to Ocean Beach where it seemed the prettiest girls made the scene. I had no intention of a summer romance, but there was a lot to look at either way!

On this particular day, decked out in our plaid Bermudas, shirts tied around our waists to show off our tanned, athletic physiques, we wandered through the countless blankets that dotted the shoreline, grinning like a pack of hyenas, giddy just to be there, with demands we could put off and illusions that we had all the time in the world. I think we all spotted her at the same time.

It was as if a white-hot beam had suddenly focused and all eyes turned to where it shone. On a soft blue blanket were four of the most beautiful girls we had ever seen. But there was one in particular who stood out—a real knockout in a way that was absolutely breathtaking. Dark, smoky eyes and great curves wrapped in a bright green swimsuit. All the guys noticed her, but it was my heart that stopped right in my chest.

When we approached with our hands in our pockets, feet shuffling like a group of eager grade-schoolers, the girls giggled and invited us to join them. There wasn't enough room on the blanket so I pulled the tee-shirt from around my waist, made a point of setting it right next to the beauty in green, and sat down. She introduced herself: her name was Barbara. "Barbara from Oakland," she said with an alluring smile. I'll never forget that name.

We spent most of that afternoon together, taking silly snapshots with my Kodak, singing songs, and sharing their strawberry wine. All the girls were vying for our attention, which was heady stuff, but all us guys were intent on getting Barbara's. It actually started to feel like a competition. We were hellbent on outdoing each other, with one story more outrageous than the next, one joke funnier, sillier, more flirtatious than the one before, but she was graciously unbiased in her attentions. When it came time to leave, she coyly gave each of us her phone number. I was disappointed—though I couldn't have expected someone like her to pay particular attention to someone like me—and I pocketed the number without a second thought.

*But when we got back to the house we all called, and it turns out I was the only one who got the right number! How about that? The one right number. The guys gave me a hard time, but they were good sports about it. I felt like I'd hit the jackpot, no doubt about that.*

*I spent the rest of that summer crossing back and forth across the Oakland Bay Bridge, rushing to her neighborhood, which was luckily not far from the bridge exit. I began to love that drive, lost in a kind of crazy paradise, feeling like the bridge magically connected me to Barbara. Initially she was shy and seemed intent on keeping things platonic. I often met her at a local soda shop or the library not far from her street. Sometimes I'd wait for her outside the ornate wrought iron gate of her family's California Craftsman, hidden by the tall bushes that framed the yard so her parents wouldn't see me. When I asked if I could meet them, she said they weren't too keen on her dating boys from out of town. I was a little disappointed, but figured we'd overcome that obstacle as things progressed. And progress they did.*

*Before long we were sneaking away to hidden spots where we could be alone and undetected. There was a small park near her neighborhood that had a particularly private area with a World War II memorial gazebo. It was tucked into a grove of large surrounding trees, and we'd spend hours in there kissing, touching, holding each other, and sharing the many deep and meaningful elements of our lives. It didn't take long for me to realize I'd fallen in love. Hard. With a woman I had no doubt was meant for me. My destiny. My soul mate.*

*I tried to explain to the guys the depth of what I was feeling but that kind of romanticism was hard to translate to goofballs intent on turning everything into a joke. But I felt emotions and sensations that summer that I'd never felt before, for a person who made me into a man I was with no one else. A strong man who could envision a future with a woman. A protective man who felt like he could conquer the world for her. A mature man, in ways that transcended boyhood notions of manliness. And certainly a lustful man, in every way a man yearns for a woman's touch. And all of that was unforgettable to me.*

*Those two months seemed to fly by and though my travel-mates* were bummed out that I wasn't available to spend the time with them we'd planned, I assured them this was no "fling"; this was the real deal. They all said they were happy for me and I believe they were.

The night before the guys and I headed back to Los Angeles, Barbara and I met at our gazebo and talked about everything we were feeling and everything we wanted: marriage, a home, even children... everything two people in love dream about. We promised to write—and wait—until the day we could be together again.

Back in Los Angeles, I was overwhelmed by my first job teaching English to high schoolers who I discovered couldn't write shopping lists much less compositions. The distractions of life occupied my mind. And yet, while the romantic high of that summer couldn't help but recede in the minutia of day-to-day life, my love did not. In fact, it grew. I could think of nothing but the beautiful Barbara from Oakland, pondering every possibility for how we could begin our life together. I wrote her often, probably too often, but so certain was I of the intensity of our love and the significance of what we'd shared, I was compelled.

Time dragged on and after sending five letters with no response, I had to acknowledge I was not only hurt, but deeply concerned that I might have somehow misinterpreted her intentions. Imagine my relief when I finally got a note, albeit a short one, but one that was at least sweet in its explanation of a busy fall and parents who rarely gave her time to think. It was only later, when I read it over for the twentieth time, that I had to admit to myself it was bereft of any of the passion we'd both expressed while together. Which mystified me. I wrote it off to the notion that she was, perhaps, someone who just wasn't good at putting her feelings into words, and I continued writing.

But soon more months went by and other than one more short, noncommittal response, there was nothing of any real feeling being conveyed. I was confused but decided to put some distance between my letters, thinking my verbosity might be intimidating to her. But at some point, with my emotions boiling, and a sense that I had to make a significant move or risk losing her forever, I put it all on the line and wrote asking her to move to Los Angeles, to marry me and be my wife.

*It was impulsive, I admit, but I felt it was all I could do to hold on to something I was absolutely unwilling to give up.*

*I never heard back from her. Clearly this was more than reticence; it was rebuff. I was devastated but then wondered if maybe, somehow, she wasn't actually getting my letters. Maybe her parents found out more about us than she wanted them to know and feared her marrying an out-of-towner who would take her away from them, keeping my letters from her as a result. I could think of no other explanation, and when I found I could no longer control this rushing train of thought, I knew there was no recourse but to call long distance.*

*Her sister answered the phone. Very affable, very courteous. And in one brutal, eviscerating sentence, she gutted me with the information that Barbara had gotten married three months earlier, just four months after our seemingly enchanted summer, to a man she'd been engaged to for over two years.*

*To describe the depth to which I fell would demand abstractions I cannot verbalize or even imagine. To merely hint at what I was feeling conjures words like crushed, shattered, disillusioned. To realize that during the entire time we'd been together she was engaged to someone else was beyond my comprehension. My friends told me to shake it off, that she was just looking for some fun before tying the knot; it was only a summer romance and they're not meant to last. But I knew my time with Barbara had been more than that. I knew it. What we had went deeper than just "some fun." I was there; I knew what we both felt. When she kissed me it was not the kiss of an engaged woman; it was the kiss of a woman wanting nothing more than to be right there in my arms. MY arms. Why she never mentioned being engaged, never intimated there was someone in her life, and always seemed so willing and intent on experiencing the time with me, was a mystery. I believe she really loved me but was a young girl who didn't know how to extricate herself from a situation to which she'd been previously bound. But whatever her reasons, whether intentional or otherwise, she had truly decimated my heart.*

*The many months since have been spent in the process of mending and finding equilibrium, as well as recalibrating my notions of love in a post-romantic reality. And I have. I've adjusted my expectations, my ideas. I've come to believe there is no such thing as "the one." A soul mate. A right person. We have criteria, we meet people, and we decide who we want to spend our lives with based on traits like dependability, integrity, responsibility, and affection. If love follows, all the better.*

*But what I originally thought was love, what I experienced that summer, what felt as real as rain, ultimately was not. It was not real. It was the fantasy of a man whose experience was so limited at that point of his life that he could not recognize, could not read, the woman between the lines. He heard her words, saw her beauty, felt her smiles and her touch, but didn't see what was really being said by the secrecy imposed, the lack of familial introduction, the unreturned letters, or the distant prose after a summer of poetry. Barbara from Oakland was a fantasy, my first big mistake, never to be repeated. Life, then, is obligated to be free of fancy, free of delusion. It is left to be, simply…reality.*

## *The End*

# TWELVE

I WAS IN my office at Joaquin's, so wound up by the story I'd read the night before that I almost paraphrased the entire thing to Zoey. With her boots up on the edge of her exceedingly messy desk, she listened, enraptured by this tale of a lost and broken heart. That this was about my cynical father made it all the more—

"Tragic. That's what it is, just tragic." Zoey had a certain lamentable view of love, either dumping or being dumped on a regular basis, so Jim's heartbreak theme struck a chord. "That must've been bizarre to read after so many years! Did he ever hear from her or try to contact her again?"

"I don't know; I wondered the same thing. I don't think so. There were no other stories about her and, according to Lucy, my mother was too embarrassed to admit she'd dragged his trash out of the pile, so she never asked him about it."

"A big, fat family mystery that's been rumbling under the surface for decades and who knows what the subliminal ripple effects have been."

"I know, right? And I can't believe he tried to get it published. It was so personal and so…maudlin, in a way. Mostly I'm stuck on the idea that my dad was ever that romantic a person."

"It sounds like he was all open and tender, and she bashed the shit out of him. I hate her."

"I hate her, too," I had to admit. "Which is kind of strange, considering I don't like my dad all that much."

"Don't say that, Dan! You love your dad!" Zoey remained inordinately close to her parents. Maybe it was a generational thing.

"Of course I love my dad. I'm just saying he's a hard case, and half the time I can't stand being around him. Which is why I find it strange that I'd get all defensive, like, 'you can't do that to my old man' kind of thing."

At that point, our boss and company founder, Joaquin Paredes, stormed into the office with a look of consternation, his usual expression. Mid-forties, I think, and, despite the ever-present frown, a great guy who waffles between fussy, serious, and affectionate. And he always, I mean always, wears black. He's a good boss—fair and reasonable—even if he does get overwrought at times when overwroughtness is unnecessary. Like now.

"Why are you two still here?! You have to be at Valley View Elementary in half an hour, school portraits, K through six! Where's the paperwork?!" If you can imagine exclamation points after everything someone says, that'd be Joaquin.

"Relax, boss; we got it and we're good to go." I tend to affect a sort of laid-back-I-got-this mien whenever Joaquin is frothing, a rebellious counterpoint of sorts, which is stupid because it usually doesn't work with him. As it didn't today.

He shot me a look that could only be described as ferocious. "Did you get a smartphone yet?"

"Don't you worry, my phone is plenty smart."

"Then maybe it's you that isn't."

This was a running dialogue with us. I'd gotten lost one or two times on a job and since then he's been harassing me about getting a smartphone so Siri or someone of her ilk can guide me. Which I refuse to do as a matter of principle. The way I see it, and as I've explained to him many times, we're at a critical juncture in our cultural evolution, a point where decisions have to be made about how far we're willing to go before we completely lose our souls. Almost every single bloody human is obsessed with technology, most specifically, the smartphone. You look in any direction, in any place, at any event, even walking down the street, and what you see are millions of heads bent in servitude to those fucking little boxes. Bob calls it Bent Neck Syndrome. But whatever you call it, it's people being seduced by the void in lieu of attachment to the humans in our midst.

Well, not me. I refuse to be a sheep. I'm a photographer, for God's sake; I've got to keep my eyes open, my scope wide, my interest attuned to the world around me. Though, trust me, I'm not a complete Luddite; I do shoot and process digital files, I use Google as much as the next guy, and I agree that email is the handiest way to get business done. But we are not obligated to throw out everything that came before to suck up to what's next. I also shoot with film when I can, and listen to actual records from time to time. We can mix it up without losing step, believe me.

And I *do* have a cellphone; it's a basic old flip model and it works just fine. I use it as needed, but what I *don't* need is to jump at the ping of every text, jangle of every call, or zing of every freaking email. And I certainly do *not* need a phone to tell me how to get to any damn place in this city, that one time—or two times—notwithstanding. I realize I'm probably the only guy in his thirties who feels this way, but what can I say? I'm my own man.

Joaquin has always been less impressed with my cultural thesis. "So your broken GPS in your car...did you get a new one yet?"

"No. I told you, it's still under warranty; I'm owed a replacement."

"Then why haven't you gotten it?"

"Because I have to take the time to get it all packaged up and sent out to this place, and I've been a little busy, as I'm sure you're aware. But, come on, I grew up in this city, I've got a great basic sense of direction, and if nothing else, there's a trusty old Thomas Guide in the trunk of my car."

"A Thomas Guide…" Joaquin shook his head as if I'd just mentioned cave paintings. "You're a talented photographer, Daniel, but a lousy navigator. And you can't be late for this one, they're tight for time." He turned to Zoey. "You have a smartphone, am I correct?"

Zoey rolled her eyes. We both loved the guy, but no one, not even Zoey, shared Joaquin's level of passion on the issue.

"Zoey, I'm asking you a serious question!" he repeated.

"Yes, Joaquin, you are correct; I have a smartphone. If he fails, I shall guide him."

"Then get, get! Off you go! And don't get lost!"

# THIRTEEN

WE COULD NOT have anticipated that Valley View Elementary was tucked into some random hills above the freeway that—smartphone or not—could not have been found without a sherpa and a pack of hunting dogs. So, yes, we did get lost, Joaquin did have a major meltdown, Zoey's phone did ultimately get us where we needed to go, and, though we were late, we did get everything done within the timeframe. And that was even with a few eight-year-olds breaking protocol to shoot the moon at the top of the bleachers. I bribed their cooperation with Magic cards and gum, which resulted in a teacher complimenting me for my "remarkable way with the obnoxious ones." It seems we all have our skill sets.

As we packed up the equipment after the shoot, I found I was still chewing on the questions piqued by "The Woman Between the Lines." It's not typically my style to spend a lot of time analyzing things, picking them apart and putting them under the microscope, but for some reason the story got under my skin. I'm not unaware that this likely has something to do with my own state of romantic upheaval, which I was also analyzing and picking apart with atypical vengeance.

Zoey caught me staring off into space for a second. "Hey, what's going on over there? You're usually jabbering after a gig. What gives?"

"Nothing. Just thinking about my dad's story."

"Aw, I know. Your poor daddy."

"Mostly I'm trying to figure out the takeaway, how this fifty-year-old event is relevant to who he is now."

"Who says it is?"

"Well, two things. One, it shows he used to have a romantic side and clearly *that's* changed. And two, his philosophy of love shared with me recently sounds suspiciously close to the one summarized at the end of this fifty-year-old story. Which suggests Barbara may have impacted his entire lifetime experience of love. Which sort of sucks for my mother."

"How so?"

"The idea that she's been married to a guy for forty years, who—I now find out—doesn't believe in soul mates, so obviously he doesn't believe my mother is *his* soul mate. And given the rest of what he had to say, I'd presume he also doesn't see her as his greatest love."

"Whoa. You got all that out of a story a guy wrote after his first big heartbreak? That seems kinda harsh. I mean, isn't it sort of a standard rite-of-passage thing? You fall apart, say a bunch of dramatic stuff, then you get over it and go on with your life…you know, have lots more romances and heartbreaks until you fall in love for real and get married?" I would guess that was Zoey's current working model.

"Yeah, sure, in most cases. But here's a guy who's *still* saying there's no such thing as 'the one' or a soul mate, so it's no wonder my mother thinks he married her on the rebound."

"She thinks that?"

"I don't know if she thinks that exactly, but according to Lucy, she's implied something pretty close."

"Wow, then that does suck. How soon after Barbara did your parents meet?"

"I think it was something like seven or eight years."

"What? That is *so* not a rebound!"

"Well, think about that right there! Why did it take him so long after Barbara to finally tie the knot?"

"Maybe he was being careful, and that's how long it took to find someone he loved enough to want to marry. Did you ever think of that?"

Her voice was more peevish than usual and I couldn't tell if we were still having a friendly debate on the topic of love, marriage, and my parents—three things neither of us had any place debating—or if we were actually fighting a little, which was strange since I never fight with Zoey. But still, I couldn't stop myself from yammering. "Or maybe, given this crap about 'playing the hand you're dealt,' poor old Esther was a consolation prize."

"Oh my God, that is so mean!"

"*I'm* not saying she is! I'm thinking maybe my dad feels that way."

"And what if he does? What are you gonna do? Return her for the mother you think you were meant to have?"

"Wait, weren't *you* the one who brought up the whole 'subliminal ripple effect' thing? That's pretty much all I'm saying."

"I just meant that heartbreak can make a person more cautious or something. I wasn't saying it changes them for the rest of their life! In fact, I bet your dad had some serious romantic years in him even after the Barbara thing. I mean, he was only twenty-two, right? And, come on, lots of people aren't romantic after they've been married as long your parents. He's probably the way he is now because he's old and retired and stuff, all bored and crabby. My grandpa's the same way."

That made astonishingly good sense, but even so... "I'm seeing some parallels between then and now that make me feel bad for both my parents. That's all."

"Well, they're still together after forty years so it can't be that heinous! Anyway, it's their life and there's no point in you getting depressed about it."

That kind of bugged me. "I'm not depressed, Zoey; I'm curious. Big difference."

"Okay, forget it! Guess I'm saying everything wrong today." She climbed in the car. Clearly she'd had enough of me.

I got in and glanced over at her. "Sorry. I've got a lot of weird stuff going on right now."

"I understand." She didn't sound like it. She also didn't make eye contact.

I started the car, feeling annoyed and a little foolish, wishing I hadn't gotten back into all this with her. Despite her nuggets of useful wisdom, the view from twenty-four isn't exactly the same as thirty-three. But, still…it was Zoey. "Zo, seriously, I'm sorry. I've been kicked out of my house for over a month, my parents are acting like they can barely stand each other, and I'm bouncing between bedrooms just trying to get a good night's sleep. Not exactly feeling the love these days. But you don't deserve my crankiness for any of that."

"Well, thanks. And *I* love you." She turned and punched my arm.

"Thank you, young woman, that means a lot." It did. I liked Zoey; when we weren't debating love, we were good work pals and she was a tough and able assistant. And now *she* wouldn't shut up about it.

"Are you seriously questioning your parents' marriage?"

"Kind of."

"Is it possible this is more about what's happening with you and Jane?"

"The thought has occurred. Lots of messages about love and marriage in all that mess."

"What messages?"

"The whole soul mate thing."

"Which, your father's or yours or…what?"

"See, there's Jane, a woman I adore but who currently hates me—or at least isn't sure *what* she feels about me. Which has given me time to ask myself the question: is she really who I want to build *my* life around? Is she *my* soul mate? Or would I be settling for what's in front of me, maybe like my dad; settling for what's easy and familiar because it's that time—or I'm that age—when these things are supposed to happen? I mean, Jane's great, like my mom's great, but I'm not so sure anymore that's enough. And that makes me not so sure Jane and I are meant to be together. Which is fucked up. But, seriously, would a real soul mate kick you out of your house for weeks on end and basically refuse to discuss it with you? I don't think so. I don't deserve that."

"I don't think you do either, Dan. And I do understand why your dad's story hit you so hard. But probably none of it means much of anything about you guys. I don't know what's going to happen, but why don't you just try to be in the moment for now? Stop thinking about all this stuff and focus on manifesting your intentions…let life reveal itself."

Zoey liked her self-help books. Zoey was probably right.

# FOURTEEN

BUT IT DIDN'T help. Right or not right, the advice didn't help. I couldn't shake it off. It *had* to mean something. Jane's banishment, the shattering of my father's faith in love, the whole point of love—it had to mean *something*!

When we got back to the office, Zoey took off for her date with some guy she'd met on Hinge (a dating app I'd never even heard of, which made me feel really old), while I stayed to eat crow with Joaquin over the earlier directional detour (again promising to get my GPS replaced). But once mollified, he showed genuine satisfaction with the proofs I printed out.

"These are very nice, Daniel! You've just got that good eye! I think people like what you do because you always give the work some artistic flourish, make it a little different, a little special, which is wonderful!" Still with the exclamations.

Joaquin often made transparent comments like these. Zoey once told me he was afraid I was too creative and skilled to stay on the job for very long. It was a compliment, surely, and I appreciated his desire to keep me on the compound, but who's kidding who about the art involved? "Not sure I see all that much art or flourish in any of this, Joaquin."

"You're just being modest!"

"No, I'm just being a generic portrait photographer. Let's not try to make it any more than it is."

He grabbed a sheet of images and held them up to the light. "Say what you will, Daniel, but look at the way you positioned these kids against that backdrop, the way you used the light. Even how you've got them grouped in different ways. That's not typical. That's artful. And people love that kind of thing!"

The shots did look good. And I did try to keep things creative, even down to researching and procuring a few arty backdrops that most hack photographers wouldn't have bothered with. I decided to make a diplomatic course correction. "Okay, I get your point. Thanks, Joaquin; I appreciate that you notice the work…and the art, wherever it trickles in!" I smiled, I meant it, and he relaxed.

"I do hope you're happy here, Daniel. You're important to this company. I have some ideas I actually want to go over with you, but I've got a dinner meeting right now so we'll talk about those another day." With that he said goodnight and left me to lock up. I wondered what his "ideas" might involve; my guess is they'd be along the lines of booking more photo booths or promoting theme weddings, neither of which stirred my Muse. But it had been a really long day, so who knows? Maybe he wanted to talk about a raise. That would be worth some anticipation.

I headed home with visions of toffee ice cream bars in my head, the perfect balm for my general angst, and something I'd looked forward to since about two o'clock. I'd get at least four, maybe even a few extra for tomorrow. Might run in when I got home to see if Bob had a taste for anything. He wasn't generally into ice cream, but I wanted to show the guy some appreciation; he'd been pretty great about all this. I knew Tomas had a guava sherbet thing he'd probably enjoy.

I was still brain rambling on the topic when I made the turn onto our street and, once past the intersection, almost screeched to a stop. WTF? *No ice cream truck.*

This was absolutely stunning to me. In the two-plus years we'd lived in the neighborhood, I'd never once found the street void of that truck. Tomas was always parked there from lunchtime until after sundown to be sure even rush hour stragglers got their supply. He was a very popular man and usually a very dependable man, so this was *outrageous*. The one time I needed him and he was nowhere to be found. Was the whole fucking world falling apart?

I barged into the kitchen like a sweating addict. "Where the fuck's the ice cream truck? Where's Tomas?" Bob, stirring something on the stove that smelled remarkably good, looked at me like I'd just been delivered from the psych ward.

"Who's Tomas?" Bob's lack of ice cream obsession had kept him from getting to know the truck driver with quite the intimacy I had.

"The ice cream guy. You know him, he's always there, for fuck's sake!"

"Calm down, I don't know him. And what's the problem? The truck's not there?"

"No, he's not there, *it's* not there. That truck is always there, every day; it's been at the end of this street since *you've* lived here, much less since we've lived here. And now it's not there!"

Bob gave me an authentically puzzled look. "And why is this so freaking tragic that you're having a seizure? It's an ice cream truck. I've got ice cream in the freezer. It's all good."

"No, it's not all good! I wanted a toffee bar, the bar I get every time I stop by that truck. I've had it in my mind all afternoon to get a shitload of bars, come in here, sit down, and enjoy the crap out of them while I ignored the rest of my crappy life. Instead I come home and there's no Tomas, no truck, and no fucking toffee bars!" I was actually yelling at this point. Over toffee bars.

"I'd say we've got some transference going on here, young fellow," Bob mused. "But hang in there; I'll put a call in to our neighborhood busybody, see what I can find out. For now I think you ought to sit down, pour yourself a drink, and enjoy a bowl of my Asian pork stew. It's so fucking excellent I bet after one taste you won't give a hoot about toffee bars."

I doubted that, but while Bob scurried off to do his detective work, I wearily took his advice, chagrined, now, at my ridiculous outburst. The weight of pile-on was taking its toll, that was clear, and I decided to mentally adjust for the sake of my roommate. And that stew *was* damn good. But when he came back to report that Tomas had been pulled over the night before on a suspected DUI and would likely be out of the ice cream business for whatever time it took to get that sorted out, I felt the loss as if the man were my brother. Which likely had more to do with his toffee bars, if I'm to be completely honest.

Later that night, after dinner and the calming of my jangled nerves, Bob and I were out playing catch in the front yard (after I made sure all was dark over at Jane's), running through our various debriefs until we got to my aborted love life. "And what's the latest with *her*?" He gestured toward the empty house across the way.

"Well, that, right there, is the problem: there *is* no latest. It just keeps rambling on, both of us recycling the same basic argument over and over. For some reason we can't seem to come up with a solution."

"Is that more her or you?"

"Her. Probably both of us. I don't know. If I'm not being flayed for my bad behavior of three years ago, I'm screwing up by saying the wrong things now. One minute it kills me to see her so sad, the next I feel like she's being a punitive bitch."

"I don't think I've ever heard you refer to Jane as a bitch."

"Because she's not inherently bitchy. But there have been moments of late when she's gotten dangerously close to full-fledged bitchdom. According to her, there's nothing I can say or do that would change the situation. I'm a disappointment at every turn."

"That sucks."

"Yes, it does. And how about we discuss the undeniable lack of balance in this situation? Jane's been calling the shots from the get-go, from keeping me out of the house, to telling me what she is or isn't feeling, right down to what she is or isn't sure about, particularly when it comes to the wedding. But if we're gonna play that game, how about we consider what *I* want or what *I* feel?"

"I'm not sure fairness is running the show at the moment."

"And that's a problem for me. I've got my own feelings about all this."

"Of course! But what are you saying…that *you're* thinking this might be over too?"

"Maybe. I don't know. I go round and round, making myself dizzy. A little hard to sort things out when the person you need to talk to acts like you're toxic."

"Yes, that is a problem, but obviously you guys need to make some decisions. As I recall, there's still a wedding on the books."

"Which sounds farcical at this point, doesn't it?"

"Points can always change." He grinned cheerlessly. "But still, it *is* sad. I was looking forward to working up my best man speech and making an ass of myself on the dance floor."

I had to smile. "Weddings do have their high points, don't they? But, to be completely honest, I'm beginning to think there really is a reason for all this."

"Yeah? Like what?"

This was the big question for me too, one I was getting closer to answering every day I was locked out of my house and shut out of Jane's life. "Not sure yet. But maybe something to do with realizing she might not be the right person for me."

"Wow, that's a big turnaround! Is this perspective from Real Dan capable of seeing the bigger picture or Bitter Dan who's been kicked to the curb for several weeks and may have temporary rage going?"

"I don't know yet. That's what I'm trying to figure out."

"And beyond the Jane conundrum, might this also have

something to do with your newly minted Jim versus Barbara Theory of Lost and Mangled Love?" I'd shared the story with Bob over dinner and he'd been properly stunned. And though his habit of titling things usually made me laugh, my mood was too weighted to find much of anything funny tonight.

"It's a different set of circumstances, obviously, but there are some connecting points. Who knows if this Barbara woman would've been any more right for my dad than Esther, but obviously *he* thought so. Which means, in his mind, he didn't marry his soul mate. I'm not sure I like the way a guy turns out when he settles for second best. And, frankly, I don't want to be that guy."

I think that was the most definitive thing I'd felt in almost a month. No idea, yet, where it might lead.

## FIFTEEN

I WISH I had a dog.

I was wandering around the neighborhood, too wound up to relax, and it struck me how much better it would be if I were traversing these dark, sprinkler-wet streets with a dog to accompany me, to give me reason to stop at certain corners or lean on chosen fence posts, a squatting, panting dog to justify the pauses.

But I like to walk either way. I particularly like walking at night when it's quieter and there's less traffic to muck up the flow of things. I do it often and I usually do it alone; though Jane loves the more arduous activities of soccer and mountain biking, she's generally less interested in the easy stroll for the sake of fresh air and a perspective shift. That's when it would be good to have a Rex or Lulu tagging along: a few biscuits in my pocket, a jangling ID, a nice leash from Petsmart, those nods and "oh, he/she's so pretty!" comments in passing. Such social things, dogs. I'll keep walking by myself for now, but I'll have to seriously think about getting one soon.

Things do change us. I believe that. Events happen and, even without noticing, we make subtle shifts, we see life differently; we alter our thinking or decide to take a different turn. I felt changed. Like I'd seen the light and come to realize nothing was as simple or benign as I'd made it out to be. I needed to pay more attention to my life, to be more protective of myself, do more than *react* to what was happening. I needed to be more of my own captain. I'd always been flexible and thought that was a good thing. But now I saw how essential it was to not just wait for the signs, for permission to proceed, but to actually decide myself what was right for me. It was a revelation.

Because no matter what anyone else tried to convince me of, there *was* a take-away from my dad's story: we all start off as open young people, ready to embrace and experience life. We're excited about it, anticipatory of it; we want to work and play and love and fuck and figure out who we are and who will be important to us, and we imagine our futures and our adventures, and dream big and loud and happy and then...life happens. And we learn to adjust.

My father was like any other young person. That litany was his as well. And losing love, his first love, had impact; it hit him at the core of his being. It changed him. Maybe Barbara *was* just a starting point to the unfolding of his particular list of life disappointments, but those firsts can be brutal.

*Am* I making too much of this, as Zoey suggests? Of course I am. Probably much like Jane is making too much of the Marci thing.

But on the other hand, I'm starting to understand why she might be, what she may be feeling. It's not so much that new information changes facts, but it changes what you *think* about the facts, how you frame them. Now, in the case of Jane and how she's interpreting my Marci betrayal, she's got me all wrong. I'm still exactly who I was, who I am, and my devotion and fidelity to her are as assured as they were when—well, at least shortly *after* the last time Marci crossed my threshold. That Jane's using that information to punish me for triggering her own insecurities is ridiculous, but it's human. I have no doubt she'll get over it. I hope she gets over it before *I* make a new set of decisions. But my dad? It seems to me he's fried for life. And that makes me sad for him. Sad for him and cautious for me.

I was now walking in a neighborhood I'd never been before. I looked around, listening, taking it all in. Music played from inside small amber-lit homes. I smelled good food and heard people laughing and clinking glasses. A child's tantrum echoed from the window of an apartment building and a mother chided in the effort to calm him. A man hollered at his TV when the quarterback fumbled a snap, and kids bounced their Wilsons off faded backboards lit by glaring porch lights. It was life. Life in a city, a neighborhood. And I felt untethered. Alone and untethered.

The phone in my pocket suddenly vibrated, snapping me out of my introspection. Lucy, in a tone as somber and terrified as I've ever heard, said, "Come to the hospital. Dad's had a stroke."

And life changes yet again.

As I rushed back to the house with a looming sense of dread, I had the illogical thought that all my churning about him over the past few days might have somehow shaken the roots of his foundation. Then I reminded myself that I'd never had that kind of power over anything…certainly not my father.

# SIXTEEN

IT'S ODD HOW shocking we find these things. They hit us so unexpectedly, as if the people in our lives will always, somehow, just be there. No matter how much we understand the facts of life—that we're all going to die, that our parents are going to die—we somehow get through each day ignoring that reality or pretending it's far too distant to earn our conscious consideration.

Then it's there, in the room: Mortality. Mortality and its ugly cohorts, Imminent Death and Probable Demise. Interlopers who always seem surprised at our surprise. They come in with looks that say, "You knew we were on our way and now that we're finally here, what's the shock?" Then one of them hip checks you so hard you drop to the floor. Mortality et al. are unruly guests.

When I got to Jim's hospital room after wending through a ridiculous maze of doors and hallways so identical one could not possibly get to or from without a map, I took in the visual of what lay beyond that door and it struck me how it was both *exactly* what you'd expect *and* the most shocking thing you've ever seen. Your big, impervious, larger-than-life father rigged up to about ten different machines with tubes and beeping lights and an unrecognizably frozen face so white it disappeared into the palette of the pillowcase. Mortality bared its toothless, evil grin as it took a seat at the back of the room.

My mother was doing her Esther thing, fluffing blankets and humming to herself as if she were here every day. Lucy, however, looked like she'd been run over. For a chick tougher than most guys I know, she'd clearly been leveled by the potential of Jim's extinction. I walked over and gave her a big hug and could feel the sob she valiantly kept in check. Esther looked up and brightened.

"Oh, Danny, I'm so glad you're finally here," she trilled. "The doctor came by a little while ago and he wants to talk to us when we're all together."

"Okay, Mom. How are you doing?" I gave her a hug too; couldn't tell if she was ready to collapse or so deep in denial she'd keep singing like a trouper.

"I'm holding a good thought, sweetheart, maintaining a smile so when he wakes up he knows I'm here and nothing too catastrophic has happened." Gotta love Esther…denial has always served her well. I steered her to a chair, and by then an official looking fellow with a white coat and a terse expression stuck his head in the door.

"You are the McDowell family?"

"Yes, we're all here now," Lucy anxiously replied. As he motioned for us to step outside, I turned to Esther.

"Mom, how would you feel about staying here with Dad…you know, in case he wakes up? We'll get the details from the doc and report back in. I don't feel like he should be left alone right now." Actually, I didn't want her out there distracting this high-ranking specialist with the typical nonsense that pops into her head in these kinds of situations. It's usually completely off the official conversation at hand—her labor pains with Lucy or that time I fell out of the treehouse—and is generally unappreciated by the official people involved (trust me…I've taken her to the DMV more than a few times).

"That's fine," she chirped. "I'd rather stay here anyway." As she settled back into the bedside chair, tapping Jim's wrist in time to whatever song was floating through her head, I slipped out to the hallway. Lucy looked at me with red-rimmed eyes as the doctor extended an introductory handshake.

"I'm Doctor Sidney Kamen, head of neurology."

"I'm Dan, the son; this is Lucy, the daughter."

Dr. Kamen smiled ever-so-slightly. "I wanted to wait until I'd had a chance to look over your father's tests before I spoke to you." He glanced back toward the room. "You don't wish to have your mother present?"

"We think it'd be best to get the information then pass it on to her," I explained. "She tends to get a bit distracted in these situations." He nodded. There was a slight pause. I filled it. "So, what is the situation?"

"Your father has definitely had a stroke; we don't know yet how significant. All his vitals are being monitored and assisted, and as soon as he stabilizes we'll be doing more tests to determine just how much brain function may have been impaired."

"Oh, God…" Lucy moaned as she leaned into me.

"How does it look so far?" I noted that I was taking the lead on this instead of Lucy; uncharacteristic, but she seemed to be letting me.

"Right now he's fighting the good fight. We'll know more in a few hours. It's wait and watch time, which is always tough on families. All I can say is, hang in there and I'll check back as soon as I have more information." He gave us what was likely his standard "sympathetic doctor" smile, another quick handshake; then he exited quickly through one of the many beige doors surrounding us.

Lucy and I looked at each other blankly and went back into the room.

## SEVENTEEN

ESTHER WAS STILL seated at Jim's bedside, patting his hand while she softly sang, "Michael Row the Boat Ashore." She looked up, quickly brushing away tears, as Lucy and I approached the bed. "He always loved when you kids sang that song."

"When did we ever sing that song?" I honestly could not remember us ever singing that song. I don't even know the words to that song.

"Dan!" Lucy snapped. I realized it was not a worthy point of debate.

"Hey, Mom," I offered warmly, "Do you want me to go get you something to eat?"

"No, sweetie, I had a little something earlier, I'm fine."

Jim suddenly stirred and we all leapt to rigid attention. His head lolled from side to side as Lucy adjusted wires and tubes to get closer. She leaned in. "Daddy, we're here, we're all here." She was outright crying at this point, something one rarely sees.

Jim's eyes popped open, no real contact with anyone, just batting around wildly like a man swimming up from some underwater vortex, frantic and completely disoriented. His mouth gaped open, his jaw working as if he were trying to get something out. The most he could manage was, "Cah...baaa...baaa..."

Esther grabbed his hand, got about an inch from his ear, then spoke as if the man were deaf. "What, honey? We don't understand you. Try harder!"

Jesus! "Mom, I think he's trying about as hard as he can."

Again, Lucy snapped, "Dan!" She got right up to Jim's face, though her approach was a tad less assaultive. "Daddy, it's Lucy. Can you hear me?"

Jim thrashed around like a trapped animal, and as I held up a few of the wires to keep him from detaching anything, he turned directly at my mom, then Lucy, then me, repeating, "Baaa...baaa."

Esther looked at us helplessly. "I have no idea what he's trying to say. What is he trying to say?" she pleaded.

And then, in the utter chaos of that moment, as nurses rushed in and we all stepped aside to let them administer to our stricken leader, it hit me like a bolt of revelation.

I knew exactly what he was trying to say.

# EIGHTEEN

LEAVING OUR SWIRLING, confused mother in the room to await further instruction, I grabbed Lucy's arm and practically dragged her out to the hallway.

Rattled by all the pandemonium, she resisted my pull with real annoyance. "What are you doing? We should be in there with Mom."

"I know what he's trying to say."

She stopped fussing. "Really? What is he trying to say?" Her skepticism was obvious but I had absolutely no doubt.

"Barbara. He was calling out to Barbara. Barbara from Oakland."

The look she gave me was so severely incredulous I don't think the word "incredulous" could do it justice. Also, her voice got a little too loud. "Are you fucking serious? Why the hell would Dad be calling out to some girl he dated for two months FIFTY FUCKING YEARS AGO?" A few of the hospital staff looked our way. I grabbed Lucy's arm and gave it a gentle "shut the fuck up" squeeze.

"I know it sounds completely random, but listen to me. I'm the one who sat up the other night reading his thoughts and words and, to be honest, I feel connected to the guy in a way I may never have been before. Which means I just might understand him a little bit better than anyone else does right now."

Lucy rolled her eyes. "Jesus Christ. I'm happy for you, bro, but could you save your Hallmark moment for a less urgent time and place?"

"I know how it sounds—I mean, who could be more cynical than me most of the time? But hear me out."

"Make it quick."

"Think about it: is it that hard to believe? He wakes up at the edge of oblivion, with no sense of time or place or what the hell is happening to him, and in that frenzied state his mind pulls up an old but obviously persistent memory: Barbara. They say you sometimes run through your entire history in the state of suspended reality, so maybe in his unconscious panic, he calls out for the one woman who may have touched him more than anyone else has since." I took a dramatic pause. "I think he said, 'call Barbara,' Lucy."

She took her own dramatic pause, though hers felt a little less conciliatory. "I think you're out of your fucking mind. You better not say one word about this to Mom, or I swear I'll kill you."

"Like I would say anything to Mom—"

At that point Esther struggled to push open the door I'd been purposely holding shut. Through the crack she whispered, "He's back asleep now."

"Okay, Mom," Lucy pulled the door open, rubbing her hair like a disturbed inmate until she looked even more disheveled than before.

Esther noticed. "Honey, stop doing that to your hair. It makes you look messy, and you're too pretty for that."

"Mom, we're at a hospital, not a beauty pageant."

"Well, let's try to look nice for Dad when he wakes up. We don't want him to think we're being sloppy now, do we? What do you think he was trying to say with all that 'baaa, baaa' stuff?"

Lucy shot me a death-ray glare as she pushed past me and back into the room. "I don't know, Mom, it's probably the drugs."

As they closed the door behind them, I stood in that antiseptic hallway with its odd noises and soft-shoed denizens and truly felt like a time portal had opened up…and into it stepped the woman from between the lines.

# NINETEEN

AFTER A HALF-HOUR nap in the ICU waiting room in the company of a dazed couple clearly dealing with their own tragedy, I was awakened when Lucy clamored up with news from the front.

"They're putting a bed in the room so Mom can spend the night. I'm going to hang around for a little while longer, and if there's nothing new in the next hour or so, I'll go home. Why don't you head out so you can spell me in the morning?"

"Okay." I stood up as if I were a hundred-years-old, all creaking joints and aching back. ICU couches are not conducive to the sort of waits ICU circumstances typically require. We shuffled down the hall and through the automated double doors to the not-ICU part of the floor, which seemed positively cacophonous by comparison. I yawned loudly. "I'll be back at seven, but call if anything happens."

"Oh, don't worry, I will. I'm not sure I can handle Mom in her current state for too long without you. She's starting to reminisce about our summer trips of the '90s."

"That's never good."

"She just brought up the time we went to Orlando and Dad

decided Disney World was too crass to patronize." Lucy cracked a smile. "Remember how insane we got?"

"I still can't think of Mickey without a shiver."

"I told her it wasn't a great memory to discuss at the bedside of said ailing man."

"Yeah, and she must have whitewashed it real good if she doesn't remember their knockdown back at the hotel."

"I think she's having some kind of secret anxiety attack. Probably doesn't even realize what she's talking about."

"Who could blame her? Okay, I'm out of here. Call me."

"Leave your phone on for a change."

"I always leave my phone on."

"You never leave your phone on. Either that or you never answer it."

"I answered it tonight." We looked at each other somberly.

"Yes, you did." She reached out and squeezed my hand.

Suddenly, approaching from down the hall, Jane flew into view, her face flushed and worried. Lucy looked at me quickly, but I made sure to register no reaction. I felt confident that, at least in these circumstances, Jane would see me as less the loser boyfriend and more the stoic son of a potentially dying man.

"I just found out from Bob." Jane panted from the rush down the hall, which I appreciated. "I'm so, so sorry, you guys. How is he?"

I let Lucy take the floor. "Pretty much out of it, but his vitals are stable for now. I'm headed back to the room; I'll leave Dan to fill you in on the rest. Thanks for coming by, Jane. Danny, I'll call you later."

Then she left and I felt awkward. "So, I'm on my way out. Are you planning to stay?"

"Yeah, I think I'll stick around for a while. I won't be able to get on the ward, but I'll see if I can be of any help to Lucy from out here. Your mom's inside, right?"

"Yeah, she's bunking in the room tonight."

"How's she holding up?"

"She's singing old folk songs and reminiscing about crappy

family vacations. It's a veritable McDowell fest in there."

Jane laughed. "Sounds like Esther."

"Yeah…pretty much." I felt excruciatingly tired and sagged into the frame of the elevator; Jane gave me a concerned look. I hadn't seen that expression in a long time.

"Are you okay?" she asked with clear sincerity.

"Just tired. Kind of rough seeing Jim McDowell down for the count. It's like the oak tree fell in the front yard."

"I can imagine how you must feel."

"Yeah. Well, I'm going to take off."

"Dan, can we talk sometime tomorrow?"

That was a surprise. Though I had a feeling it was more a sympathy move than anything else. "Sure. I don't know what my day will be with all this going on, but call and we'll see what happens."

"Okay, I will. Try to get some sleep. Bob said he made you a nice beef and barley soup." She smiled.

We'd often talked about the culinary skills of our favorite neighbor and how he put us both to shame. Weird, that shared reference at this particular moment. It made me feel sad. Sadder. Not that I let her see.

"I've always said the man's gonna make some guy a great wife. See ya, Jane." I stepped into the elevator with a wave. Before the doors closed, I caught her face in a flash of melancholy.

# TWENTY

LATER, AS BOB cleaned up after my late-night dinner (the soup, as expected, was incredible), there was little conversation between us, which was unusual. I presumed he was being sensitive, knowing I needed both to talk and not talk, whatever that means, but he just did his thing, said goodnight, and went to bed.

Sleep would not come easy for me; that was clear. I put on my favorite B.B. King album and lay back on the bed, staring at the ceiling while the bluesman echoed my pain. After a few minutes, I decided maybe reading was the prescription and picked up *Crime and Punishment*, lately on a Dostoyevsky jag, but even Raskolnikov's travails couldn't keep me from inventorying my own list of upending life circumstances. I finally gave in to compulsive thought:

Obviously, there was Jane. I'd be curious to see what she wanted to talk about tomorrow. I suspected her sudden willingness to engage was not only about my dad's situation, but also a response to the void I'd created with my recent silent strategy. I wished the idea of talking to her made me feel better, a little more victorious, but some of the air had seeped out of the "getting us back together" bubble. It was starting to feel like maybe, just maybe, we'd gone too far, let the separation go on too long. But tomorrow's meeting would give me opportunity to find out.

The bigger issue for me was the Barbara scenario. That one was sitting in the middle of my mental living room like an elephant playing the bagpipes, so much damn noise going on there. Now that I was hours away from my revelation at the hospital, I decided to check back in with my psyche to see if I felt any differently after mixing time and distance into the equation. Nope. Nor did I have any clearer sense of what I should do about it. Or if I even *should* do anything about it. Probably not. What would that be anyway? Some kind of lame statement to Mom about what I thought Dad was really trying to say? What would that do? She'd already been hurt enough by that fucking story; why would I choose to reopen the wound? There was no option that made sense other than to let it go. Barbara from Oakland was a specter that didn't need dredging up. I guess I would just let my dad die with those words on his lips.

Fuck.

*Let my dad die.* That was a stunning combination of words to think out loud. I realize there is no *letting* or *not letting* on my part, at least not at this point—dear God, hopefully not at *any* point—but putting "dad" and "die" in the same sentence was a mind fuck.

I used to think about death all the time when I was a kid, pondering what it felt like, if you knew when it was happening, if it was terrifying or as freeing as some have reported. I wondered what happened if you died in your sleep—if you were aware that you'd transitioned out of your dream state and into the actual expiration of your physical self, or if you thought you were still happily dreaming. It remains a topic that looms in and out for me. When you have older parents you know it's likely to be upon you sooner than your peers with younger parents, but it's something I can't quite wrap my brain around in real life. Death in real life. Strange paradox.

But older parent or not, Jim still seems too young to die. Seventy-three is the new fifty, right? He's always been so strong, the kind of guy who'd be impossible, really, to kill. Why now, when I'm struggling with my own crises, would my old man die? I know that's a stupid, selfish, utterly narcissistic question on so many levels, but really, why do I have to deal with that major fucking milestone when I'm already dealing with so many others?

I don't want to. I don't. I don't want the opportunity to discover how much I love the grumpy old fuck just because he's no longer in this world.

## TWENTY-ONE

JANE'S KITCHEN. OUR kitchen. Strange that it felt so foreign to me already. It had only been a few weeks. I used to eat breakfast at this table every day; now I was sitting here like a stranger picking at cherry pie and feeling like it was time I be on my way.

I looked up at Jane, chattering in some nervous manifestation of her discomfort, and observed her like I was watching a movie with the sound off. She swirled around the kitchen making coffee and wiping down the counter, sitting down, getting up, chattering on top of more chattering about whatever it was she was chattering about—I didn't know, I wasn't listening—and all I could think was, why did she make cherry pie when she knows apple is my favorite?

At some point I realized I needed to tune back into the conversation or this would surely take longer than I wanted and likely be less productive. So I tuned back in.

"...so then Gordon tells Tina to call Shandi and say he needs the spreadsheets on his desk, with her evaluations, no later than the next morning, and Tina just freaks! I don't know if you remember me talking about it, but she's been trying to fix these two up for—"

"I don't care." If I'd thought more about it I might have said something less abrupt, but it was all I could muster at the moment.

She stopped talking, startled. "What?"

"I don't mean to be ruder than usual, Jane, but I really don't care about the mating rituals of your adolescent boss, a man I can't stand, who has more money than me despite the fact that he's a moron, a crappy CPA and, from what I hear, has a really small dick." I immediately felt bad about embarrassing her but I was serious. I could not listen to one more word of this stuff.

Her face reddened. Which made me cringe. "I'm sorry. I was just trying to make conversation."

"I'm sorry, too. But I'm really fucked up right now."

She reached over and took my hand. "I know."

I suddenly felt confused and a little impatient. The schizophrenic nature of our relationship was not only unsettling, but starting to chafe. This time I pulled my hand from hers. "Listen, I've actually got to get to the hospital soon, so…what did you want to talk to me about?"

She took a somewhat dramatic pause then gazed at me with the kind of soft eyes I hadn't seen in over a month. "I miss you, Danny. That's really all I wanted to say. I'm sorry I've been so crazy. I know it's been hard and, now with your dad sick, I didn't want you to feel completely abandoned."

I looked at her without a shift in expression. I'd been waiting to hear some version of those words for a long time. And my first response?

"I want to take a break." This declaration surprised even me, but in the second it took to check my emotional pulse after the words popped out, I realized it was exactly what I wanted to say.

She, however, appeared confused. "We *have* been taking a break."

"We've been taking a break because *you* wanted a break. I want a break now because *I* want a break."

"What, is this a competition?" Her eyes were no longer soft.

"No, it's confusion. It's frustration. It's a lot of things. Maybe it's just that I'm not so sure about anything anymore either."

"What does that mean?"

Interesting that she'd ask me that. I'd been asking her the same question for weeks and getting nothing in response. But I was so sick of this deadlock. I wanted to do things differently, which was why I really had to think about my answer.

What *did* it mean? How much did I want to say to her right now and how far did I want to push this? I took another quick pulse check; yep, it was real.

"To be completely honest, and after a lot of time alone going over everything, I'm not sure anymore how right we are for each other. When I think about your response to what happened, about my disagreement with that response, think about what appears to be a disparity in our worldviews on these really important issues, I'm not convinced we're in synch. Or that there isn't somebody else out there who'd be a better fit, more authentically the person we're meant to be with."

That was a mouthful....and pretty much all of it had originated from Lucy's mouth.

Jane looked at me like I'd hit her. "I thought you said I *was* the person you were meant to be with," she said in a very small, stricken voice. Which sort of killed me—though not enough to doubt what I was feeling.

"I know. I think we both thought that about each other. I mean, we were planning a wedding, for God's sake! But at this point, after everything that's happened, there's nothing left to do but be honest with each other. And, Jane, I'm not trying to point fingers, but you *were* the one who forced this separation. It really pissed me off, as you know, but it also forced me to consider some things I might not have otherwise. And, like you, I've come to some different conclusions."

She appeared sideswiped by the unexpected turn in the conversation. "I never said I came to any conclusions; I just said I was feeling insecure and unsettled—"

"Actually, you said, and I quote, 'everything's changed.' That's a bit more than 'insecure and unsettled.' And look, that's your prerogative. It kicked my ass to hear you say it, but obviously it's your prerogative. All I'm saying is that right now it feels like everything's changed for me, too."

There was a beat of silence as she sat staring at her hands. "I'm wondering how much of this you really mean…or how long you'll decide to really mean it."

Odd comments. "Trust me, this isn't an overnight hissy fit or something I'm doing to create an effect. We've been in a serious separation that came with lots of time to reassess things and make new decisions, and I've taken the time to do exactly that. Isn't that what people are supposed to do in these situations?"

"Yes, to figure things out. But they don't necessarily see them as reasons to just end things!"

"I'm not *just* anything. It's been almost five weeks! I'm a little confused about what you thought would happen if you kept ignoring me and keeping me out of my house, with no communication, no nothing, for five weeks and who knows how much longer after that!"

"I thought we'd get past it. I thought we'd ultimately figure it out."

"Well, so did I, for maybe the first three weeks. Then it felt like we'd gone past the point of no return. Which sucks, but we wouldn't be here if there wasn't a reason." Yep, I was convinced of that now.

"A reason? Of course there's a reason."

"I don't mean the Marci thing. It's bigger than that."

"What do you mean?"

This, right here, tapped at the crux of my emerging epiphany. "I think if we were really right for each other none of this would've happened. At least not the way it has. You wouldn't have reacted the way you did. The separation wouldn't be into its second month. Neither of us would be feeling like 'everything's changed.' I think when there's an authentic soul mate connection, a concept I've never fully explored before, these things—"

She cut me off without a blink. "*Please* tell me you're not going to use that pathetic line as an excuse!"

I was taken aback by her vehemence. Clearly the soul mate theory did not resonate with her. "It's not an excuse; it's an ideal."

There was a pause. She looked at me as if she didn't know who I was. But, then again, she'd been looking at me like that for five weeks.

"What?" I finally asked.

"Are you punishing me for kicking you out?"

"No."

"Really? Because that's what it feels like."

"I'm not and I'm sorry you feel that way. But this is not as much about you as it's about me." Even I winced at the depth of that cliché.

She rolled her eyes. "How original!"

Suddenly a wave of fatigue washed over me. I didn't want to do this anymore. I didn't want to sit here dissecting our relationship for the eight-hundredth time. I wanted to get to the hospital and spend a little time with my dad, I wanted to shake this off and stop feeling so damn shitty on a day-to-day basis, and none of this recycling conversation was getting me any closer to any of that.

"Jane, it may be clumsy, the way I'm putting all this, but it's what I'm actually going through, what I'm feeling, and I don't know how else to say it."

But just as our relationship had probably gone past the point of no return, this conversation had hit a similar marker. The law of diminishing returns applied itself with a vengeance.

"Oh, what you're *feeling*, what you're *going through*." She said these as if they were diseases. "Well, I'd *feel* real sorry for you, Dan, but let's not forget how all this started."

"Oh, how could I, with your constant reminders?"

"So, you're going to go from Marci to me to whoever else is next, over and over, until you're a sad, stupid old man, all by yourself, always hoping the next person you stumble on might be 'the one,' your soul mate, is that it?"

"Well, if you think my need to explore who might be more right for me than you means I'm destined to be a sad, stupid old man, I'd say you're a little bit full of yourself." I had no idea why I was getting so snarly. It was completely unnecessary, and I knew I should get up and leave before this got really ugly.

But she did have a way at times—like right now—of minimizing my stated feelings, of doing what she could to make me feel as small as I could possibly feel, and I was *so* not in the mood for that size at the moment. I started to stand and she quickly beat me to it, almost knocking her chair over in the effort. I couldn't stop from rolling my own eyes.

"Really, Jane?"

"You're an asshole, Dan, you know that? I started off wanting to fix things with us and now I just think you're an asshole."

"Then I guess we're right back where we started."

"I guess so! So let's not belabor the point; I'm sure you have better things to do. Don't want you to lose any time on your soul mate search, unless, of course, you've already started!"

Then her eyes welled up, and once more I felt like crap. This was so nuts. And not remotely my plan. "Jesus, Jane…let's not do this. I'm too tired for this, and all I'm trying to say is that everything that's happened, including a bunch of stuff with my dad, has had its impact. I need a break from trying to figure out this relationship. It's not working right now, that's all I know. Maybe you've decided that even though things suck between us it's still somehow enough for you…but it's not for me. My father says life is about settling for the hand we're dealt, but I think that's a pretty cynical way to look at things. I think we each get to explore our options until we find true happiness. And I think it's my time to do that." There, I said it…though none of it sounded as good out loud as it had in my head.

Apparently she agreed. Jane marched to the door, flung it open, and declared, "Then take your break, take your options, and take your ass out of here."

I paused. This felt monumental. But there was nothing else to say. So I walked out, defiant, head held high. Me, the bludgeoner of hearts...but a man taking control of his life.

Her...slamming the door.

## TWENTY-TWO

HOSPITAL ROOMS ARE, from my perspective, the least calm and healing places a sick person could possibly be. Beyond the entrapment of machinery with its incessant alarms and whirring and popping, I have not witnessed as much sheer traffic since the last time I got stuck on the 405 Freeway. But he was still alive. They were doing at least that right.

I'd relieved Lucy an hour earlier and sent Esther home for a shower and some fresh clothes, and, sitting now at my dad's bedside, I realized it was the first time I'd ever watched him sleep. Or whatever it was he was experiencing in that shadow state of suspension. Strange, feeling like he was so vulnerable and weak and I was there to protect him from…what? Death? An errant nurse? Bad hospital food?

The drive over from Jane's had been hammered with fleeting doubt mixed with the general conviction that I'd handled it all pretty badly. But I was also relieved. It was done. A period at the end of the sentence. At least now I knew what my next move was; I wasn't waiting for her permission to make it. I love Jane; I will always love

Jane—she's the first woman I ever asked to marry me—but whatever happened in these last five weeks happened because we really *aren't* right for each other. That seems evident. We're both good people but our individual neuroses just don't mix, don't click into place. Over time I think she'll be grateful we made the break when we did. No one wants to live in a relationship where every challenge becomes a catastrophe.

Jim stirred a bit and I sat up, alert. There was some general twitching and jerking under the sheets, but ultimately he quieted down. Again I found myself gazing at him, trying to figure out who was in there, in that colorless shell of the robust man who'd rather see me crack my skull on a clay court than ever give up a point. I was strangely compelled to pick up his hand. It felt dry and cold, the flesh mottled with bruises from the attached intravenous tubes and various blood tests. I laced our fingers together like we used to when he'd walk me across the street to my kindergarten class, and the gesture felt intimate and strange after so many years of distancing and batting away. I squeezed but no response was forthcoming.

His breathing was labored and seemed to be getting faster, and just as I was about to get up and see if a nurse should come check him, Jim's eyes fluttered open, again with that wild, disoriented look of someone waking from a bad dream. I reached up and put my hand on his forehead, thinking it might calm him. "It's okay, Dad, it's okay," I said over and over.

In a sudden, startling burst, he snapped out of the fog and his eyes locked onto mine. He held the gaze for a silent moment, which unnerved me, not sure what to do; then he opened his mouth in an attempt to speak: "Aaah...caaa...baaa...baaa...ah caaa...." The effort exhausted him and he closed his eyes again, clearly drained.

Once more I felt my gut knot with the visceral certainty of what he was trying to say. I leaned in close to his ear and said as clearly as I could, "Dad, are you saying 'call Barbara'? Is that what you're trying to tell me? You want me to call Barbara?"

Jim opened his eyes and looked off wildly, teary and confused. I felt him try to lift his arm to make a gesture but he wasn't able to. "Baaa....baaa," he repeated over and over, looking as tragic and terrified as a man drowning in the middle of the ocean. Then he drifted back to unconsciousness.

That was it. My mind was made up. I squeezed his hand tightly. "Dad, you can relax; I got it. And I'm going to take care of this for you, okay? I'm going to keep it to myself, but I'm going to take care of this. You can count on me."

I leaned my forehead on the edge of the bed and felt the wheels turning.

## TWENTY-THREE

I DROVE TO Lucy's house. I knew she wasn't home, but I wasn't looking for her; I was looking for an accordion file with a yellowed, rejected manuscript about an event that happened in 1965. I shoved through the door, rushed to my designated bedroom, and grabbed the file from the closet where I'd stashed it nights earlier. I rifled through the old magazines until I found "The Woman Between the Lines." I pulled it out, sat down on the bed, and started scanning through the lines and paragraphs until I got to her name: Barbara. From Oakland. Okay, Barbara from Oakland, where could you be?

I'm not sure if I thought staring at her name would somehow reveal more information than was actually there, but I read that line over and over, hoping some cogent idea would jump into my head and lead me somewhere. It didn't. I was going to have to do a cold search, figure a way to find out if this woman still existed, if she was still in Oakland, and, if she was, *where* she was. Clearly I needed more than "Barbara from Oakland," and given the passage of time since this event occurred, odds of finding anything else were not good. Particularly without a last name or address.

I pulled everything from the accordion file and literally turned that thing as inside out as an accordion file will go. Random slips of paper fluttered to the bed and I grabbed each one as if it were gold, hoping for clues about something, anything; I didn't even know what I was looking for. There was one slip with a couple of scribbled names, completely illegible; a crumpled receipt from what appeared to be a gas station; another that looked like the ripped portion of a magazine page, no idea why it was there. But nothing of any particular usefulness.

I skimmed through the story yet again, like a code breaker trying to ferret out patterns, salient words or phrases that stood out, thoughts or ideas that might mean something. And this time through one line did jump out at me: "We spent most of that afternoon together, taking silly snapshots with my Kodak..."

*There were pictures.* Specifically from *his* camera. Had he kept any of those? It was a pivotal summer for a twenty-two-year-old guy falling in love for the first time. He didn't even write the story until over a year later. That was a good long time of some serious mooning, so he surely would have kept any pictures he might have had of the girl he was mooning over. But if he threw out the story, why wouldn't he have thrown the pictures out as well?

Unless he'd tossed them somewhere way back when and just forgot about them or didn't want to take the time to find them. Both my parents tended to stockpile souvenirs and mementos. The various storage spaces in our two homes always had stacks of photo albums, scrapbooks with trip pamphlets and train tickets, even boxes of loose photographs that never made it into any of those albums. There were so many that, at one point, my mom attempted to identify and categorize them by year. I don't know how far she got with that project, but if my father held on to any of those "silly snapshots" from the summer of 1965, it's likely they'd be in one of those dusty boxes.

I felt my pulse quicken at the thought of doing some bona fide investigation. I had a plan; I had a purpose; I was going to my parents' house to see what I could find. And I had to do it without Lucy's awareness. She was not exactly tracking with me on this whole Barbara angle, and yet I was feeling increasingly convinced it was the most essential angle to pursue.

I checked the time and realized I needed to get to a gig. I tucked the Barbara manuscript into my camera bag, put everything else back in the accordion file, and stood up. When I did, a small piece of paper drifted to the floor from my lap. I bent down and picked it up; it was a ripped corner of a larger piece of yellowed paper. Like the paper of the manuscript. I quickly pulled the story from my bag, flipped through it and, sure enough, the third page had a missing corner. The piece of paper fit exactly into that space on the page.

I turned the piece over and could make something out: words, maybe numbers, in the faintest of pencil. This was significant, but the writing was so faded I couldn't read it clearly. I held the torn corner up to the light and…unbelievable. It was a phone number. No area code, just seven digits with a dash in the appropriate spot. Seven digits of a phone number on the back of a corner ripped from a page of the manuscript about my dad's summer with Barbara from Oakland.

What were the odds those seven digits were her phone number?

# TWENTY-FOUR

SOMETIME BETWEEN THE discovery of that number and the rush to my gig, I called 411 and determined that the area code for Oakland was 510. Just to have it. You never know. It might come in handy.

But despite the pull of my evolving investigation, despite my obligations to Lucy, my dad and my mother, the burgeoning demands of my job were not to be denied. I'd gotten backed up on appointments, with a slew to keep, most of which I'd actually sold and set up myself. This was not the time for distracted behavior, as much as I felt distracted. I stayed admirably focused the rest of the day.

And the good will this hearty workflow garnered from Joaquin was something to behold. I actually saw the man smile when Zoey and I staggered in from an exceedingly long series of photo sessions—though half the reason Zoey staggered was the foot cast she'd acquired after an unfortunate yoga accident. That girl could still sling a tripod, though, and Joaquin giddily referred to us as his "Dream Team," not a particularly original assignation but certainly an appreciated one.

As we sat at our desks getting through our various paperwork and computer uploads, I was aware that the strange thoughts nipping at my brain since my discovery of that faded phone number were once again in full nip. In fact, those nipping thoughts never seemed to completely stop; they just receded in times of necessary focus. But now they were back, like rabid Pac-Men making their way through my synapses, chomping madly and refusing to be ignored. I pulled my wallet out of my back pocket and removed the ripped corner of the manuscript page. I set it on the desk. Circled the number. Wrote "Barbara?" next to it. Then "Oakland/510?" I took my phone out of my pocket and set it on the desk as well, peering at it as if some action would be forthcoming.

Zoey looked up. "Waiting for a call or are you as amazed by the patheticness of your phone as we all are?"

I threw a pencil at her.

"See, that's how you take out an eye." She threw it back and missed.

A few quiet moments went by, then, in a spastic jump, I picked up the phone and punched in the number, adding the Oakland area code. It rang and rang and rang, and then…someone answered. A woman answered. I opened my mouth to speak and nothing came out. I snapped the phone shut and set it down like it was on fire.

Zoey said nothing, and didn't need to: her eye-roll spoke volumes. But when I'd heard an actual voice, the tremulous "hello" of a distant stranger, the shift in the time/space continuum knocked the wind out of me. The woman who answered—soft, welcoming, and, quite possibly, older—likely expected a response, but I had no idea what to say.

## TWENTY-FIVE

BY THE NEXT day, Zoey's ankle had swollen to the size of a small child so Bob stepped into the rest of the week's assignments, grateful for the work during a lull in his fine art and wedding photography gigs. Again, I'm not jealous, just observant. And happy to throw some income a friend's way.

We were doing portraits for a very wealthy family at their Holmby Hills mansion, and I was once again astonished, as I so often am, that this one-percent world existed not all that far from my still-homeless state in the valley. But hey, I'm thrilled that someone has the lifestyle; what would I aspire to otherwise?

It was a fairly formal sitting, one Joaquin booked through his more politically oriented contact list, so my usual sassy style was sublimated for the demands of a sport-jacketed portraitist somberly capturing several generations of well-heeled Los Angelenos. It was exhausting. I was glad Bob was there to offer the exact right tone of deference and professionalism. Zoey would have been like a zoo animal in there.

And they were pleased, the one-percenters, which pleased me, and would no doubt please Joaquin. With a job well done, and it being Friday night, Bob and I spryly wrapped up with plans to hit a nearby microbrewery for dinner and decompression.

"Thank you, sir, for your kind assistance," I said as I handed him a rather impressive tip.

"No problem. And thanks! I'm happy to help, but hope Zoey's ankle mends soon. That thing looked nasty."

"Too bad our insurance doesn't cover tree pose failures."

"Wow. Insurance, huh?"

"Yeah. See how fun these real jobs are?" Any time my full-time perks trumped his artistic freedom was worth pointing out.

He laughed. "Well, I'm happy to plug in when I can. No weddings until next month and you know how magazine work goes."

Actually, I *didn't* know how magazine work went, but I got the point. "You could always go out on your own with portrait gigs. You've got that fine art angle, and Joaquin tells me people love that."

Bob wasn't the entrepreneurial sort, as we'd often discussed, so he just looked at me with a smirk. "Let me know when you're ready to go into business, and willing to do all the hard labor, and we'll talk."

As we headed out, we chatted in that comfortable way we had with each other, me assuring him I'd be looking for an apartment next week, him reiterating that I was welcome to stay as long as needed; me complaining about the state of music on the radio, him changing the station from my preferred blues to his current Nashville predilection.

"Country music is not allowed in my car," I remarked as some twangy fellow carried on.

"What, you don't like a guy in cowboy boots and a fishnet shirt?"

"Not unless he's an old black man with twelve bars and a banjo."

"Hey, remember that girl I told you about, the one with the Canon 5D for sale? She called and wants to know if you're still interested."

"It's the Mark III, right? Still under warranty?"

"I think so."

"Yeah...I'd like to get it, but with all the upheaval with Jane and the fact that I've got to get my own place coming up, I don't think throwing four grand at a camera I don't absolutely need is a good idea."

"She said she'd go to three."

"Still."

"Yeah."

"Besides, the one I've got is doing fine, so I'm good for now."

"You always were one for hanging on to your stuff. I admire that in you, my friend. I can't believe this old beater of yours is still kickin'. What is it, a '92?"

"You sound like my old man. Actually it's an '87. Quattro Coupe. Mint, as you may have noticed."

"You do take stellar care of it, that's a fact. Speaking of your dad, how's he doing?"

"Same."

"Jane?"

"I think we broke up again."

"So...same?"

"Pretty much." I grimaced. We'd become *that* couple.

"Lucy hanging in there?"

"Like the soldier she is."

"Esther?"

"Still singing the '70s."

"That's my girl."

"I'll pass that on."

"So everything's pretty much status quo?"

"I called Barbara yesterday."

He sat straight up, eyes popped like a cartoon double take. "Barbara from Oakland? You called the woman from 1965?"

"I don't know if it was her."

"Why, what did she say? What did you ask her?"

"I hung up before I could ask her anything."

"But you actually found her number?"

"I found a number on this piece of paper ripped from the story manuscript. What are the odds it's hers?"

"Not good? Hardly possible? Probably not? Was it even an Oakland area code?"

"There was no area code, just a number. I don't even know if they had area codes in 1965. But, come on! Doesn't that seem a little too coincidental?"

"Does it? Seems to me it could be, oh, so many other possibilities."

"I'm getting a gut thing."

"Man, you are truly wigged out."

"Seems so."

"I cannot believe you did that!"

"I can't either. Feels like I might be fucking with the time/space continuum."

"You just might be! But I'm kind of impressed. Also wondering if you're getting a little creepy with this."

"I was kind of wondering that, too. But I'm compelled."

"Then fuck calling; drive on up to Oakland and track her down!"

I looked at him, incredulous. "Are you kidding me?"

He practically barked. "Of course I am, Dan! Jesus Christ. Why? *Would* you?"

"No…of course not."

"You got that right, brother."

Thankfully the bar was up ahead. Drinks were needed all around.

## TWENTY-SIX

ON MY WAY into the office Monday morning I swung by a couple of places I'd circled on Apartment Hunters, deciding to get a jump on my pending relocation. A quick drive down the designated streets made clear neither would be neighborhoods I could tolerate. Frankly, I was having a hard time getting it up for the task, figuring since Bob was in no rush to get me out I could be lackadaisical about it. The word "lackadaisical" sounded like something my old man would say, which reminded me of him, leading to a stab of anxiety about his continuing state of suspended unconsciousness.

Lucy and I had brought this fact up to Dr. Kamen last night, concerned about what it meant that, other than his two "caa…baaa…baaa" moments, there'd been no real progress. He said this was not uncommon and was often the body's way of healing and calming down impacted nerves. But we were almost two weeks in, with Lucy and me both spending time there daily, and we were feeling the strain, emotionally and logistically, on every level. Esther, meanwhile, seemed simply to have shifted her normal, perky, Jim-ministrations from home to hospital. Her imperturbability, one assumes, was a result of enduring the man for the last four decades.

Waiting at a light, I glanced to my left and noticed a billboard advertising a condo development on the good side of Ventura that Jane and I had planned to look at after we got married. There was a rush of…what? I didn't know; I couldn't tell what I was feeling half the time. There were moments when I found myself pondering and missing and hating and being glad I was no longer with Jane all in the same swirling mass of conflicted emotion. And it amazed me that, despite proximity, I never saw her. Ever. It was as if she'd vanished into the vortex of the house across the way. It was either intentional or I was coming and going at remarkably non-conflicting times. The fact that I was enmeshed in all this speculation told me I really needed to find my own place.

But on a day-to-day basis, I wasn't missing her all that much. Shouldn't I be missing her more? I hadn't had sex in over six weeks and, frankly, sex with Jane, making love to Jane, feeling Jane's body next to mine, was, well…quite something. Always had been. So shouldn't I be missing that more? I mean, I was *missing* it, but shouldn't I be more systemically upset about it all? There was just a weird emptiness when I thought about her most of the time, weird because only weeks earlier we'd been actively planning a wedding. To say, "I do." To promise to love each other for the rest of our living days. How do you go from the precipice of that promise to the void of detachment in a few short weeks?

When I mentioned this to Lucy she said it was probably some kind of protective disassociation. I figured it had more to do with awakening to the soul mate theory, the blessing and/or curse handed to me by my quixotic sister, who now had me convinced of the invisible hand of Divine Intervention. But I did wonder if and when I might wake up in a puddle of screaming grief over the realization that Jane and I were no more.

I was headed into the studio a little earlier than usual. I'd gotten a text from Joaquin the night before asking if I could come in early to discuss some business matters—I presumed it was regarding the "ideas" he alluded to a few weeks ago. When I arrived and found neither Zoey nor any of the freelance staff in attendance, I sat at my desk with the faintest sense-memory of waiting outside the principal's office.

Suddenly his door swung open and Joaquin invited me into his large, eclectically decorated sanctum where I found lattes, scones, and Craig, the portly, soft-spoken studio accountant who rarely made personal appearances. Craig smiled cordially and I wondered again, as I often wondered, if he and Joaquin were a couple. Or if Joaquin was, in fact, even gay. I didn't know these things. Much was assumed but one didn't know. Anyway, the breakfast spread and the atypical grin on Joaquin's face were harbingers of good things to come, so I unclenched and grabbed a cranberry scone.

Joaquin stood behind his desk, fingers splayed to affect a lawyerly pose, and cleared his throat. Very dramatic; very Joaquin. "Daniel, Craig and I have been going over the books, assessing the status and trajectory of the business as a whole, and, to be completely honest, we were quite surprised to see just how much business you've brought into the studio over these past four years."

My shoulders relaxed about two inches. "Well, thanks, guys. I'm glad it's working out. It's good for all of us."

"Frankly, I feel I should apologize for not recognizing it sooner. I don't think there's anyone here who's been as instrumental in helping us grow this business since we opened, and we'd like to offer our enthusiastic gratitude! So, thank you, Daniel!" At this point he bowed like a visiting dignitary.

I had to squelch a grin at the pomp of it all, but since Joaquin rarely got this gushing when it came to the business end of things, I also had to acknowledge it was a really nice gesture, and said so. "I appreciate that, Joaquin. It's very nice of you to mention it, and I can't say I mind the scones either." I grinned. He grinned. Then he continued:

"But I want to do more than offer thanks, and that's why you're here. I've been doing a lot of thinking about where I want to go in my business life, and Craig and I have been meeting lately to brainstorm ideas. Craig?" Joaquin turned to Craig with a prompting nod.

Craig stood up as if preparing to address to the court, and since I'm not sure I'd ever heard the guy utter more than a few words, nor could I imagine what he was about to say, my curiosity was at fever pitch.

"Dan."

"Craig," I said somberly, as if we were meeting for the first time.

Craig paused and cleared his throat, another very serious sort. I could see why he and Joaquin made a good pair. I mean, if they were a pair. Outside of business. Anyway, Craig peered down at his notes and began his summation. "Joaquin is looking to branch out into some new ventures; some of the things he's considering may even be outside the realm of the photographic businesses." He stopped. I stifled the urge to smirk as he shifted through his notes with all the flounder of a rookie attorney. "But he's also looking to expand this studio, perhaps with franchises, perhaps with just one other location to begin with. But he cannot do any of that on his own. We've been involved in a hearty due diligence process with a number of potential candidates, and over and over we kept coming back to you."

That surprised me. To realize anyone had been thinking about me, specifically, was astonishing. I found myself flattered and alarmed at the same time.

Craig looked up as if to gauge my response; I smiled, knowing my pleasure was the expectation. He smiled briefly in return, then continued (interesting how, with only a few sentences, he'd managed to make this speech seem very long). "You know the business, you have exemplary technical skills, and you've shown an aptitude for solid and consistent sales. Additionally, and most importantly, you've already been here with us for four years, you've built up a prodigious client list, *and* you have the confidence of your fellow workers, so we could not imagine a better choice than you." He stopped.

Now both Joaquin and Craig gazed at me expectantly. And still I had no idea what, exactly, they were talking about.

"Wow. Thanks, you guys. You made my day. But, to be honest, I'm not exactly sure what you believe I'm the best choice for."

Joaquin jumped in at this point, speaking almost as if I were a silly child. "Daniel! I want to make you a partner, that's what! It's time I expand my horizons and get out to try some other things, but this studio is my baby, so it's very important to me that it thrives and flourishes. So I need a partner, a partner in this studio. To grow with it and participate in its potential expansion. We believe you'd be a perfect fit!"

I was stunned. I had zero idea he'd been thinking along these lines. A raise, maybe, but this?

"We'd start with a seventy/thirty split. You're the thirty, of course!" He grinned as if the clarification was both essential and superfluous. "There would be no expectation of capital input—your client list suffices for that—but I want you involved enough financially to take a proprietary interest in where we go from here. We'd offer full benefits, a significant salary bump with commissions, stock options, the whole ball of wax!" He paused briefly, peering at me for response. "How does that sound?"

I was honestly and completely bowled over. "Wow, Joaquin, I'm...I'm speechless."

"Well, you *are* getting married—"

Yep, hadn't brought him up to speed on that yet.

"—but more than that, you're at that time of life when—"

Here it comes, something about thirty-three, being a man—

"—what are you now, thirty-three?"

Bingo. "That's right, thirty-three."

"Which is an age when a man usually makes some pretty big decisions regarding his profession and his family life. And before you know it..." Again with the grin.

Before I know what? Oh, dear God...*that!* "Oh, I don't think there'll be any of them any time soon!"

"Well, at some point there will be, and you'll want to have built a solid financial foundation for that family of yours! I cannot imagine a better situation for either of us than you growing that foundation right here. I want you here, Daniel; I hope you will join us!"

This was so completely unexpected I didn't quite know how to respond. "Well, Joaquin, this is…great, and…I want to, obviously, I want to give it some serious thought. Of course, I want to talk it over with…Jane." I swallowed hard with that one. "See how she feels about the idea."

"I understand. If you both want to sit down with us and—"

Just then my phone rang; it was my mother. My heart stopped. "Joaquin, it's my mom. I've got to take it."

"Of course. But please come back in when you're done so we can wrap this up."

I stepped out to the hallway. "Mom, what's up? Something happen with Dad?"

"No, honey, I wish something had—I mean, something good. But he's the same. I called to ask if you could stop by the house and pick up my red slippers on your way in. These floors are so cold and I keep forgetting to bring them."

I couldn't help but feel a pang of tenderness for poor Esther. She'd spent every single day in that place since the old man fell, with not a complaint nor criticism expressed. Well, other than the cold floors. "Sure, Mom, I'll bring them later tonight. I've got to go now, though; I'm in a meeting."

"Oh, sorry, honey!"

"No worries, Mom. I'll see you a little later." She didn't hang up. "Is there something else?"

"I wanted to be sure you emailed everyone about the anniversary party being canceled. I know Lucy's been too busy to get it done but it's important that people know so they can rearrange their plans."

"I got all those out a few days ago, Mom. Everyone I've heard from so far has been very understanding and they're all sending their best. I'm keeping copies of the notes so you can read them later."

"Oh, thank you, sweetheart. I appreciate that."

"Okay, Mom, I gotta—"

"I'm feeling so helpless today, Danny. Your father had another one of those waking up things, where he looks around and keeps yelling 'caa baaa baa' or whatever it is he's saying, and I'm just so upset that I can't understand him."

It jolted me that he'd again called out Barbara's name. I could tell Esther was holding back tears. I realized I hadn't seen her cry, I mean really cry, even once since this whole thing started. "Aw, Mom, I understand how you feel, but it could take a while for him to be able to communicate clearly, so don't be so hard on yourself."

"It breaks my heart that I can't help him...mostly because I have no idea what he wants."

But *I* did. My emotional pulse was racing again and I felt a new surge of conviction. Now it was getting to her, which was getting to me. We said our goodbyes and I walked slowly back to Joaquin's office.

"Everything okay, Daniel?"

"Yes, she just needs her red slippers."

Joaquin smiled, then immediately got back to business. "Well, I'm sure we all need to get going with the day, so let me ask what you're thinking about our proposal at this point."

"It's an incredible offer, and I'm going to give it some honest, serious thought. Can I do that and get back to you?"

"Of course. This is a big commitment. Take your time."

"Actually, I do need time...some time off."

"Time off? Really?"

"Yes."

"When?"

"Right now."

"Right now? Oh, well, that's a problem, Daniel. You're booked with a very heavy week, what with both Kaiser and Occidental College and—"

"I know, Joaquin, which is why I've got Bob Fiedler on line to fill in. Zoey said she's ready to get back to assisting tomorrow, and things are pretty light for him at the moment, so I know he'd appreciate the work." And was, hopefully, available. "Any problem with that?"

"Well...no, Bob's an excellent photographer. But what's going on? I haven't heard a thing about this. Is there something we can help you with?"

"Thanks, but no; it's about my father. Some things I need to take care of for him, things I can't put off any longer. I'll be taking off tomorrow morning and, presuming Bob can cover the week, I'll be back for the charity gig on Saturday."

"Yes, good, because we need all hands on deck for that one."

"I know, I'll be there. And thanks, Joaquin, for the time and the offer. I appreciate both."

Until the moment I was offered that partnership, until my mother's growing angst hit my radar, and until I heard that my father had called out Barbara's name again, I had no idea I was going to ask for time off. Now it seemed like the only thing I could do.

I was going to hunt her down. I was going to hunt down Barbara from Oakland like she was the last woman on earth.

## TWENTY-SEVEN

THE REST OF Monday was a busy shooting day—Bob was on board and we covered one high school and two corporate gigs—but I managed to find time to get the small spiral notebook out of my camera case and start making lists of what I needed to find, what I needed to pull together, and what I needed to get done before I took off in the morning. I begged off lunch with some random excuse about a dentist appointment, but in truth I wanted to step away briefly to gather, ponder, and organize my many tumultuous thoughts. I grabbed some In-N-Out and sat at a park bench making notes and going over my strategy.

First of all, and let's be frank, there was no strategy. I had no idea what I was doing. None at all. I was driving to Oakland. That was as specific as it got. And Oakland is a big city, with lots of people, and I needed lots more information to go on: landmarks, clues…pictures. I had to find the pictures.

I'd already planned to stop by my folks' house after work to pick up Esther's red slippers, so after we wrapped our last shoot and Bob took off for his evening plans, I headed over to their place with the intent of ransacking every inch of that freaking house until I found something, *anything*, that offered clues to Barbara from Oakland. I wished I could've talked to Lucy about it (couldn't). I really wished I could've asked Esther where the photo boxes might be (couldn't). And, of course, there were the voices in the back of my head sniggering that this was the most irrational and deeply misguided plan ever. For now I was ignoring those little fuckers.

It was weird being in my parents' home with neither of them present. I couldn't remember the last time I'd been there under those circumstances. Maybe never. I paced the house flipping on lights and looking around: my old room (still with workout equipment that looked generally unused); the "treasure chest" that was Lucy's room (a strong candidate for items useful to the investigation), and the basement (surprisingly messy, given Esther's proclivity for neatness). I even got a ladder and climbed up to the attic (also a strong candidate). I wanted to get the full lay of the land before I invested too much time in any one spot; the urgency of my schedule was unforgiving.

The attic. Dank and dusty as one would expect from a place rarely occupied by seniors with little reason to risk a ladder, the attic held particular promise. There were countless stacks of scrapbooks, and boxes of various shapes and sizes strewn everywhere. I had an instinct this was the right spot to focus, the exact kind of place one would find random collections of loose, old photographs. I began pushing aside furniture and mounds of old sports equipment, and, as if the gods were smiling upon me, I hit pay dirt after only a few minutes of searching.

Behind racks of hanging clothes and old shoes were about fifteen small filing boxes with the years scribbled onto their sides: "1978-1979, 1982-1983," and so on. I wondered if there would even be a box from the '60s, a time before my mother came into my father's life, but as I continued to push and shove things out of the way, I found it. A box with "1960s" scrawled on the side in red marker. My heart started racing.

I cleared a space on the floor, ignoring the clouds of dust skittering in the shaft of light from the window above, and essentially climbed inside that decade of images. Kneading my fingers through the worn and weathered Polaroids, Kodak prints, and crinkle-edged snapshots, flipping them over to see notations, names, dates, locations, whatever I could find, my eyes were attuned for anything Kodak that read "1965," or looked like it had been shot at a beach during summer. Given that the era was not one shared by us as a family, this particular box was mercifully less abundant than the rest, but still, there were hundreds of photos to go through.

About two-thirds of the way into the pile, however, I started seeing images of sand, beach towels; umbrellas. Girls in swimsuits. Vintage shots of another time, another cultural moment: Beatle cuts, "mod" fashion, lots of plaids and headbands, even the whiff of imminent hippiedom.

Then I saw it: a photograph of my dad sporting a goofy grin. Handsome in his early twenties, he was seated on a tee-shirt next to a blanket of young girls, smiling up at the photographer…with a beautiful dark-haired girl sitting provocatively nearby.

Barbara from Oakland. Had to be.

I felt a bolt of discovery, the sense that I was truly onto something. This must be the rush detectives feel when they hit a bona fide, undeniable clue. Though I had no idea if the girl sitting next to my dad really *was* Barbara, it seemed hard to believe it could be anyone else. I started shuffling through the box more diligently now, pulling out any Kodak prints that looked remotely like they could be from the time and place. There were several. One of a bunch of guys standing together near the surf line, another of two fellows in shorts huddling with their arms around my dad, still another of my dad, bare chested, caught in a silly pose flexing his muscles. In one shot I could actually see the big rocks of Ocean Beach in the background, so this was definitely the right location.

I grabbed an empty shopping bag from a nearby chair and started filling it with the photos I wanted to take with me. I found three more with the same beautiful dark-eyed girl and by now I was utterly convinced she was Barbara. One captured her smiling widely under a Fisherman's Wharf sign; in another she was demurely seated on a bench in a very wooded park area; in still another, a darkly shadowed image that was hard to make out, she appeared to be seated inside a gazebo, likely the one my dad mentioned in the story. And then I found the picture that was the golden ticket.

Having read the story over countless times by now, I remembered another specific line from the manuscript, one that described the family's house and a particular gate at the end of their walkway. And at this moment, in my hand, was a picture of Barbara—in front of a bank of shrubs bordering the yard of a majestic California Craftsman—off to the side of what I could only assume was the *"ornate wrought iron gate of her family's house."* Unreal.

This picture was a stunning clue, one that would be of great value once I located the neighborhood and the street. There simply could not be that many houses with that kind of gate. Now all I had to do was find that neighborhood…and that street…and that house…with that gate…in the great big city of Oakland. Shouldn't be too difficult, right?

I didn't have time to ponder the absurdity of the question; I was already too far in either way. And finding the "silly snapshots" *was* as good as finding gold. That was worth at least a second of celebration.

# TWENTY-EIGHT

BOB TENDS TO be a calm, reasonable guy no matter what the circumstances, but as I packed my bag for the road trip north, his incredulity was notable.

"You don't know if the phone number is hers, you don't have an address; you're just going to drive up there with no fucking idea of where you're going or what you're doing and that's supposed to make sense?"

"I don't think any of this makes sense, Bob, but I have to do it."

"You understood I was kidding the other day when I said you should go up there, right?"

"Yes. I know you were kidding. I'm not."

"You may be truly insane."

I turned and looked at him with all the fervor I was feeling. "I get it; it's nuts. We both know that. But this is not a normal time in my life, in any part of my life, and when you read a story written by your old man in a voice you've never heard from the guy, then you *do* hear him calling out this woman's name while lying on what could be his death bed, and *then* someone answers at the number you have that might belong to the woman in question, tell me: what would you do?"

Bob sat down for the first time in thirty minutes. "I'd drive up to Oakland."

"Exactly. Look, if it turns out to be a lost cause, I'll basically have wasted some driving time and a few days away. My dad's status has been unchanged for weeks, but if anything happens I can be back here within hours. The point is, I have to *do* something that might actually have some impact. Right now all I can do is go to that room and look at him lying there…there's nothing I can *do*. *This* is something I can do."

"I have a feeling Lucy might see it otherwise."

I had yet to share my travel plans with Lucy. And Bob was right; it was unlikely she'd think highly of them. "Yeah…me, too." I was now rifling through the photos I'd taken from my parents' house.

"What's all that?" Bob asked. "You're planning to do a little scrapbooking before you head out?"

"I'm taking along some photos of my dad from 1965. Memory joggers, so to speak, in the event I find her. There's actually a few here of Barbara."

"Jesus, really?" He came over and started looking through them. "Amazing. You think?"

"Well, look at these." I fanned out the photos on the coffee table. "This is definitely Ocean Beach—look at the rock formations. And these were all in a box labeled '1960s.' There's my dad sitting next to this girl, as beautiful as the one he described in the story. That can't be coincidence."

Bob sifted through the pictures with a hint of awe. "Wow, you might actually be better at this than I've given you credit for. You really think these are Barbara?"

"Yeah, I do. But I'll call the number again tomorrow and see if it's hers. I have a strong feeling it might be. But, either way, something will shake loose. I just gotta get started."

Suddenly Bob was up again. "I don't know whether to strap you to a chair or pack you a lunch, but if you're set on doing this, let's be clear about the mission." He was now pacing like we were in the war room. "Are you leaving tonight or tomorrow?"

"I'll head out at the crack. Probably before you even get up."

"Okay. Tomorrow's Tuesday; I can cover you until Friday. I've got my Saturday booked, so you'll have to get back here for that big gala thing."

"I know; I already talked about it with Joaquin."

"Good. You've got four days, tops, more than enough time. You get up there, you find her, however you find her, you pick her brain and—wait, how exactly do you plan to pick her brain?"

"I don't know yet. I'll give that some thought on the ride up. Basically I want to be able to bring something back, something real for my dad, you know? I want to be able to tell him that I called her, I saw her, and she remembers him. I'm hoping I can report that the great love of his life mattered…and not just to him. That she understands what they had was special and rare, and whatever forced her to do what she did, well, she knows it was a mistake; that she threw something real away and she's sorry." I had no idea where all that came from, but it was ardent.

"Wait, are we still talking about Jim and Barbara?"

I looked up sharply. Bob was giving me the raised eyebrow. I rolled my eyes. "Yes! Of course we are. Who else would we be talking about?"

"Uh huh. But, okay, that's some serious brain pickin' to get done. So you do all that, however all that happens, then you get your ass back down here as quickly as possible."

"That's the plan."

"If Jane asks me anything, what do I tell her?"

"Well, we're broken up so it's really not—"

"I'll tell her you're on a vision quest or something vague like that. Now, with Lucy and Esther—"

"I'll figure something out. Leave that to me."

"Absolutely. As for me, well, I think you're nuts and…sort of cool at the same time."

And that's why I loved Bob. He didn't fully grasp my fixation on Barbara—he saw her reemergence as disruption rather than romantic nostalgia, and certainly wasn't as enthused as I was about revisiting the past. But in spite of that philosophical difference, he could make the switch when needed. He got unequivocally on board, particularly once he knew the decision was made and I would not be talked out of it. I appreciated that flexibility…and his way with provisions: I hit the road with a cooler of meatloaf sandwiches, sparkling water, and enough apples and protein bars to get me through to Friday.

The only thing I didn't have was a handle on how to explain my pilgrimage to Lucy or Mom. I was confident I'd come up with something that sounded good enough: an out-of-town job, a meeting of some kind, scouting shoot locations. This was a time when Bob's theory of truth finessing had some serious merit.

# TWENTY-NINE

HITTING THE ROAD by the dawn's early light gave me a rush of what...freedom? Considering the circumstances, there was some guilt in that realization, but I hadn't been out of town in a long time, and the thought of detaching from the madness of my life, particularly for the sake of a worthy cause, seemed a grand and noble aspiration. Maybe even a little fun. Though that remained to be seen.

Of course, once on the Interstate 5 North, I was reminded of how long and dull a stretch it was past the Grapevine but at least traffic was light. Three hours in, I stopped at The Harris Ranch for much-needed coffee and the best chocolate-dipped macaroons in the state of California, then took a quick look at the bonsai road stand, thinking a house gift for Barbara, assuming I found her, might be appropriate. Decided against it. Back on the freeway, I rolled up the windows as I flew past the dusty cattle ranches that stretched for miles to the north and east, considering briefly the merits of vegetarianism. When I started to feel sleepy, I turned up the radio and warbled along to "B.B. King's Bluesville" on Sirius, munching corn nuts and slugging back Dr. Pepper Cherry. YEAH...road trip!

The phone rang. Bob. "Did you mean to leave your laptop here?"

"No. Why? Is it there?"

"Why would I ask if it wasn't?"

"Fuck! Where did you find it?"

"On the foyer table."

"FUCK! Obviously I need it, if nothing else, for Google."

"Well, buddy, that ship has sailed, unless you want to pop back here and get it."

"Are you kidding? I'm four hours out!"

"Then you'll just have to find an Internet café. It's not the end of the world; they're everywhere."

"Yeah…thanks," I said glumly, hanging up. A major snafu. I'd been so vigilant about my list—checking off items as I'd gotten them done, keeping notes on the order of remaining tasks—it was unfathomable that I'd left my most essential tool on the foyer table. I swerved off the freeway to a rest stop and sat there for a few minutes, seething. Which led to eating; I pulled supplies from the car and assuaged myself with a picnic table lunch.

Working on my third half of a meatloaf sandwich (damn, these were good), I took out my notepad and scrolled through the order of priorities set for myself once I finally got to the city. Though I still had no clear-cut destination, I knew I was looking for a neighborhood near the Oakland Bay Bridge exit, I knew there was a library nearby, and somewhere in the general area was a park with a little gazebo. I'd taken time to do some map questing the night before and had jotted down directions to the residential neighborhoods nearest the bridge exit. I also made note that the library closest to that exit was the Oakland Public Library on San Pablo Avenue. So that would be the starting point. I'd drive around there for a bit and see if, by some wild stretch of happenstance, I found the neighborhood with the house with that notable gate. What could be easier, right?

But easy or not, I had my trusty map, a focused attitude, and hope that Lucy's Divine Intervention would help lead the way. It was generally an easy five-, maybe six-hour drive—depending on traffic, which, in California, could never be depended on—so I was now over halfway there.

Before I pulled back on the freeway, I flipped open my phone and thought about calling the "maybe Barbara" number again. Nah. It made sense to stick with the original strategy of surprise; show up at her door without any notice to allow time for concocted defenses or conjured theories. Try to catch her emotionally red-handed, as it were—off guard enough to get the real, hardcore, honest-to-God skinny on things.

Then again, it *would* make life simpler if I called, found out if it actually was her, and, if so, how to get to exactly where she might be. Maybe surprise needed to take a backseat to time and logistics. I had the number saved in my phone at this point, so I pressed the designated button and waited, my hands shaking a little.

Voicemail picked up this time. I'm pretty sure it was the same woman's voice from the earlier call. Hard to tell the age; could be an older woman. Pleasant, soft, nothing particular about it. She offered no identifying name, just the standard "thanks and leave a message." I didn't. I got back on the road.

Turns out Divine Intervention was as directionally challenged as me. Despite my best-laid plans, somewhere around that confusing mess where Interstate 5 hits the I-580, or whatever it is that happens right there, I got all turned around and ended up on a wrong exit ramp and stuck taking surface streets in the general direction of Oakland proper, a rather hefty time suck, given the traffic. But I stayed strong, kept focused, sweating and chewing apples from street to street.

If you've never been, Oakland is less the distant sibling of the shining sister that is San Francisco and more the creepy, pockmarked cousin who sells smack and is regularly picked up for street fighting. According to Bob, during that hour in which he tried desperately to talk me out of the adventure, Oakland has been designated as "the third most dangerous city in America," its reputation that of a drug-riddled, poverty stricken, cesspool of violence. Though I imagine *Forbes* magazine, the reference material he waved in my face while making these pertinent points, was somewhat less caustic in its assessment. Bob did, however, read verbatim that "the city across the Bay from San Francisco ranks first nationwide in violent robberies." Good to know. I'd be watchful. But I'd done my own research and rebutted that Oakland was also "one of the top cities in the United States for sustainability practices." Bob was unimpressed, remarking dryly that if I got robbed I could expect the involved paper and plastic to be responsibly recycled.

Though none of this dissuaded me from the mission, the fact remained that this was not only a city with which I was completely unfamiliar, but a place I'd be wise to not ramble injudiciously. I'd conceded that point to Bob the night before, as well as made it part of my general strategy, yet now, after finding the Oakland Public Library on San Pablo Avenue, I was doing exactly that: rambling injudiciously from one scrubby street to the next.

It's already been established that orienteering is not my strong suit. And obviously I hadn't had time to get my car's GPS replaced (though, without an address, how useful would that have been anyway?), but I figure men have been finding their way around the globe since time immemorial, so I could surely get Oakland sorted out. And, contrary to stereotype, I'm happy to ask for help as needed. Okay, maybe not *happy*. But I will. I will ask. And as I rounded another corner that looked to be nowhere near anywhere I wanted to be, I now had to. Ask, that is.

I was exceedingly aware that the neighborhood through which I was slowly driving was a particularly sketchy one—certainly not the high end of town (and research convinced me there *was* a high end of town). The street was stacked with shoddy apartment buildings and faded bungalows, all of which looked like they'd once been nice little buildings that had gone seriously to seed: peeling paint, crappy lawns, and grafitti'd exteriors abounded. I wasn't thrilled to be lost in a location I wouldn't want to stop my car, but I was now so low on fuel I had to pull into the nearest gas station, Kenny's Gas & Mart, which, of course, was also sketchy.

Standing at the greasy counter area with a few market items in hand and my credit card out, I started my pitch to the grubby attendant as cordially as I could. "Listen, I'm in a bit of a quandary. I'm trying to find a house I don't have an address for, but I do have some local landmarks, so I was wondering if maybe you could help me out."

A combination of the annoyed tilt of his head, along with an utter lack of customer service warmth, set the tone immediately. "Street."

"What?"

"What street do you want?"

"That's what I said, I don't know the street—"

He looked up at me with a blank stare. "How do you find a house without a street?"

I attempted some jocularity. "Exactly, right?" He didn't smile. "But I know it's somewhere near the bridge exit, in the general vicinity of the library, and I guess there's a little park nearby with an old gazebo."

"Gazebo?"

"Yeah, you know those little, round, sort of open bandstand kind of things? This one is an old World War II memorial. Do you know about any of that?"

"Maybe." That was it. He said nothing else.

"Well, do you think you could direct me to the place where you think that gazebo may *be*?"

"South of the 580, east of Broadway."

"Okay. But could you be a bit more specific? I've been driving around all day and—"

"What I said, south of 580, east of Broadway, there's a little park, that's it." He turned and walked into the garage. The impulse to pop this asshole in his cocky, sneering face was strong, but I believe

I've already mentioned I'm not a fighter. I also figured violence was not a particularly evolved way to start my vision quest.

Welcome to frikkin' Oakland.

# THIRTY

AFTER REINING IN my pugilistic urge, I headed south of the 580 and east of Broadway...wherever that was. Where it *was* was as hard to find as, so far, everything else in this city. It was getting deep into rush hour so traffic was slow-going and I stumbled over a number of logistical dead-ends, but finally there was something to celebrate when I got to a scruffy neighborhood that appeared to have a little park at the end of the block. Hallefuckinglujah!

I surveilled the houses as I made my way down the street, hoping no one would find my slow-moving car suspicious in any way. But in looking around, I'd say odds were good nobody would find anything about me and my old Audi noteworthy. If anything, they'd assume I was some yuppie eyeballing for the local drug dealer, which I hoped wouldn't inspire any unwelcome tapping at my car window.

Fact is, I was searching for that wrought iron gate. It did look like most of these houses—the ones that hadn't suffered hideous '80s refurbs—had held on to at least some measure of their architectural flourish. I was hoping to find the one with that unique, vintage gate captured in my dad's snapshot. But, no; no gate. That would have been too easy.

When I got to the end of the street I parked the car and got out, walking through the trash-strewn gravel toward the park. Certainly it was little: one rusty swing set, a slide that shook like a death trap, and a sandbox that appeared to have less sand than discarded candy wrappers and cigarette butts. And no gazebo. Not that I'd have expected a war memorial in this shithole. Christ!

A young Hispanic woman was seated on a nearby bench rocking a baby in a stroller and I figured she might know the area well enough to offer some guidance. "Excuse me," I called out as nicely as a strange man should call out to a young woman with a baby.

She glanced up quickly, a little startled, but my smile eased the moment. "Yes?"

"I'm trying to find a park somewhere near here that has an old gazebo, a war memorial, I think. Are you at all familiar with that?"

"No. I'm sorry. I don't know about anything like that in this neighborhood."

I thanked her and sprinted back to the car, deciding, against my better judgment, to pay a return visit to Kenny's Gas & Mart, where that surly fucker *had* to have known he was sending me off on a wild goose chase. After the long day of driving, and with my electrolytes precipitously low, I was feeling irrational enough to tangle once more with the local crank.

He was standing at the counter when I pushed through the door; gave me a vacant stare with that same condescending tilt to his head, and, once again, I felt the urge to smash my fist into his face. Something about the head tilt. I kept my voice modulated—though odds were good my state of peeve was busting out all over—and made a point of peering at his nametag this time. "So, Frank, I went south of the 580, east of Broadway; I found what I presume was your 'little park,' and guess what?"

By now he was back to whatever he'd been doing over by the grease-smudged cash register, and didn't seem keen on further interaction. His sheer imperturbability was awe-inspiring.

"It hardly qualified as a park, Frank, it was more of a trash pit, and there was not a gazebo to be found. I believe you said you were aware of the gazebo, and you implied you were sending me to the small park where the gazebo was, but it turns out that was not the case, which I did not appreciate. So I'm back, wondering if you'd like another shot at it."

Probably not the best way to frame the challenge, given the brewing disdain between us. He lifted his head as slowly as I've ever seen a man lift his head and then said nothing, staring at me with dead fish eyes. I snapped.

"Oh, I see…you're not going to speak, is that it? Do you think that's excellent customer service? There's a sign above the door that says you give 'excellent customer service.' I hate to say it, Frank, but I'm not seeing much of the excellent stuff. So maybe I should speak to Kenny at this point. Is he around?"

Still he said nothing, squaring off as if we were posturing for a fight.

"Really? You're not going to say anything? Seriously?" I must have had too much adrenaline rushing around to see the folly of this tactic, since odds were good he could gut me with a ballpoint before I'd do him any damage. There were also two or three burly mechanics in the adjacent garage who kept walking in and out, checking the status of our repartee, and they didn't seem all that friendly either.

Frank finally spoke up. "There is no Kenny. And I'm not gonna say nothing to you because you got a bad attitude."

"*I've* got a bad attitude?" That was rich.

"You want some gas; go pump it. You want chips; they're over there. You want a tour guide; call the Chamber of Commerce. They love guys like you."

Yep, Frank continued to make me want to rip his fucking throat out. Which was so unlike me. I came to the conclusion I was too tired to behave any better than a yawping teen with sleep deficit, so I just threw him the hardest glare I could manage and stormed out. No doubt he was crushed.

# THIRTY-ONE

LODGING ARRANGEMENTS HAD been efficiently handled at an earlier rest stop, where I'd pulled out my weathered AAA guidebook and looked for something in my price range that didn't appear too hideous. I booked a small but charming hotel with 4 stars and a list of amenities that covered the gamut (the Jacuzzi tub sounded particularly comforting after the day I'd had). I was very much anticipating a relaxing night at the Lamplighter Inn, "Oakland's best kept secret," as their promo so enthusiastically touted.

As I pulled into the parking lot, however, a quick scan of the property suggested the Lamplighter might be secret for all the wrong reasons. *Seedy* would be a good word to reference at this point, maybe "bad '60s rundown," if you want to go with real estate jargon. The pool looked like it hadn't been cleaned since the 20th century and the smell of something meat-like and pungent practically knocked me over as I walked into the sad little lobby. There was a shower curtain hanging between the counter and the back area, which was just wrong, and I could hear a baby caterwauling somewhere in the tinny distance. I thought about turning around and walking right back out, but I was so tired and testy I opted to give the Lamplighter a chance, hoping for the best.

The sixty-something, slightly brassy receptionist had a nametag identifying her as "Rita," but as we went through the requisite paperwork and credit card ritual, she was happy to make the introduction more formal, reciting from a script that had been personalized on my behalf.

"Hello, Mr. Dan McDowell, my name is Rita, your red-headed receptionist for the evening," she offered with a gap-toothed smile. "I want to welcome you to the Lamplighter Inn, Oakland's best kept secret." Apparently this point needed emphasis, though I might have suggested a less cryptic catch phrase. "Now, how many nights may we be delighted to provide service for you?"

I decided to err on the side of self-protection. "I'm not sure. Can I keep it open?"

"Why, of course, honey. It's our slow season, so that should be no problem." I suspected their slow season was on a year-round track. As she set the room key and various receipts on the counter, she droned on. "There's a continental breakfast of muffins and juice from six till ten. And you're definitely going to want to take advantage of that, because the muffins we put out are those scrumptious Costco kind! When you do decide to leave, be aware that checkout is at eleven, but while you're here, please enjoy your Jacuzzi tub and the real wood-burning fireplace." She plopped a Duraflame log on the counter. "Sleep tight!"

I headed up to Room 427 on an elevator that creaked and jostled so alarmingly I couldn't help but lean forward to check the inspection report: 2007. Apparently the pool guy and the elevator inspector were on a similar schedule. At one point, it lurched to a brief and unexpected mid-floor stop, and I had a split-second urge to call 911. But once it wheezed back to life, and with only one more floor to go, I gritted my teeth and hoped a cable wouldn't snap. My focus was on the Jacuzzi tub and waiting bed.

Despite hope and need, however, my entrance to the room

made clear we were still trending on the downward slide: questionable carpet stains, holes in the walls where one assumes pictures once hung; even the fireplace, wood-burning or otherwise, was filthy and likely not big enough for the proffered Duraflame. But it was after deciding a hot bath and cold beer would heal all traveling woes and I went in to get things started, that events hit a nadir from which they could not recover. After filling the noted Jacuzzi tub high enough for the jets to function, I flipped the switch and the resultant black sludge that spewed from those foaming spigots was enough to make me, seriously, want to vomit. All good will evaporated.

After descending the four flights of stairs with my duffle and bag of beer, and rather vociferously alerting Rita to the health and safety infractions of Oakland's best kept secret (as she nervously processed my demanded credit card refund), I made my way to that bastion of generic comfort and lodging: the nearest Motel 6.

## THIRTY-TWO

ONCE ENSCONCED IN my tidy and predictably unimaginative new room a few miles down the road, I showered up, grabbed a not-so-cold beer, got out my notepad, and sat back against the rickety headboard of my California king to review the day. It had not been an auspicious start. Not having my laptop was a blunder of epic proportion. If it were here, I'd be Googling that gazebo as we speak. And though I don't know whether Motel 6 chains typically provide computer rooms for their Internet-needy customers, this one, in this grungier section of Oakland, did not. There *was* free Wi-Fi in the room, but…yeah…no computer.

The receptionist behind the counter seemed like a nice enough person; I asked, but she had no awareness of a park with a gazebo anywhere nearby. Beyond that query, I didn't want to rely any further on the kindness of strangers; the charming fellow at Kenny's Gas & Mart had put me off the strategy. Besides, we were a little outside the presumed Barbara-area anyway, and odds were good no one around here would know what I was talking about.

For once in my life I was begrudgingly in step with Joaquin on the point and purpose of smartphones…oh, to have one at this moment! I even tried to see if my flip phone could get me online and was startled when it kind of did…almost. But after search upon search yielded nothing but the spinning circle of death, I finally gave up in defeat. I'd track down an Internet café in the morning—or maybe break down and get to an Apple store. At this point my Ludditism was less a charming quirk and more a wrench in the urgency of the mission.

I checked my messages; there was one from Lucy asking where I was and why I hadn't called at any point during the day (something I'd done religiously since this saga began), additionally relaying how annoyed she was that she ended up late to work as a result of my inconsideration (despite Esther's assurances that she was fine by herself and Jim still floating in the netherworld). It was a long message. Lucy was capable of leaving very long messages. As if you were conversing. Or even just listening while she conversed. This was long even by her standards. Too late to call back (thank God), so I texted her, apologizing for not being in touch, sowing the seeds for my lie about "a long job," and promising to call tomorrow.

It was also too late to call the "maybe Barbara" number again.

Nothing left to do.

One more sip of lukewarm beer and lights out. Day one sucked.

# THIRTY-THREE

SOMETIME DURING THE night I was awakened by the sound of loud men yelling at each other in the parking lot across the street. I peered out the window at a grimy dance club whose a tilted marquee promised, "Every Night Is Ladies Night!" If only I'd known.

A quick check of the clock told me it was closing time and it seems this bunch was put off by the schedule. Or perhaps a drug deal had gone wrong. Or maybe someone dissed someone's girl and chest butting was in progress. Whatever the impetus, there was lots of shouting and squealing. Someone banged something that, for a moment, sounded like a gun but was just a bottle being cracked over the hood of a car, which was bad enough and appeared to spark further outrage, given the increase in general volume. More people got involved. Girls were screaming as drunk girls do. Suddenly police cars swarmed in, and by then I was so fully awake I knew it was likely I'd never get back to sleep. But once the melee was sorted out and the crowd was cleared, a *Cops*-like drama I watched from behind the safety of my hotel curtains, I fell into a deeper sleep than I'd had since Jane threw me out of the house. I awoke renewed and ready.

Wednesday morning. Day two of the hunt.

While brushing my teeth and checking myself in the mirror (I needed a haircut, that's for sure), I made a mental declaration that today was the day I was going to find Barbara. I wanted to get the goal accomplished as quickly as possible and get the hell out of this hellhole. I went so far as to put on a tie, deciding it was something a seventy-something woman would find a polite touch and was, therefore, a token of positive thinking. Everything else in my available wardrobe was wrinkled, but the tie made the point.

Before I headed out for breakfast (Motel 6 did not offer scrumptious Costco muffins), I called the studio to make sure nothing had gone sideways in my absence. Luckily Zoey was there, still limping, she reported, but eager to fill me in on the previous day's activities.

"I have to tell you, Bob is so great; we had so much fun together!"

"Yeah, he's a good—"

"He's fucking hilarious! We laughed through the entire gig, almost gave me a laugh headache. I just love him."

"What, like I never make you laugh?"

"Not really that much, Dan. You're fun, you've got a cool playlist, but you're not that funny."

This annoyed me. What would a goofy twenty-four-year-old know about my particular brand of humor? "Well, lucky for me, lots of people *do* think I'm funny." I was debating this? I sounded like my mother.

"Well, good, then. We all need people who think we're funny. So Bob was telling me about this—"

"You do know he's gay, right?"

"Ah...yeah! Why would you ask me that?"

"Because you sound like a girl with a crush. Just wanted to be sure."

"Oh my God, Dan, you're jealous because I said he was funny! Jeez, grow up, wouldja?"

"Whatever. I'm glad you two are finding such bliss together. Anything useful to report?"

"No, Mr. Grumpy, life went on without you." She laughed. Apparently humor was now her thing. "Oh, wait, Jane came by."

"Jane came by?" That was strange. Jane hardly ever came by the studio when we were together; why would she suddenly find her way there now? "What did she want?"

"She said she was looking for Bob, seemed to know he was filling in for you."

"Oh, okay. Was he there?"

"No, he was out getting stuff for the Kaiser shoot. I told her that and she said something about a weird message that you were on a 'vision quest.' Did you really tell him to say that?"

"No, Christ, that was his idea. I didn't actually think he'd go through with the specific verbiage. And he was only supposed to say something if she asked, not offer it!"

"Yeah, that's lame. Especially since 'vision quest' couldn't sound less like you anyway."

I wasn't sure what she meant by that, since this *was* sort of a vision quest and I *was* the one on it, but I figured it was better to let that one go. "So anything else I should know?"

"About what?"

"About Jane!"

"Oh, I thought we were done with that. Okay, more about Jane. Um…I guess I thought she'd leave after I told her Bob wasn't around, but she actually sat at your desk and started talking like we were BFFs or something. Which was weird, since I think I've said three words to her in my entire life." An exaggeration, but I got the point; they were definitely not from the same tribe.

"That *is* weird. What'd she say?"

"She got into this thing about not knowing what was going on with you these days, that she knows you're worried about your dad but you've also been so strange lately, stuff like that."

"What'd you say?"

"I don't know, Dan, I was busy and just wanted to get her out of here so I could get back to work. I think I said something like, 'yeah, he's been a little zoned out lately,' thinking that made sense considering your dad and all, but then she got all interested, like, 'Really? What have you noticed?' and then I was completely stressed because I didn't want to say the wrong thing and, really, I'm not even sure what *is* going on with you, so it was basically weird!"

"You didn't say anything about my dad's story, did you?" Did *not* want Jane in on that chapter right now.

"Of course not! I know how to keep a secret; I'm not eight!"

"I know, Zo, but I can't remember the last time she stopped by the studio so—"

"What *is* going on?"

"With what?"

"With you and Jane."

"Well, she and I are officially over so, really, nothing is going on."

"Wow. Then I'm sorry. I didn't know it had gotten to any kind of official point. I thought you were still on that hiatus or whatever it was you were calling it."

"We were and then it sort of turned and I decided to pull the plug. Got tired of being in limbo. But I haven't said anything to anyone yet, so keep it to yourself for now, especially with Joaquin. I don't want him to think I was bullshitting about something he and I talked about the other day."

"Oh, do tell! What did you talk about?"

"Nothing, just some work stuff. Anyway, was that it?"

"Well…pretty much."

"What?

"I noticed her kind of looking around your desk while we were talking, sort of casual-like but obviously trying to see if there was anything worth noticing. Then she picked up this piece of paper and looked at it real funny, like she was trying to figure it out. I have no idea what was on it, and I'm not sure, but I think she might have taken it with her. Thought I better warn you in case it was classified."

I could not imagine what had been on my desk that would have been of any interest to Jane. But then again, I couldn't have imagined much of anything that's happened with Jane lately.

## THIRTY-FOUR

FOOD WAS NEEDED and luckily there was a Denny's nearby. There's always a Denny's nearby, especially in questionable neighborhoods. Not that I particularly like Denny's—in fact, I don't like Denny's at all—but when you don't know where you are and the local dining options are hard to predict, at least Denny's isn't. I've always said it's pretty hard to fuck up an egg.

As I waited for my two over easy with bacon, I decided I could no longer put off calling Lucy, who was likely standing in a hospital hallway screaming a message into her phone in her latest attempt to get a hold of me. I got queasy just thinking about it but had to man up; these were trying times for us both.

"You're *where*?" Yep. Screaming.

"Yeah, I know, not exactly great timing. Joaquin's got me up here shooting the Oakland Fire Department. I planned to call last night but there was so much going on it was too late by the time I got back to the room."

"You lying sack."

"Which part, the shooting or the calling?"

"Tell me where you are or I'll start screaming." Warning that seemed redundant.

"Okay, okay…I'm on a vision quest. It's important and could ultimately be life-changing." I thought something spiritual might strike a chord. Not so much.

"Cut the crap, Dan. Are you really in Oakland?"

"Yes…I am."

"Why are you in Oakland?"

"I've got some clients up here and—"

"You don't know a freaking soul up there."

"All right! Jeez. I'm in a Motel 6." I said that as if it were all I needed to say. A guy can hope.

"Really, Dan? A Motel 6. In *Oakland*? Do you think I'm an idiot? I let you read one stupid story, you decide our comatose father's ramblings mean any damn thing and—Jesus Christ, you really needed to do this RIGHT NOW?!"

I imagined people at the hospital were running for security guards at this point, she was so damn loud. "God, Lucy, bring it down a notch before they drag you off to the psych ward! Look, could you just have a little faith in me for a change? Believe it or not, there *is* a purpose to what I'm trying to do up here."

"You are so full of shit. Do you realize I've been in this fucking hospital for most of the past two weeks *while* trying to keep my restaurant running? Do you *not* see how ridiculous and selfish you're being right now, with your *vision quest* bullshit?" Her sarcasm was flaying.

"Hey, I've also been there most of the past two weeks while attempting to stay on top of my job! Let's not forget that. And, yeah, maybe my being up here seems selfish from your perspective, but it's not. Trust me, I have a plan. I'm only going to be gone for few days, and you never know, unbelieving sister, I might bring back something that could shake Dad out of this. That is the goal, for your information."

She groaned. "You are so delusional. Seriously. I'd be more

upset but this is so pathetic I actually feel sorry for you, up there in Oakland like a wandering idiot looking for some fantasy woman. Are you planning to anoint her the 'mother that should have been' if you find her? Because, you do realize, if you want to look at your insanity with any spiritual logic, you wouldn't even exist if Dad had married her, how about that?"

"You don't know that! Maybe, expanding on your whole soul mate theory, children are meant to be with certain parents too. Maybe I would've existed either way!"

"Or *maybe* you would have been assigned to Mom instead of Dad and wouldn't even know him right now, with or without Barbara. Or, we could have each been assigned to completely different sets of parents and wouldn't even know each other! Which would be fine with me right about now. But, oh, *so* many options, which to choose?" Her derision was dripping through the phone.

"Jesus Christ, restrain yourself," I snapped. "I just want to talk to the woman. Taking everything into consideration, I don't think that's so stupid, sorry to disagree with you."

"Well, listen, it's been a blast having this existential debate with you, but I've got things to do that are actually useful, so, whatever the fuck it is you're doing, keep your fucking phone on! I may need to call you because, you know, our dad's in the hospital!"

"Lucy, come on, you don't have to be such a—" She'd already hung up.

My breakfast arrived. I was wrong; you *can* fuck up an egg.

## THIRTY-FIVE

I WAS NOT immune to my sister's disapproval. There was guilt, without a doubt. I could justify this expedition all I wanted but there was no denying the timing of it sucked. But even so, I remained convinced it could ultimately be a game-changer...life altering and wrong-righting. I know that's not a word, but it felt like the exact theme of my mission: wrong-righting. I was going to hold on to that noble concept no matter what Lucy said.

Back at the motel room, I grabbed my notepad and the photo envelope, spread the pictures out over the bed, and just stared at them. There had to be more visual clues in all this that would help me. I picked up the one of Barbara in the gazebo and examined it, hoping to see some details or additional landmarks in the background that might be noteworthy, but the image was too dark and nothing stood out. The one of her in front of the gate was golden, but until I found that street and that block, what use was it?

I thought again about the phone number. I had to call. I had to make contact. As much as I wanted the element of surprise, it was starting to feel like this would take too long otherwise. I had no choice but to play the card. I pulled out my phone and pressed the button with a sense of unnerving anticipation.

"Hello?" A woman answered. She sounded like the woman who'd answered the first time, the same woman whose voice was on the outgoing message: high and sweet, with a timber that *might* belong to an older woman. I was hopeful.

"Hello! I'm sorry to bother you, but I'm trying to find someone who once lived in Oakland, someone who was very close to my father, and I found this number in his personal belongings. Her name was Barbara. I was hoping this might be the right number."

"I'm sorry, what are you're asking me?" She sounded completely confused and not particularly warm.

"I realize this must seem so random. But my father is really ill and we need to find someone who might be at this number."

"I'm the only one who's been in this house for over a year, so I don't think you've got the right number."

My heart sank. "So, there's no one there named Barbara?"

"No."

"Do you know if there ever was anyone there named Barbara?"

"I don't know about before I lived here, but there's no one named Barbara here now and, as far as I know, the people who rented this place before me were two guys. And I think they'd had it for a pretty long time. Sorry."

She quickly hung up, and I literally felt as if I'd been kicked in the gut. For some reason, and despite the odds of that number being nothing more than ancient reference to a long-ago contact, quite possibly in another city, part of me held hope that it really *was* her. It really was Barbara behind those numbers. I felt stunning disappointment.

No other option; time to find an Internet café. Also, I was hungry again; my half-eaten Denny's breakfast had sorely disappointed and I needed…what? I needed pie.

I got in the car and made my way to a commercial area not far down the road, which—while not exactly the inner city—wasn't one of your more gentrified spots. Not a Starbucks in sight. I noticed a small coffee shop that didn't appear too dingy and pulled into a convenient parking space in front. Actually, there were several convenient parking spaces in front, testament to either the post-breakfast hour or lousy food yet again. I went in anyway.

As expected, there wasn't much going on in there, plenty of open tables, but I decided to sit at the counter, thinking I could keep an eye on the car through the overhanging mirror. And in the time it took me to glance down at the menu, find the pie section, make my choice, and glance back up again, there were three rough-looking dudes literally *on* my car: one propped on the bumper, another leaning on the door, still another literally *sitting* on the hood. A tableau of urban cliché if there ever was one.

Now, I'm tall and in decent shape, with moderately developed musculature and edge to my demeanor when necessary, so idiots don't typically mess with me. In Toluca Lake. Here in the grittier environs of the third most dangerous city in the country, I felt a little out of my element. But it didn't look like the Three Musketeers were going anywhere soon, and I didn't like the potential of where this could be headed. I stuck a toothpick in my mouth, strapped on my best streetwise 'tude, shook off a burgeoning wuss factor, and sauntered out the door with faux bravado.

"Hey, guys, appreciate your visit but time to hop off."

They looked up, all deadpan stares and macho posturing. They appeared not much older than teenagers and didn't seem particularly interested in any kind of street cordiality. Not surprisingly, no one moved. I felt a mix of alarm and aggression.

"Tight ride, man." The one leaning on the door spoke first. I'll call him Dude One. "And we be three homies who know how to appreciate a fine set of wheels."

My first thought was, "Did he really just say *homies?*"—not sure if that was still current vernacular or he was just messing with the white guy. Second, I wondered if my old Audi, despite its vintage classiness, was really the kind of wheels considered "fine" by urban street toughs. Next, I wondered if "street toughs" was still part of current vernacular.

At this point, Dude Two stretched out like he was setting up for a tan. I was not having any of that. "Hey, come on! This is a nice old car, and I'd appreciate you not putting dents in the hood. Could you please get off?" He made no move other than to close his eyes and lean into the sun.

Dude Three, the one sitting on the bumper flipping through what looked to be a porn magazine, decided it was time for him to throw in. "We're just chillaxing, man, so why don't you go back to your chef salad or your Perrier or whatever you were doing in there and leave us to it. Besides, I ain't done with my book yet, and they say us disadvantaged youths need to read more."

I could not figure what the play was here. Did they intend to steal the car, gut me with a shiv, see if they could horn in on my chef salad; what? They did have a bona fide air of menace, but, on the other hand, we were in broad daylight, they were being viewed from inside the coffee shop, and so far, I didn't seem to be inspiring any particular urge to violence on their part. I decided to go with the casual/funny approach. "Listen, I'm with you, and I hear that issue's got some great articles, but I've actually got to get going and—"

"Oh, you ain't goin' nowhere, home." Dude One again. I felt my first jolt of real fear. He jerked his head toward the right front tire and I looked down. It was flat as a pancake with an obvious slash through the sidewall.

"Oh, that's real nice." My implication was plain. They didn't appreciate it.

"Don't be trippin', man, we didn't do it." Dude Two hopped off the hood with his chest puffed. "You racist moes always jumpin' to conclusions."

"Well, considering the circumstances, it's not exactly a stretch, is it?" I puffed out a little myself, thinking it might be the appropriate body language, like yelling at a bear. Besides, I was a lot taller than any of them, though presumably less well armed. That thought was probably racist, too.

Dude Three had something to share on the point: "Yo, you might be surprised. We saw some crazy old white bitch come by, said she was lookin' to snag a ride. We say, cool, check it out, she kicks the tire and snap…it popped, just like that." All three laughed, slapping high-fives all around.

"Yeah, that's real funny, guys."

"For reals, man! We tried to snatch her but she clocked outta here real fast, like a goat." They all laughed and fived around one more time. Apparently goats were funny with the younger urban set; I'd have to work up a goat routine and dazzle Zoey.

Dude One gave me a look of commiseration. "Ain't it wack what's happenin' on the streets these days?" He held my gaze for a long moment, making some point; what, I didn't know.

"Yeah," I agreed. "It's…wack."

The door of the coffee shop swung open and a large man with a face that looked like a boxer's came out, his newspaper tucked under his arm. He stopped a few feet from the curb to light a cigarette, then just stood there, smoking and…just standing there. The message was clear, and I felt a wash of relief come over me.

There was some shuffling amongst my three visitors. Dude One, either intimidated by the smoking bystander or satisfied that I'd gotten whatever point he was trying to make, turned and sashayed down the sidewalk; the other two jumped to follow. Dude Two flashed a peace sign in the direction of me and my silent bodyguard, while Dude Three made an obvious point of slipping a knife into his pocket—clearly he'd been the muscle—tossing back one summarizing thought:

"You have a nice day, now, sir. We'll keep an eye out for that lady, but you know how hard it is to find crazy old white bitches in this neighborhood." And off they went.

Need I point out the irony of that last statement?

I turned to thank my rescuer but he was already halfway down the block.

## THIRTY-SIX

AAA GOT A tow truck out there faster than I might have expected but, wouldn't you know it, the man behind the wheel was fucking Frank, the misanthrope from Kenny's Gas & Mart. Was he the *only* auto wrangler in this entire area? It was a big city, dammit! True to type, he was as warm and fuzzy as remembered.

"What are you doing around here anyway?" he growled, banging on my hubcap as if wishing it were my skull. "Just asking for trouble, like every other fucking tourist?"

I wondered how AAA might feel about a representative of their fine organization using the "f-bomb." If he hadn't been swapping out the tires on my car I think I might've decked him, plainly a recurring theme with this fucker…though given his blatant antipathy, I'd guess the impulse was mutual. It was also quite possible my current level of antagonism was bleed-over from the three amigos of earlier. There was no shortage of unlikeable people floating around my Oakland circle these days.

"Well, since you're so interested, Frank, I had a lousy breakfast at your local Denny's, and after doing some serious research on this place I'm trying to find, decided I needed food that was a step up from lousy. So I came here for some pie, and to see if they had a computer I could use, maybe ask for help from someone with a little more consideration than you, and, well, there you have it. I didn't know I was in the Seventh Circle of Hell."

Frank stood up, wiping his hands with a dirty rag, and looked at me like I was a first-class idiot. "You talk too much, you know that? And I don't know what your problem is, but why don't you have a smartphone like every other motherfucker in this world?" His ease with profanity was surprising from a service professional.

"What is this with you guys?"

"What do you mean, 'you guys'?" He actually snarled.

"Take it easy. I mean you guys who think everyone is obligated to have the latest technology. Have you ever heard of consumer anxiety, the compulsion to chase after the next best thing even if you don't need it?"

"I'd say you need it."

"My phone is fine, thank you. I did intend to bring my computer—yes, I *have* a top-of-the-line MacBook Pro, thank you very much—I just happened to forget it. But I'll find an Internet café, I'll get on Google, and everything will be right with the world, Frank, don't you worry." No idea why I was getting into all this. He not only didn't like me, he clearly could give a shit.

"Okay, Grandpa," he snorted derisively. "Sounds like you got it all figured out. But you must be some kind of cheap-ass fool to not go get a fucking iPhone or whatever. But not my problem. Good luck and goodbye." He packed up his gear, hopped on the truck and drove off, shaking his head. I sincerely hoped this was our last, *very* last, goodbye.

## THIRTY-SEVEN

I AM MANY things, but I am no cheap-ass fool.

Before I took off with my shiny new spare I asked the counter waitress at the coffee shop if there was an Internet café nearby. She didn't know of any in the immediate vicinity (of course) and they (of course) didn't have a computer for public consumption. So I was on my way to the mall (she *did* know where that was), ready to finally succumb to the needed convenience and handy Internet features of a smartphone. I was done traipsing around this city like a blind man.

Traffic was heinous for some reason and as we sat, packed bumper-to-bumper with little appreciable progress, I had too much time to think and too many things to think about that stirred my anxiety. I sensed the creeping fumes of futility wafting all over my mission but shook it off, reminding myself that I'd not even been here a full twenty-four hours. There was still time to pull this out.

But, speaking of time, ten minutes had gone by and I realized I hadn't moved an inch. The guy in front of me got out of his car and stormed up to the corner. Returning with his jaw clenched, he yelled out to us all, "There's a fucking big rig sidewise on the road. We'll be here all day!"

As luck would have it, I was close enough to an alley entrance to shimmy back one or two inches, then pull a hard right to get the hell out of there. Winding through the now-crowded detour route, I circumnavigated around the accident intersection as best I could, and, within minutes, was completely lost, with no idea how to recalibrate the directions to the mall. Yep. This was when a working GPS would've been a grand thing.

I pulled into the parking lot of a neighborhood grocery store, took out my map, and scanned to see if I could find the mall where I'd been headed. For some reason, as I sat looking at the unfamiliar streets and designated points of interest, the numbers and letters swarmed like fire ants and I could make nothing out of any of it. This was startling. Either my weariness was taking its toll or I was in serious need of glasses. I closed my eyes tightly then opened them up again. Okay…better. But the tiny lines and letters seemed too small to read and I felt lost. Literally and figuratively.

It struck me that I never got my pie.

# THIRTY-EIGHT

GIVEN THE DRAMATICS at my last food stop, I drove until I was in a decidedly better section of town and looked for a place that seemed simple enough for my hunger needs and safe enough for my physical well-being. A small diner with a particularly artful sign drew my attention, but it was the flashing neon "Fresh Pies" that got me in the door.

By the time I had coffee and a slice of apple pie in front of me, I was overcome with a familiar wave of exhaustion and the gnawing sense that my mission had become a rabbit hole of circuitous blunders. I couldn't tell if this assessment was due to the fact that the adrenaline high I'd been on was leaking out like a pin-holed balloon after a party, or if I really was the selfish, delusional idiot Lucy had suggested. Likely the latter. Maybe both. I don't know. This pie was good.

And then something utterly incredible happened. I'm not sure if it was the haze of the incoming sunlight or just my overwrought imagination, but in a moment of what seemed to be tantalizingly slow motion, the most beautiful woman in the world walked into my view and all time stopped. For. What. Seemed. Forever.

You know how you see photographs of women—in magazines or on celebrity websites, on TV shows or in movies—who are so impossibly beautiful you just know that Photoshop or great makeup or lighting or lens filters or something beyond human DNA is responsible because there simply *can't* be a woman on this earth that impossibly, breathtakingly, unfathomably beautiful? You know that thing? Well, the woman walking toward me with a coffee pot in her hand and a smile so radiant it seemed to have sparkles of sugar dust on its edges *was* that kind of woman. I felt the axis tilt.

Curls that could only be described as lustrous, in the color of summer wheat, tumbled across her shoulders and swung sassily as she strolled down the aisle pouring coffee for eager customers. Dimples made an adorable accent to her incredible smile; eyes were gemstone amber, skin warm gold, and the shape of her face and body too perfect and symmetrical to be anything but divinely designed. She was truly a walking work of art…and she was walking in my direction. Then she was there, right there in front of me. I might have been holding my breath.

"Hi, my name is Fiona, and I'm taking over for your waitress for a few minutes. Can I refill your coffee?"

"Yes, absolutely." I couldn't take my eyes off her. I hoped I didn't outwardly appear as slack-jawed as I felt.

"So how are you today?" she asked.

"Today…well, so far I'd say I'm caught between fatigue and confusion."

She laughed, a twinkling kind of laugh that, if this were a Disney movie, would have been illustrated with golden stars and little ribbons of pastel light. Then again, even her name sounded like a Disney movie. "It seems like you might need more than pie and coffee."

My heart took the tiniest skipped beat, wondering if there was even a hint of flirtation in the comment. Her innocent (albeit, stunning) smile disabused me of the idea.

"Yeah...more like therapy and a smartphone."

She set the coffee pot down and leaned on the counter, ever so slightly closer to me. "And now I'm intrigued. How do those two things go together?" she asked.

I wasn't sure how far to get into my sad story, realizing how inane I could sound to a perfect stranger (and, oh, this stranger was perfect), but the urge to make contact with someone who wasn't sneering or screaming at me was powerful. "It's an odd little story, that's for sure, but, in a nutshell, I'm trying to find my father's old girlfriend for reasons even I suspect at this point, and I've discovered you apparently can't get there from here. Or anywhere else in Oakland, for that matter."

"That does sound confusing! Do you have an address?"

"No, and before you ask, I also don't have a smartphone and the GPS in my car is broken. I do have a map and some unusual landmarks, so I remain convinced I can piece this thing together in some kind of way. My next stop is an Internet café."

"Is there a number to call for some directions?"

That *would* be a logical question. "The number I had, the one I thought might be her, turned out to *not* be her. Which was very disappointing."

"Oh, that's too bad! Well, listen, I'm off in about fifteen minutes and you seem like a nice enough guy. Why don't you walk over to my shop with me, and you can use my computer to find whatever you can? I'm just a few blocks from here."

"You have a shop?"

"Yes, herbs and tinctures. Maybe you can pick up something calming for yourself while you're there...might do wonders for your stress."

Again she smiled that smile, and my stomach lurched like I was on a roller coaster. "Stress? What stress?" I smiled too, though I doubt mine had quite the same effect. I reached out to shake her hand. "Dan McDowell, by the way. And that sounds like a plan."

"Fiona Nielsen. Enjoy your pie and I'll come get you when I'm done."

Other than my smoking, anonymous protector at the previous coffee shop, this was the first really nice thing to happen to me since I got to Oakland. And she was definitely a lot prettier.

Life, I could just feel it, was about take a turn in my favor.

# THIRTY-NINE

THE WALK THROUGH Fiona's neighborhood adjusted my view of Oakland from hellhole extraordinaire to a place where sane people might actually choose to live. Stately trees lined the streets and each home we passed was architecturally appealing and nicely kept. Of course, it's not as if a woman like this would choose to live in the slums, but my general attitude about the city ascended with each passing block.

I kept stealing glances her way, transfixed as she pointed out the various places of interest in the neighborhood while asking general questions about where I was from and what I did. We talked a bit more about why I was in Oakland, but she commented that she wanted to wait to hear all the details over tea, when she could pay better attention. I liked that she was that interested. Every time I looked at her I found myself newly awestruck. If I could have drawn a cartoon of myself during that short walk it would have involved gobsmacked eyes and lots of drooling. I'd literally turned into man jelly.

Which is just so shallow, isn't it? And I hate being shallow, particularly about women. I count myself a feminist in the purest and best sense of the word, believing, without question, that women are not only equal to men, but often smarter and certainly as deserving of anything the world has to offer. Our partners and collaborators, not to be victimized, minimized, or objectified by anyone for any reason. And yet there I was, staring at this woman with such a gnawing sense of beauty-awe I felt like an ass who'd lost all sense of civility. But I'd never before been in this kind of proximity to this kind of beauty, which made me wonder if she experienced men acting like idiots around her on a daily basis. If so, and probably, that must get tiresome. Or maybe a beautiful woman is so aware of her particular power that she enjoys the responsive display and doesn't let it get to her, maybe even finds it validating in some way. It's strange, though, the impact that a beautiful woman has. It's also strange how many times the word "beautiful" has rattled through my head since the moment Fiona approached with that coffee pot.

We got to her place and it was exactly as charming as I'd pictured it: a tiny Victorian with bright little flower pots everywhere and some weird, arty metal sculptures set in various spots in the picket-fenced front yard. Very whimsical landscaping—wild flowers, twinkle lights, and other charming doo-dads. It was just…well, charming. No other word. Even the sign above the door that read "Fiona's Fine Herbs and Curios" was charming.

While I stood there appreciating all these adorning touches, she opened the front door to a closed-in porch. "So, this is my shop."

She flicked a switch and the room, warmed by soft, well-placed lighting, popped to glowing life. I stepped in to see shelves filled with tiny brown bottles with raffia ties; there were scented candles, dried herbs, all kinds of little things that smelled good and looked pretty in a Hippie-Chick-meets-Martha-Stewart kind of way.

"Wow, very nice."

"Thanks! I love this room." She smiled sweetly. "I'm only open on the weekends—unless someone really needs something during the week. I'm kind of an herbal pharmacist: I've got a Facebook page,

I'm on Twitter and Instagram; I've even got a call-in number, the whole thing. I wish I could afford to do it full time, but until then the waitress job is perfect."

"Yeah, that has to be convenient with it being so close."

"It is! And I actually end up handing out lots of cards to people I meet there. Some of them have become my most loyal customers."

Well, I'd imagine so. And somehow thinking about that gave me a most irrational twinge of jealousy. I wondered how many of her "loyal customers" were fawning men. Like me.

"I'm sure it isn't hard for you to attract new customers, Fiona. I mean...look at all this great stuff!" I was browsing through the bottles, reading labels with such bizarre names—tribulus, sea buckthorn, astragalus—I felt like I'd wandered into Diagon Alley. She reached over my shoulder, a move that inspired a jolt to my midsection, and grabbed one of the bottles.

"Here, try this, Avena Sativa. It's an oat tincture. Four drops under the tongue three times a day. You'll be amazed how much calmer and less stressed you'll feel."

"Okay, Miss Herbal Pharmacist, I'll give it a shot." Which I did. And if I ever had to guess the taste of mulch, that'd be it.

She smiled at my unavoidable grimace. "It'll grow on you."

"I'm thinking it'll grow *in* me."

She laughed that laugh I'd already fallen in love with—the laugh, mind you, just the laugh—and opened the inside door to the rest of the house. "And here's my home."

As expected, it was a charming extension of the charming shop: cozy, enchanting, and whimsical, like walking into a little girl's fairy princess bedroom, though, happily, without the preponderance of pink. She set her bag down on the table and headed into the kitchen.

"I'm going to make some tea. Would you like a cup?"

"Sure, that'd be great." I stood awkwardly in the main room feeling unsure of where to sit or what to do with my hands. Fiona came out with a bowl of fruit and some crunchy-looking crackers and pointed to a computer across the room.

"It's already on. Please help yourself."

I sat down and quickly pulled up Google Maps while running a short internal interview with myself: What am I doing here? Why am I sitting at this desk? *This* particular desk in *this* particular house? Yes, I need some logistical guidance, but couldn't I have simply asked where to find an Internet café? Something to relax me is warranted, a cup of tea is always nice, but come on…*look at this chick*!

Just as I turned to gaze her way, Fiona glanced up from where she was making tea as if she could hear the jabbering inside my head and, right at that moment, the light filtering in from the gauze-curtained windows hit her face and she looked like the kind of painting I could never afford to have in my home. I wished I hadn't left my camera in the trunk. Breathtaking.

"Any luck?" she called out.

"Um, not yet…but let me see…" I snapped back to the task at hand.

Frankly, I wasn't sure how to approach this search of mine. I was staring at the screen when Fiona walked over and leaned in to take a look, her hair wafting close and exuding an intoxicating scent, likely something she sold in her shop. Musky and slightly herbal. Very erotic—I mean, exotic.

"So what have you got so far?" she asked.

"Well, based on things my dad wrote in a story I have, I know the neighborhood I'm looking for is near the bridge exit, also near the library that's near the bridge exit—"

"The library on San Pablo—"

"Yes, which I've already found. And apparently there's a small park nearby with a gazebo, a World War II memorial. Do you know anything about that?"

"No, I'm sorry, I don't."

"I have a picture of the woman sitting in the gazebo, but it's not a very good shot, so there's no other visual markers to pull from it."

"So, somehow you've got to find the park, and then maybe you can triangulate the bridge, the library, and the park, and at least lay out a basic area to explore."

Wow. So incredibly *Law & Order*. "Impressive, Fiona; are you sure you're not more than an herbal pharmacist? CIA, maybe?"

She laughed as she took over the mouse, leaning closer to the screen. "I think I just spend too much time on the Internet. Why don't we pull up Google Earth and see if we can find the park with the gazebo? If it's still there, it should be visible."

She sat next to me on the computer bench and, like two investigators drawn to the thrill of the hunt, we pored over the emerging images near the bridge and the library. When she started inputting search words like "park," "gazebo," and "World War II memorial," I felt my heart beating faster and couldn't tell if it was her proximity or the fact that we were honing in on something that could be significant.

"What's that?" she suddenly asked. She zoomed in on a green wooded area not far from a crowded neighborhood street. "Oh my God, look."

She'd closed in on a small area with tightly packed trees and overgrown bushes and as the image expanded, a small white structure of some kind was visible amongst the encroaching foliage. It was so enveloped it was impossible to determine exactly what it was, but surely it *could* be a gazebo.

I was stunned. "That's amazing. Like finding a needle in a haystack. Thank you, Fiona, that's incredible!"

"Well, we can't get too far ahead of things. You still have to find out if it *is* the gazebo you're looking for."

"Absolutely. My next move will be to drive over there and take a look."

"But first, come, sit; we'll have our tea." She walked over to a very nicely set table.

I quickly jotted down the address and directions to the park and joined her. It felt odd to be sitting with a woman who wasn't my sister, my mother, my workmate, or…Jane. It had been a very long time since this sort of scenario played out in my insular little world.

Fiona and I both did the requisite tea ritual without a word: a little honey, some stirring, some squeezing of the tea bag. All very quiet and undeniably charged. And given her smiling glances my way, I felt convinced, at this point, that it wasn't just me. That thought rattled me enough that I needed to talk again.

"So, Fiona, you live here alone?"

"No, I have a roommate. She's a massage therapist, works at a spa across town. When she gets home later you should let her give you one; she's a masseuse nonpareil."

I couldn't remember the last time I heard someone say that word. It was not a word even my very literate father kept in his verbal toolkit. In fact, I wasn't sure I'd ever heard *anyone* use that word. Beautiful and cultivated…an enticing combination.

"Do you like massage, Dan? I know not everyone does."

"I do. I don't get them often, but I've enjoyed the ones I've had. A massage might be nice." Apparently Fiona assumed I'd be around long enough for her roommate to administer said treatment "when she gets home later." Was this further flirtation or just a healthful suggestion?

"So I'd love to know more about why you're looking for your dad's old girlfriend."

I figured if we got into this I *would* be around long enough for that massage. "Well, it's a long story, and, to be honest, I'd like to get out to that park before sundown. You want to come with me? We could talk in the car."

# FORTY

WHILE I WASN'T really sure why Fiona would take time from her day to go off searching for a total stranger at the behest of another total stranger, she seemed fully up for the adventure at hand. Glancing over at her in the passenger seat, I made note that she had to be one of the prettiest navigators I'd ever had. What's more, I was sincerely grateful for her time, her computer, her perspective, and her familiarity with the city. She'd input the park's address into her phone and was now, quite expertly, leading us there.

The sun was getting dangerously close to setting and I felt an urgent push to get to the park while there was still enough light to see. With the skill of a local cabby, Fiona took us off the more traveled roads to the less burdened side streets, which helped us make better time than I might have expected. As we made our way closer to the park, I found myself once again scanning the passing homes, hoping against hope to see that very particular wrought iron gate. I wished I'd shown the photo to Fiona so she could check from her side of the car, but for now I was happy just to have her steering us in the right direction.

"There it is!" she called out, pointing to a wooded area off to the left. It was, indeed, a small park amongst a profusion of tall and overgrown trees. It didn't look any better maintained than the park I visited yesterday, nor did most of the surrounding neighborhood. I pulled to the side of the road and we both disembarked, the tension of hoped-for discovery high.

With few words between us, we walked past the rusted playground and deeper into the small but glutted forest beyond. It was approaching dusk and, in the snarl of unkempt trees and bushes, it felt as though we were making our way through a jungle, pushing through thickets of lowered branches and overgrown shrubs. At some point we came upon a slightly more opened area, almost crescent-shaped, where dilapidated benches covered with leaves, branches, and pinecones were curved around a small structure literally wrapped in vines and blighted by neglect.

The gazebo. The one from the picture.

Fiona and I turned to each other with wide eyes, stunned to have actually found the location we'd just pulled up on a computer screen. I couldn't have felt more like a true detective than I did in that moment. We brushed aside the rotted branches and decaying leaves piled across the stairs and walked into the small, circular interior. Looking up, I could see gaping holes in the roof that let in both the elements and swooping birds, but the charm of the architecture peeked through at certain spots, evidence that this had once been a lovely place to sit and spend time, to talk, to dream…to fall in love. I felt a pang of sorrow at its decline, particularly since this was a place my father had, long ago, found some joy.

"Look." Fiona had pulled away some ivy tendrils at the arched entryway and underneath was a corroded brass plaque that read: *In Honor of Those From Our Fair City Who Fought In World War II*. "I can't believe they'd let this fall into such decay."

I agreed; there *was* something dispiriting about a monument, however small, being so abandoned, but that's what you get with an economic downturn, a limited budget, and a tough city with much higher priorities to manage.

But even that could not diminish my powerful sense of "destiny found." It was too random to be anything else. I felt a calmness descend. Now I could do exactly what Fiona suggested and triangulate the area to search. From there, I would surely be led to Barbara from Oakland.

## FORTY-ONE

IT WAS DARK by the time we got back to Fiona's, allowing her the opportunity to plug in the many strands of twinkle lights she had stretched across every available wall, affecting a cocoonish, almost Christmassy vibe. Very festive and celebratory.

After an hour of enjoying the exceedingly wholesome meal she put together (vegan, gluten-free, organic, and moderately twig-like...but, still, tasty!), all while running down The History of Jim and Dan And How Love Has Eluded Them Both (one of Bob's titles offered in recent conversation), I found myself checking my watch more than I'd like, concerned about Lucy and the imminent earful. Still, I couldn't seem to break from my rather leisurely telling of the tale. That I was one step closer to Barbara, especially after the amazing events of the day aided by the amazing Fiona, only added to the thrill of my burgeoning besottedness. I decided to shove thoughts of Lucy aside for a bit longer.

Fiona had been immersed in the story from the get-go, genuinely curious, like so many others in my life, about how so brief a romance of fifty years ago could have horned into the present with such a punch. "Has your father actually been unhappy all this time without her, do you think?"

"I don't know. I wasn't aware that he was. But maybe if I'd read the story years ago, I'd have framed things in a different light: his gruffness with my mom, his general sense of dissatisfaction. But he's always been a tough guy for me to read, so I'm not sure how much of it is just him or how much could be about Barbara."

"My father is also pretty mysterious, so I think I understand."

"Yeah, is he?"

"He is, but I want to keep talking about this right now."

It amazed me how incredibly, authentically interested she was in me and my life, a balm after weeks of Jane slamming literal and figurative doors in my face.

"That's really nice, Fiona. I guess I haven't talked about this all that much with anyone." Something I'm sure Zoey, Bob, or Lucy might take issue with, but I meant in the sort of intimate, thoughtful way one does with a woman. And I realize Zoey and Lucy are women, but you get the gist.

"I think it's amazing how you put it all together and then made the decision to come up here."

"Yeah, kind of crazy. At least my sister thinks it is. But the tipping point had to be what he kept trying to say at the hospital. How do you ignore that?"

"Which is why you're here, and I can understand why you're here. You're a good son."

That moved me. Not too many other people were making that point these days. She went into the kitchen for more hot water (I'd now consumed more tea than I had in my entire life), and while she was gone, another orbiting thought moved to the forefront of my slightly addled brain. When she came back in, sat down and filled our mugs yet again, I took the pause…then threw it out there.

"So let me ask you something, since we've been talking about my dad and Barbara, and you seem to be a person who's willing to look at life from all its many angles."

She smiled. "I think I am."

"I'm curious if you think our romantic connections in life are random, or if we're meant to be with one specific person. Someone who's destined to find us and recognize their soul mate status with us." I said this casually, as if it were part of the general sociological analysis of my father's situation. In truth, it felt so transparently loaded with meaning that, along with my rising temperature and the fact that if I inched any closer I'd actually be *on* her lap, I was sure she'd presume I was coming on to her. Which I wasn't. Of course not. Just curious in a strictly hypothetical way.

She, meanwhile, smiled as if taking the bait, and with a hint of coquettishness said, "I think there *is* someone I'm meant to be with…and it's just a matter of us finding each other."

I smiled, our eyes held, and there was the craziest moment when I thought I was going to lean forward and plant my lips right smack on that gorgeous mouth, when WHAM! The front door flew open and a very large, very striking woman with purple hair, jet-black skin, and clunking Doc Martens stomped in like a giant in drag. Fiona and I both popped upright as this bear of a woman yelped in our direction.

"HOLY FUCK, Fi, did *not* know you were home! Turn the damn lights on, wouldja? I thought PG&E got us again!" With that, she flipped on the overheads and the mood was immediately snapped. She also took notice of me at this point. "Oh, shit—sorry, didn't know you were having a tea party!"

"It's fine, Maris; Dan was here using the computer—Dan, this is my roommate, Maris Bagely. Maris, a new friend, Dan McDowell. Dan's in town looking for his father's old girlfriend."

Maris shook my hand with the heft of a quarryman. She leaned in to grab a hunk of bread from the table while shooting me a sly grin. "I'd usually pull up a chair after a statement that riveting, but I'm tired as a dog and you two looked like you were about to clinch. Have at it, kiddles, and good luck with your scavenger hunt, Dan." She thumped up the stairs, and Fiona and I were left to look at each other awkwardly.

"She certainly knows how to make an entrance." I offered with a meager smile.

"She does. She's a wonderful roommate, but she tends to be noisier than I'd like." As if on cue, the wailing of some unidentifiable kirtan music wafted through the floorboards from above, sending the mood from snapped to shattered.

I started shuffling things around the table. "Well, I should probably get going anyway. I told my sister I'd call and it's getting late."

Fiona reached over and took both my hands in hers, giving me one of those soul-melting gazes from which eyes cannot avert. "You don't have to leave."

"Thanks, Fiona, but I—"

"I'd *like* you to stay."

My heart literally jumped in my rib cage; I actually reached up to my chest wondering if I was about to have a heart attack. Nope. Just swooning. "And I'd really like to stay, but I don't think I'm ready for that yet."

"Ready for what?"

The leaping-in-the-sack part. "The implications-of-staying part."

"No implications, Dan. Just a little tenderness between friends."

Jeez, really? She was going to make it *that* easy? "Fiona, there is nothing I'd like more right now than a little tenderness, specifically from you. But I've got way too many people clanging around in my head to honestly give you my undivided attention. Let me clear up some of that first and then let's see what happens. Can I do that and call you tomorrow?"

She smiled and took my hand, walking me out to the front porch. "Absolutely. And I completely understand. Remember to take some Avena Sativa before you go to bed tonight, okay? You'll get a good night's sleep and then you'll wake up ready to go find Barbara. I'll look forward to hearing about it afterwards. What an adventure!"

She smiled like the angel she was, gave my hand a squeeze, and closed the door. All I could think as I stumbled down the stairs was: "She's the most beautiful woman I've ever not slept with."

# FORTY-TWO

DRIVING BACK TO the Motel 6 after an evening of surreal bliss at Fiona's felt like descension from a place of mystical heights. It also felt like it was about three o'clock in the morning, so when I checked the time I was surprised to note it was only ten. This had been one long, jam-packed day, but luckily it was still early enough to get in a call to Lucy. As I made my way down the hall and unlocked the door to my gray-walled home away from home, I felt so utterly discombobulated by the evening's events I had to sit for a moment and take stock of my evolving situation.

It had been a good day in terms of progress, a great day even, but I couldn't deny it: I had lost perspective. I couldn't readily remember Jane's face, I hadn't thought about my father for at least two hours, and I'd reprioritized the mission to the point that all I wanted to do now was suck herbs, eat oat cakes, and see that beautiful woman naked. I was aware that none of this was appropriate, given why I was up here instead of down in Los Angeles helping my sister.

But not only did the time of the day feel oddly out of whack, it also felt as if I'd been in Oakland for about a month instead of two days. Why was that? Maybe because I was spatially disoriented and completely detached from my normal life; I didn't know. But there was a sense of now living on a different planet, far, far from home, about to enter a portal from which I might never return. Either that or I just needed sleep and some food with heavier nutritional value than anything I'd consumed today.

Chomping on a protein bar, I flipped my phone open to face my daily comeuppance with a sense of dread and obligation. I'd had it on mute the whole day and could now see three messages from Lucy. This was not going to be pretty. And, more critically, she might have called with news of importance related to Dad, frantically trying to reach me while I was out mooning over my new friend. You idiot! Answer your damn phone; these are urgent times!

"So nice of you to check in, brother; it's been lonely here in the emergency room without you."

My heart jumped. Then I got confused. "Why is Dad in the emergency room when he's already in ICU?"

"Oh, not Dad. I'm not sure you're going to believe this; I know I didn't. Oh, and by the way, you did *not* leave your phone on as promised because I called you three times today and—"

"Actually, I *did* have it on, I muted it when I was at...at a meeting and forgot to turn it back on."

"Semantics, asshole. You didn't answer. That's the point: answering." I suddenly heard my mother in the background.

"Is that Danny? Let me talk to my boy—"

Before I could suggest Lucy *not* confuse things further by putting Esther on the phone, Esther was on the phone.

"Danny, where are you?"

"Mom. What's going on?"

"I'm better now, honey. They said there was no gangrene and it turns out the poison hadn't worked its way far enough into my system so, thank goodness, no permanent damage! I get to keep the arm!" She said all this in her gleeful Esther way...as if I had any idea what she was talking about.

Just as I was about to make that point, Lucy jumped back in: "Mom, they need you to go read some instructions about your bandage. I'll tell Dan what's going on." She was back on the phone. "You're not going to fucking believe this," she hissed.

"What? Would somebody tell me what's happening?"

"She got bit by a brown recluse."

"WHAT?"

"She actually got bit by a fucking brown recluse spider, is that insane? At first I thought she was being dramatic, maybe trying to get a little attention, complaining about a goddamn spider bite while Dad's up there drooling through his never-ending coma—"

"Jeez, Luce, take it easy—"

"Says the guy who's not here! The point is, one of the doctors asks her to show it to him, she does, and you'd fucking die."

"What?"

"She's got this rancid-looking speckled mass on her arm, swollen up like something out of *Alien*, the doctor practically freaks. Turns out this thing is unbelievably toxic, could cause paralysis, could be fatal, she has no idea when it happened. So I've got her downstairs in the ER on an antibiotic IV, Dad upstairs wired for sound, AND WHERE ARE YOU?"

That could not have been louder. She was not even bothering to disguise the strain at this point. In fact, she may have already snapped. I felt as guilty as I could feel. "I know, Luce, I'm so sorry. But I am making headway; it won't be long."

"I'm exhausted, Dan, you need to come home right now. I mean it."

"I will, I promise. One more day and I'm there. Is she going to be okay?"

"She'll live. I actually think she's thrilled to have a big old bandage on her arm. Everyone'll ask, she'll get to tell the story; it'll give her something to talk about besides crap '70s music and delusional family fun."

"You are a cruel girl." I couldn't help but laugh and was relieved when she did too.

"Yeah, and you're the one tracking down fantasy mom."

"Hey, you could be a tad more supportive about this. He's your father too."

"Oh, shut the fuck up before I get really mad."

"There's more mad to get?"

"Don't start with me, seriously."

"Okay, fine. So no news with Dad?"

"Nope. Which sucks. But the party line seems to be that it's still acceptable at this point, that things are busy righting themselves while he's off floating wherever he is. I don't know. But so far nothing new."

"I'll take that as good. Or better than what could be worse. Or whatever. Listen, tell Mom I love her, keep her away from elevator shafts and flammable liquids, and give Dad a kiss for me."

"Just get back here…and be good."

"I will."

"I mean it!"

"I will, jeez, goodbye!"

Why did she say that? "Be good." What did I have to *not* be good about?

Fiona, you asshole, that's what! Beautiful, magical Fiona.

My sister was now, apparently, reading minds.

# FORTY-THREE

SOMETIMES YOU JUST make the move. You decide to leap for something even if it might not be right, it might change your life more than you want, it might take you places from which you'll never return. But you leap because the pull is so strong you can't resist. And you refuse to think too hard about it, analyze it too lavishly, because you want the heat of sensation, the tactile, tangible realization of what it is you've dreamed of.

And just as I'd imagined her bedroom, once there I discovered it to be a wondrous place filled with flowers and candles, textured fabrics hanging like tapestries from the ceiling, and lace curtains draped across the windows. It was so *her*, this space, even as little as I knew of her, and I felt as if I'd entered a sumptuous domain that made the rest of the world seem dim and pale by comparison.

In the blue glimmer of moonlight creeping in from behind those lace curtains, I stretched out on Fiona's canopied bed and gazed at this woman now straddling my hips, feeling deliciously lost, seriously, sensuously lost in the intoxication of her touch, the heat and weight of her body on mine, the sheer artistry of her impeccable form.

She arched back, luscious and beautiful. Her breasts swayed to the rhythm of our motion, her hair a tangle of curls, her lips opened in unrestrained desire.

As my eyes fixed on her gorgeous face, my hands caressed the satin of her skin and we moved together in perfect tandem, as if we'd been making love to each other all our lives. *This* is what "soul mate" feels like, this pure, instinctive connection. I pulled her to me, longing for her eager mouth to envelope mine…fevered by the glow of what felt almost too perfect to be anything but a dream, until the sound of wailing sirens pierced the cloister of our ecstasy, and loud men started throwing beer bottles against brick walls, and I jerked up to realize, GODDAMMIT, THIS *IS* A DREAM! FUCK!

Awake now, my heart pounding, feeling as if I couldn't swallow for my thirst, I looked around the darkened, utterly uninspiring motel room for a bottle of water and all I could think was, "Tell me I am not really in THIS room…SHIT!"

But I was. In *this* room, not that one. In the one by the freeway entrance near the commercial district where that fucking dance club was still in high gear given the *thump thump thump* of Euro-trash disco and the squeals of drunk, chain-smoking, "Ladies Night" females. Those were *not* the feminine squeals I'd been enjoying moments earlier and I felt a deep resentment that my fucking head was far more exciting than my fucking life. For whatever reason, this sentiment compelled me to pick up the phone and call my roommate, a man who is often up at this hour and might be the only one to whom I could express my prurient frustration.

"Hel-lo…Bob's big boy, get 'em while they're wet!"

"I'm gone two days and you've turned the place into a bath house?" I heard a man's voice singing opera, very loudly. I imagined even Jane could hear it. Things must be going well over there.

"Oh, buddy, it's been party time since the day I was born!" Clearly he'd been drinking. "Why are you calling me at one-thirty in the morning? Is everything okay?"

"Bob, why is my fucking head so much more exciting than my

fucking life?"

I could sense his immediate tone shift. "Oh God, you found her!"

"Who?"

"Who? Barbara! What do you mean, 'who'?"

"Oh, yeah…I'm closer but, no, not yet. It hasn't exactly been a cakewalk. Now I know why I don't live in Oakland."

"Screw Oakland, what's up with Babs?"

"I found the gazebo, the one in that picture I showed you."

"I have no idea what you're talking about. Have you called her yet?"

"Yeah, I did. Big letdown there. The number wasn't hers."

"Whose was it?"

"Why does that matter at this point?"

"I don't know. Maybe the person could give you some information."

"She was a renter. She had no information."

"Okay, fine. But remember: tomorrow is day three. Day three out of four. You're a man on a mission, Dan, let's not forget that."

"I haven't forgotten."

"Wait. What was this about your fucking head versus your fucking life or whatever all that was?"

"It's complicated."

"Do not start with the time/space crap. You're not twelve, buddy, and you've only got me for two more days. So go find her, ask your questions, and git on home. Simple."

"Nothing is simple."

"What does that mean?"

I couldn't help but sigh like the twelve-year-old he just said I wasn't. "It's a mess."

"Oh, man, is it your dad?"

Now I felt like an asshole. "No, no. It's Fiona."

His pause felt judgmental. So did his voice. "Who the hell is Fiona?"

Suddenly it all burst from me like a tumultuous dam of repressed...tumult. "I met this girl, Bob, this warm, gorgeous, generous girl, who gave me tea and herbs and let me tell her the whole story without one snide comment. She had a computer that saved my life, she helped me find the gazebo, her house is full of dried flowers and herbs, and her butch roommate is apparently a masseuse nonpareil. I think she might be my soul mate." Deep breath.

"The butch roommate?"

"No, fool, Fiona."

"I don't think I've ever heard a straight person use the word 'nonpareil' before."

"Fiona said it and, trust me, she's a *very* straight person."

"Okaaaay..."

"I mean...*Fiona*. Even her name is special. Have you ever heard a more poetic name?"

"I'm not even going to mention that you now sound even gayer than your last statement, but let's get real: there are plenty of Fionas out there since *Shrek*, my friend."

"That's not really the point, Bob."

"What is the point? Shall we presume you've slept with her?"

"No. Didn't want to. I mean, I *wanted* to...oh, God, if you could only have been inside my head a minute ago—"

"Please don't make me."

"I'm just saying I *want* to sleep with her, but I've decided to wait."

"For what? The Barbara showdown? Permission from your ex? A note from your mother?"

"No. Until I know it's more than a one-night, up-in-Oakland, out-of-town, leaving-tomorrow hook-up."

There was a reverential pause from the most sexually active man in Toluca Lake. "Then, good God, man...this *is* serious."

# FORTY-FOUR

UNBURDENING MY ANGST to Bob, however brash and boozy he might have been in response, had a certain cleansing effect. Or maybe it was the reminder that he was only covering me until Saturday. Whatever it was, after I got back to sleep for a few hours, sleep sadly bereft of any sequel to the interrupted dream of earlier (one I'd likely be replaying for years to come), I woke up Thursday morning, day three, ready to make some serious headway.

Showered, shaved, and as nicely dressed as my second unpressed shirt would allow, I slugged back a shot of Avena Sativa with its reflexive grimace, pocketed my phone, grabbed all the necessary photos, my notepad, and a handful of protein bars. Most importantly, I made sure I had my copy of the "triangulation map" Fiona and I created the night before: the library, the bridge exit, and the gazebo. Somewhere in the middle of all that, I felt absolutely convinced, was the house where Barbara lived. Lives. Hopefully.

Of course, just running that thought through my head reminded me that the odds of her or anyone from her family still living in that house were really quite slim. Who stays in their childhood home once they're an adult? I didn't. Lucy didn't. Bob didn't. We grow up and we move on. We buy a condo or build something in an emerging neighborhood. We drive by the old house from time-to-time and reminisce about our high school pool parties as we notice the new owner mowing the lawn. But we don't *live* there.

I slumped back down on the bed and felt buffeted, yet again, by the weight of futility. What the fuck was I thinking? Even if I found the house near the gazebo and the library, the house with the ornate wrought iron gate, it was highly unlikely Barbara would still be living there fifty years later.

Then again, Bob's parents live in the house where his father grew up. I have a softball buddy who lives in a house handed down from his grandparents. It *does* happen. And, frankly, what did I have to lose at this point? I'd made the trip to Oakland. I'd located the likely area. If I did every single thing I could and still didn't succeed, no one could fault me. Not even Lucy.

I readjusted my attitude and headed out to the day of reckoning…or whatever the day would end up being by the time it was done.

## FORTY-FIVE

MAP IN HAND, I stood inside the dilapidated gazebo and looked outward, surveying the surrounding neighborhoods like a bloodhound with a scent. I had a gut feeling I needed to somehow intuit my way through this exploration. I wasn't exactly sure what that meant, but I was convinced I had to tap into some psychic connection to my father's history, the history of the woman to whom he'd pledged his heart, feel the pull of energy they'd created together and let that guide me...like a divining rod.

Oh, fuck me, I needed to get boots on the ground and march up and down every street within the triangle to see if a one of them had a house with a gate that looked anything like the house and gate in the photograph, period!

And so I did. I tromped up and down what surely must have been every single damn street anywhere within walking distance of that park and when I was so tired I could barely walk, I found a tamale cart and enjoyed a late lunch of some spectacularly good pork tamales, vegan be damned.

Once fed, I had a hearty surge of optimism. The sun was

shining, I was focused on the mission, and I'd been unusually efficient with my usual obligations: I'd already called Lucy; she didn't pick up, but I was pleased to have gotten to her before she left her first message of the day. I'd checked in with Zoey, who was still laughing it up with my roommate—whatever; all was going swimmingly over there. I even texted Fiona, confirming that her map had, so far, been very useful, though I'd not yet had any luck finding the house. She texted back something appropriately cheerful and encouraging, enough to buoy my spirits for another round of pavement pounding. I downed my Jarritos Tamarind soda and hit the sidewalk for another round.

After two more hours of walking, however, I was nearing a point of both exhaustion and hopelessness. I turned onto Chantry Avenue, a small, one-block street that dead-ended on the other side of the park, and stopped to pull another soda from my backpack. Once quenched, I popped the empty bottle into a nearby recycling bin (Oakland *was* remarkably green!) and looked around. There was nothing notable about this street, certainly not more than any other I'd been up or down. I made my way past about six houses of varying degrees of curb appeal, turned to my right, then to my left, and then…I saw it. I shook my head, blinked a couple of times, and looked again. My God. There it was—rustier, darker, but undeniable: *the ornate wrought iron gate.*

I practically ripped the manila envelope from my backpack and pulled out the photo in question, staring at the fifty-year-old image of a young woman, with beautiful eyes and a sensual smile meant for the man behind the camera, posed in front of a gate. I looked up from the picture, and there was no question…it was the very same gate. I felt a rush that almost took my breath away.

Flushed with excitement, I crossed the street and peered beyond the gate; I was not disappointed. There it was, as if emerging from the fog of time and history: the house. Though shabbier, with a yard that needed the hand of a good gardener, it was the same beautiful old Craftsman captured in the photo—a house, I'd guess, that had once been the crown jewel of the neighborhood. Slap on a sepia filter and it was golden.

I stood for a moment in existential awe. I could not believe I'd actually found it. The place where it happened. Where my dad stood, helplessly falling in love with the lithesome Barbara, who would scurry from that house to this gate to join him for a stroll down Oaklandian lanes. This was also where he'd been kept hidden, behind this same row of bushes where I now stood, unwelcomed inside because the woman of his dreams was the lying, cheating fiancée of another man—

Okay, *not* a line of thought to get into while prepping to meet the fabled woman who would hopefully solve the mysteries of the romantic universe. I shook it off and looked around, assessing my options. Unwilling to make myself too visible at this early stage of exploration, I thought it might be a decent idea to take a peek through the bushes. I discreetly shoved my arm into the rather tightly packed foliage (what *was* this stuff?), hoping to pry it apart just enough to glimpse at the front of the house without detection. Too dense. And, of course, as I attempted to quietly extricate myself, a branch snagged the strap of my watch and within seconds I was flapping around like Jim Carrey trying to escape the bullying bush. It would have been funny were I watching; experiencing it was a lot less hilarious, particularly since I was trying to blend in with the scenery, not be consumed by it.

I finally got myself detached, but as I sputtered under my breath, pulling small branches out from my cuff and wristband, I felt the distinct sense of detection. I glanced nonchalantly to my right. It seemed the woman across the street might have been peering in my direction from behind her own flank of shrubberies, but she now had her back to me with the hose going. Probably just doing her gardening. And I was probably just being paranoid.

Turning back to the house, it was clear I was going to have to make a frontal assault, no getting around it. I stretched my neck a few times, adjusting my face to, hopefully, affect an expression of casual friendliness, opened the noted gate, and strode up the walkway to the house. I knocked. There was no response. I sidled up to a window bordering the front door…interesting treatment going on there. Behind a draping of beads was a collection of brightly colored ceramic statues: a couple of clowns doing who-knows-what and the bust of a smiling wide-eyed woman in black. Oddly artistic. Either someone inside had an eclectic sense of decorative humor or this was *not* the home of a seventy-something woman.

I went back to the door, knocked again, harder this time. Nothing. I considered leaving a note—maybe my business card—then decided against it, thinking the name might give away the mission and I was still fixed on the advantage of surprise. Particularly since I had no idea if Barbara or anyone who even knew Barbara was actually living in this house. I headed back to my car and, again, noticed the woman across the street. Yep, she was definitely looking my way, hose still in hand.

"Excuse me," I called out to her.

She turned to me with a decidedly unfriendly glower. "Can I help you?"

"Do you happen to know if a woman named Barbara lives in that house over there?" I motioned across the street. "Or if anyone in this neighborhood might have known the woman named Barbara who lived there?"

"Why is that any of your business?"

Her tone inspired a fleeting thought about Frank from Kenny's Gas & Mart. "She was an old friend of my father's from many years ago, fifty years ago, actually, and I'm trying to find her. I don't want to bother whoever lives there now if it's not her, so I wondered if you had any information."

A dogged glare conveyed her disinclination to help. Perhaps the "she was an old friend of my father's" was a well-worn scam for people of her generation, but I was just trying to be informative. And accurate. And getting nowhere.

"I'm not at liberty to say, thank you very much." And with that she turned her back to continue watering.

Fine. But I took her snippy dismissal as an affirmative. I'd be back in the morning. Oh, this was going down.

## FORTY-SIX

FIONA INVITED ME to dinner at her place, insisting we celebrate my considerable progress, and the woman had done it up right. Though not quite as gauzy—or naked—as my dream, the setting was still pretty dreamy, with scores of candles lighting the living room where we were currently ensconced, gazing at each other like two lovesick puppies. In the glow of candlelight she seemed even more beautiful than she had the day before. How was that possible? I found myself imagining how I'd like to photograph that gorgeous face; the angles, the softness, even the tiny lines in the crinkles of her eyes made her all the more alluring. She was visual perfection...from both a photographic standpoint and a romantic one. I felt like I could stare at that face for the rest of my life.

With the remnants of dinner and dessert on the coffee table, we talked for some time about my day, mutually gleeful that our detective work had led me to the exact spot I'd hoped to find. I have to say, I *was* impressed with myself. Undoubtedly, I was impressed with her. And since it was definitely time I got to know a bit more about her, I asked the questions this go-around.

I learned that she was twenty-three (I don't think that's too young), of Danish and Puerto Rican descent (a compelling combination), transplanted from Santa Cruz a year earlier in the thrall of a traveling musician who'd later hit the road without her (she made the cliché sound romantic). She was close to her four siblings and amicably divorced parents, all of whom remained in her home state of Indiana, a place she'd left to attend the University of California, Santa Cruz. I couldn't help but feel profoundly grateful for the twists and turns in her road that had somehow led her here, to this moment, with me.

Aware of a warm surge of contentment, I took in the room, feeling all kinds of cozy. "It's so nice in here tonight: the food, all the candles..."

She laughed. "This time we really *can* thank the electric company. I never seem to get the bill paid on time and today they pulled the plug. But I think candles are so much nicer anyway, don't you?"

I looked around and realized the twinkle lights were, indeed, not twinkling. "I do. In certain circumstances they put lights to shame."

Fiona smiled coyly and reached across me to a stack of books she'd piled on the couch; she handed me a small paperback. "I wanted to share some books with you; they're favorites of mine. Do you like to read?"

"Yes, mostly the classics, sometimes more contemporary fiction. What about you?"

"Oh, I like lots of different things. Have you read this one, *The Four Agreements*?"

"No, I don't think so. Good?" It looked like something you'd pick up at the Psychic Eye Book Shop on Ventura Boulevard.

"Very. It's a really beautiful, simple book. Kind of a road map to enlightenment and freedom. I wasn't sure if you were into that kind of thing and don't want to make any presumptions, but I thought someone as fearless as you might have read it at some point in your life."

Fearless? I don't get that attribute thrown my way too often. "To be honest, I can't say I've spent a lot of time investigating spiritual matters, but it's not something I'm adverse to exploring either." Certainly I'd been relying on Divine Intervention with more enthusiasm than any time previous. "And thank you; 'fearless' is kind."

She snuggled in closer. "I think a man who can defy convention and reach back into his family's history to reclaim something precious for his father is fearless."

All I could think was: I wish the other women in my life could hear me described with such open admiration. "Well, thank you, Fiona. That's a really sweet thing to say."

She smiled again. God, that face. Suddenly she sat up and looked at the table. "You haven't eaten your pie!"

Yes...the pie. I'd mentioned to Fiona that I loved pie, probably not long after actually meeting her over a piece, and so she made this pie today with her sweet, beautiful hands. And now, set before me was a hearty piece of thick-crusted pie I had ever-so-briefly tasted, then set aside in my laser focus on Fiona (at least, that's what I told myself). Topped with a heavy dollop of vegan whipped cream, it was a well-intended offering I could no longer ignore. But this pie—she watched as I took a bite and swallowed thickly—*sucked*. How a pie could actually suck, I don't know, but this one did, lacking in sugar, flavor, or a crust that had been baked to any degree of actual crustiness. I grabbed my ever-present cup of tea just to get it down, telling myself it was not necessary for this dazzling woman to be good at *everything*. "Now, what is this, boysenberry?"

She clapped her hands. "It is! You guessed it!"

"I can't believe you made it...for me!"

"Just for you."

"You are a true artist."

"It takes one to know one."

So sweetly second grade, all this. Was it acceptable to feel seven and horny at the same time? Anyway, now that we'd gotten past the pie discussion and I could safely put it aside as if there were plans to get back to it later, I was hoping for further conversation or, perhaps, even some of that tenderness she'd—but before I could put my arm around her, she reached back into the book pile and pulled out another selection.

"You'll love this book, too. It's been around a long time, but it's still so completely relevant I think it will amaze you. It's called *The Artist's Way*, a sort of manual on how to tap into the artist inside. It might inspire you to reach beyond what you're doing now to try something more artistic."

That hit me oddly. "What's wrong with what I do now?" I tried not to sound as defensive as I suddenly felt.

"Oh, Dan, there's nothing wrong with what you do," she was quick to answer. "I just think a man like you should be doing something with that incredible imagination of yours, that sense of adventure. You should be taking fine art photographs, beautiful pictures that reveal something of who you are, your unique view of the world. Have you ever thought of that?"

Seriously? "Of course I've thought of that, many times. I think every photographer does. I just never found there was much of a living to be made in landscapes."

My defensiveness could not even pretend subtlety. She took my hand and moved in very close. Ahhh…better. "I don't mean to insult you. Of course a man has to support himself. I'm only saying you've got this really special sensitivity; I feel it in everything you do and I imagine it could lead you to being a really successful fine art photographer, that's all."

She smiled, caressed my cheek, and I melted, thinking to myself: gorgeous, profound, and perceptive. Who needs flaky crust?

We talked further about books, art, our individual jobs and what they entailed, all while holding hands like teenagers with parents in the other room. Which was strange in a way, our chasteness, since Maris was not even home. I think, after my dream, I'd expected something of a more libidinous nature to carry over into real life, something more ardent driving the energy of this evening, but, for whatever reason, I wasn't making the moves. Then again, I was also repeatedly checking my watch, not able to fully squelch the pressure of the nightly Lucy report, and that, no doubt, had something to do with my reticence. I made regretful noises about having to leave, and we once again took that slow walk to the front door, me with my new books under my arm.

Outside we stood at the top of the stairs, and in the golden light thrown off by the street lamps, with the fog swirling all around, Fiona looked movie star gorgeous. A feeling of honest adoration grabbed at my heart. She leaned into my shoulder, and I buried my face in the crook of her warm, fragrant neck, mumbling. She pulled my chin up. "What did you say?"

"I said I want to stay."

"Then stay." Very direct, no equivocation. She took my face in her hands and kissed me in that long, deep way that makes men's knees buckle. Our first real kiss. My knees buckled.

I had to step back for air. "Oh, God…you are so incredible and I have to go."

She cocked her head as if slightly confused. Which was not hard to figure, since I was more than slightly confused myself. "Have I done anything to—"

"No! You have done nothing but charm me off my feet. Thank you for dinner, for the pie, the books, the candles, the electric company." This time I pulled her to me, kissing her again, but gently. There was no point in stirring further ardor until I could do something about it.

As she stepped up to the top of the porch, she gave me a wistful smile, as if we were saying a real goodbye. Which made my stomach drop. Because, though I had no idea what, exactly, I'd be doing in the next twenty-four hours, it was certain I'd be leaving this fine city shortly thereafter.

"Night, Dan. And good luck tomorrow. The big day, finally, right?"

"Yes, right…the big day. Finally. Hopefully."

"I'd love to hear how it turns out."

"Of course! You'll be my first call."

She smiled again and went inside, softly closing the door behind her.

As I turned and shuffled down the steps yet again, a hollow, lonely feeling descended.

So *this* is what smitten feels like.

## FORTY-SEVEN

"SMITTEN? *PLEASE*...IT'S mission creep, dude!"

I was on the phone with Bob. Who was starting to sound like Lucy. Who I'd already called. She, thankfully, had been in the thick of things at work, and after an uncharacteristically pleasant and quick status report on Dad and Spiderwoman, left it that we'd talk more after I wrapped things up Friday. Now it seemed Bob was filling in on the surly front.

"What does being smitten have to do with 'mission creep'?" I snapped back.

"My point is, Dan, you set out to do one thing, now all of a sudden you're all caught up in another. You're majorly distracted, your focus is shot, you're all busy falling in love…or whatever it is you're doing with Miss Gorgeous Oakland Flower Child."

"I admit this was not anticipated, obviously, but, trust me, I remain utterly focused on the mission!"

"With a little collateral damage on the side, is that it?"

"Would you stop with the military-speak? Man, I thought you'd be thrilled for me."

"Did you really? Okay, I'm thrilled. Especially after getting my sixth phone message today from your recently dispatched fiancée and me fresh out of lies."

Jane was still on the warpath? What the hell? "I'm sorry about that but, come on! She's responsible for her own situation, including the initial dispatchment...which lasted long enough to lead to my more recent dispatching. Let's not revise history."

"Look, all I'm saying is, I'm being cornered here, and I'm not sure what to say at this point."

As annoyed as I was at the moment, I did genuinely regret getting Bob mixed up in whatever it was Jane was doing. "Sorry, man, obviously this is not your problem. I didn't expect it to *be* a problem. Just tell her you're out of the loop. I don't know why she's bugging you about anything right now anyway. Our last conversation should've made things pretty clear to her."

"Apparently not," Bob sighed. "Or maybe she's seen the light since you left. But she's definitely got a new agenda going. Oh, and by the way, in one of her many calls she mentioned that she'd been at your office and found some piece of paper with 'Barbara' and 'Oakland' written on it. That seems to have piqued her curiosity."

So *that* was what Zoey caught her taking off my desk! The torn corner with the phone number. A little invasive, maybe? "Well, odds are, like so many other things between us lately, she's either misinterpreted it or blown it out of proportion."

"Yeah, as if you had a secret someone in Oakland. Imagine that?"

"Really, stop."

"Just sayin'."

"Okay, fine; point taken. But please tell me you didn't get into any of the Barbara stuff with her. So not interested in her opinion of how stupid I am right now."

"I played dumb. Last thing I want is to get involved in trying to explain your life to anyone at the moment. I'm pretty sure even *you* couldn't explain it. But she's riled up, Dano. Does she have any idea about this Fiona chick?"

"Fuck no! You're the only one who knows anything about this Fiona chick, so it better stay that way. But I'm telling you, Jane and I officially ended it. Which means any discussions about what I do from here on out are none of her business."

"I hear ya, bro, but I'm not sure *she's* convinced it's really over. She seems to think it's just been about bad timing or something."

"Okay, I'll get to her tomorrow and see if I can call off the dogs."

"So sensitive."

"Give me a break, man!"

"I've given you a four-day break—hey, my doorbell just rang. That's weird; I don't have plans tonight."

"How unique."

"Fuck you. Wait; let me check, make sure it's not a home invasion or a gang of Witnesses. Okaaay…I'm looking through the dining room window and…"

"Let's call it a night and you can—"

"Fuuuck. You're not going to believe this." Suddenly Bob was whispering into the phone. "It's Jane."

Now she was chasing Bob down to chase after me? We were such a cliché. "Are you kidding me? What is up with her? Never mind…look, tell her—"

"I got it, dude, trust me. You take care of your end and get your ass home. After that she'll be all yours."

"But wait—what are you going to say to her?" I was whispering, too, not sure why.

"I'm going to reemphasize that you're out of town working. Maybe I'll suggest she move on with her life. Then I'll feed her; that always works. She's still ringing, gotta go."

"You're a good man."

"You have no idea, McDowell."

Jane. Wow. Sitting here in Oakland, having just come from Fiona's house, the thought of Jane ringing the doorbell at Bob's in search of answers about me felt like a page from another time, another place, and a very different chapter of my life. Was that normal? Feeling that way? It wasn't that long ago we were excited about a July wedding. Was I being callous? Retaliatory? Male? How did this happen?

It happened. We turn pages, don't we?

## FORTY-EIGHT

FIONA'S WORDS STUCK. The ones about how I should be doing something more artistic with my "incredible imagination." It was a little insulting on the one hand; on the other, I liked that she framed my work in a more creative light. I once did, too.

I'd thought a lot about things like *artistry* and *creativity* when I was in school. I was one of those passionate students excited about everything I was doing, whether learning to shoot with film or working with the piles of digital equipment we had at our disposal, whether attending master classes on studio lighting or running the streets with guerillas of the new technology. Everything is potent and possible when you're young, particularly when you're embedded in one of the best art schools in the country, and, like every other kid with a camera, I had a finely tuned plan to be the next Ansel Adams, Helmut Newton, or Henri Cartier-Bresson. At twenty, my "incredible imagination" was in full swing.

Then school was over and it was time for life. I worked hard those first couple of years out, taking any kind of photography jobs I could get, focused on establishing a portfolio and expanding my network. I interned with a number of well-established pros and went after whatever fine art commissions I could get. Bob and I were sharing an apartment in Culver City at the time, and I remember being impressed by how committed he was to his own path. We were both good, each with our individual style and sensibilities, but frankly, he did a lot better on the work front than I did, which probably had to do with his ease at selling himself and cultivating a wider pool of contacts. I was always more restrained with all that. We both lived like paupers, though, very artist garret and the like, but then things shifted for him. He got a major gig apprenticing with an eminent fine art photographer who showed in places like MOMA, the Met, and the Smithsonian, and the trickle-down for him was powerful. He didn't get to shoot much at first, but I could see he was learning a lot, and he hopped from there to a couple of other high profile gigs, leading to some prestigious exhibits of his own in Los Angeles and New York. Me, I was raking it in with the portraits.

But in the decade or so since we graduated, the industry has changed—a lot. The rules have slip-slided all over the place, and while there are still (probably) plenty of lucrative, highly regarded opportunities for the elite sector, for the rest of us, most of the old paradigms have been blown to bits. The "perceived value" of our work, and certainly of *us* as professional photographers, has been trumped. The greater photo-crazed public now considers anyone with an iPhone, an Instagram account, and a web page an "artist," and not a lot is being paid for. Some of the work is good, some of it is awful; you can make a buck here or there, then you find your photos all over the Internet without a dime changing hands or even a credit to your name. No one seems to know what to do about any of it, but the general *think* about art—how it's monetized, how it's valued (or not), even what *is* art—is being debated and ripped apart by the artists themselves, as well as every commenter, blogger, or Tweeter with a mouth, brain, or set of eyes. The prevailing message seems to be, "The wave's too big, you can't stop it, quit your whining, grab a GoPro, and hop onboard." It's the wild, wild west out there, whether we like it or not.

The point is, in reference to Fiona's suggestion, I have no fucking idea how to be a "really successful fine art photographer" at this point. Bob made some kind of workable accommodation when he got into wedding photography, and I'm dead serious when I say his wedding photographs are some of the most beautiful work I've ever seen. His subjects tend to agree. He gets calls from across the country and works about as much as he'd like during the busy season, but he still mixes it up with his fine art stuff. He's relentless about keeping all his plates in the air, and, in that regard, he's my idol.

I've been lazier, maybe. Less motivated. When I got the job offer from Joaquin, I took it reluctantly, with a sense that, by taking a full-time gig, I was selling out my artistic soul. But the bargain I made with myself was that I'd follow Bob's lead and get out on free days to shoot the more artistic stuff. I even had this one very cool theme I wanted to shoot around, something inspired and artistic enough to hopefully show some of my contacts in the better galleries around the city. And I did get out some, set up a few studio sessions, shot some interesting stuff to see what I could come up with, but it never caught fire. *I* never caught fire. I felt uninspired, unconvinced that I wanted to do the dance just to get a show now and again and spend the rest of my time hawking my website on social media.

Eventually the money I was making with Joaquin became the drug; the more I worked, the more I made, and I worked a lot. I told myself I wasn't a complete whore because, like Bob, I *did* bring art to even the most mundane of sessions. Just as Joaquin pointed out, I made those damn eighth grade portraits as arty as time and the Los Angeles Unified School District would allow. And parents got it; my portraits *weren't* your average grade school shots. I got referrals, the business boomed and…well, here we are, with Joaquin offering me a partnership and Fiona suggesting I be more courageous. As ever, I am confused.

The point to this analysis on this particular morning, Friday, day four, the last day of my Oakland sojourn, is that I got up early, strapped on my camera, and hauled over the bridge to Ocean Beach. Yes, *that* Ocean Beach, the very place Jim McDowell met Barbara from Oakland and started this long, bizarre journey. A place I wanted to view through my own lens. I also wanted to see if I felt inspired enough to take some shots of what I was observing, rather than what I'd arranged on a bleacher or in a boardroom.

It was cool and foggy when I got there, typical weather for this part of the world at this time of year. It was a weekday, so there weren't many people around, which was good. I'd left my shoes in the car, intent on fully embracing the beach experience, something I don't do often enough and used to enjoy. The crashing surf and squawking gulls made a quintessential soundtrack for my seaside jaunt; I rolled up my cuffs, pulled my jacket tighter, and headed out.

My first thought was that it was too gloomy for inspiration, what with the wind kicking up and the fog thickening. My second was that I was getting sand in my cuffs, which would likely be hard to completely shake out later, and the grit between my toes was…well…gritty. My third, which came just as a pelican dived into a wave and tufts of sea foam skittered across the beach like little girls in tutus, was…this is fucking beautiful.

For a while I just wandered, trying to envision the scene Jim described in his story, its accompanying images memorialized in the photos: Barbara and her giggling friends perched on their blue blanket, Jim and the boys strutting across the sand, the heat of summer sun, the buzz of young life with its intoxicating conviction of being on the brink of something open-ended and important. Though it might have been different for Jim's generation. It was a strange time, 1965: fear of the impending Vietnam War, guys worried about leaving college to be pulled into the draft, early signs of the cultural revolution ready to break. Or maybe it was all the more electric for that heightened anticipation. Maybe Jim and his buddies were eager to push against the boundaries of what came before to get started on all that was to come for them. It's hard to picture my dad being particularly revolutionary about anything, but those *were* the times.

When I focused the lens and took my first shot, I felt as though I could actually *see* those images, the ones Jim remembered, the ones he didn't even see. Shot after shot: the Cliffhouse in the distance, the rock formations off the shore line, the pelicans skating across the galloping edge of water, the handful of surfers braving the morning waves.

It felt good, like a familiar muscle being put to use after too long a rest, a muscle that quickly found its way back to rhythm and pace. I walked farther than I planned but it was invigorating. I felt grounded, connected to my shooter's eye, my sense of composition, my confidence that what I was capturing was a story and the story I was capturing was art…of the finer kind.

Meaning that I, Dan McDowell, photographer of wiggling grade-schoolers, well-heeled socialites, and bored corporate drones, was out in the world on this glorious day taking some damn beautiful pictures.

# FORTY-NINE

TWO HOURS LATER, with feet colder than I'd like and, yes, persistent sand sticking to the folds of my jeans, I was back on the Bay Bridge to Oakland. Traffic at this hour was far worse than the commute earlier but certainly better than what was happening on the other side, where cars headed toward San Francisco were stacked up for the westbound toll. I turned on the radio and slowly made my way to Chantry Avenue.

Given that it was now my last day in Oakland, I was more than poised for the next inevitable step: contact. Period. No more delays. Please. I pulled onto Barbara's street, parked the car, and marched up to the gate like a man with a mission. Which I was...though I once again felt the knot of anxiety that came every time I imagined myself facing the mystery woman. GET A GRIP, MAN, AND GET ON WITH IT! (Even my psyche was yelling at me.)

I made my way up to the porch and knocked as loudly as one does when actually hoping to arouse someone from inside. Nothing...again. I knocked twice more. As the seconds ticked by with no response, I thought, "Is this woman *ever* home?" There was one brief instant when I thought I detected motion at the front window, the one with the odd beaded treatment and weird statues, but a second look proved otherwise. I knocked one more time for good measure but still no one answered.

A frustrating development. I hadn't considered any scenario in which I found the house but was never able to make contact. Now it seemed like a very real possibility. Barbara's actual presence—or at least my access to her presence—was ultimately out of my control, but returning to LA without even talking to her would obviously make my reason for coming seem all the more flawed to my selected detractors. But leaving in the morning was non-negotiable.

Shaking my head, I walked back to the car and just sat there, thinking. An idea popped up: what about a stakeout? What if—instead of coming and going—I sit here for a while and watch who else comes and goes? Why not? What could it hurt?

So, okay; that was the plan. I determined, however, that it might be wise to tuck myself off to the side a bit, rather than perched front and center. As I pulled slowly from the curb to drive around the block and park on the perpendicular street, I couldn't help but notice the curmudgeonly neighbor once again stooped over a line of bushes, peering at me sideways through the slats of her fence as though I couldn't see her. Which reminded me of those toddlers who cover their eyes and presume they're now invisible to the outside world. She was not only *not* invisible, her rather hefty carriage made her impossible to miss. I waved as I drove past.

I parked far enough down the block to be out of her sightlines but close enough to keep an eye on Barbara's house. It seemed an excellent vantage point. Now I'd wait.

As I sat there studying the house with its interesting flourishes and noticeable attempts at exterior maintenance, I once again pictured young Jim McDowell parked on this same street, waiting, just as I was now, for Barbara to appear. What does it say about a guy when his life is tracking along a parallel route with a father he barely understands and often finds impossible to tolerate? I would never consider me and my dad to be similar men, but damn if I wasn't doing a good job of disproving my own theory.

I must have fallen asleep, and for quite some time, because when a sudden and startling rap at my window jolted me awake to the ferocious visage of the cranky neighbor, I was stunned to note the darkening sky. I sat up quickly, got my bearings, and rolled down the window.

Before I could utter a syllable, she squawked, "I'm warning you right now, mister, if you don't move off this street instantly I will be calling the police."

"Ma'am, I think we've gotten off on the wrong foot. I'm not a threat to anyone, I'm just trying to find this woman named Barbara who lived here fifty years ago and I haven't had any luck, so I'm sitting here hoping she'll show up and I can talk to her."

She seemed unimpressed by my explanation. "I don't care what your excuse is, you're breaking the law by loitering, and it will not be tolerated."

"Okay, well how about this? I'm going to go back up to the house and knock on the door again, and if no one answers, I'll take off. How's that? Nice and friendly, no need to get yourself in a tizzy, I promise you."

With that somewhat cocky retort, I climbed out of my car, marched up to the door and knocked. Knocked several times. Louder. Louder still. No response. Damn.

With the snarling mistress of the neighborhood overseeing from the sidewalk, arms folded and the countenance of a prison warden, I came back through the gate, climbed into my car, gave her a smartass salute, and drove off. Looking back through the rearview mirror, I swore I saw motion at that beaded window again. I had a distinct feeling Barbara really was in there, which only exacerbated my sinking realization of opportunity lost. So close...but my last card had finally been played.

# FIFTY

AS INCONGRUOUS AS beauty may be in the generic gray environs of the average Motel 6 room, Fiona was, in fact, in such a room, my room, stretched out on my bed being a beautiful, sensuous anomaly. She had decided I needed some cheering up, especially after hearing that my Barbara attempts of the day had been unsuccessful and I had no choice but to leave first thing in the morning. Since Maris was hosting a massage clinic at their house, Fiona insisted she come over to the wrong side of town to share this precious last night with me. It was a delightful gesture, and the fact that it was happening in this slightly tacky motel room made it all the more decadent. Which only added to the buzz.

I wasn't sure exactly what might, or even should, transpire in this room over the course of the evening. I'd expressed to Fiona the need to clear my head before launching into actual honest-to-God sex, but I was now wondering, considering I'd be leaving in the morning, if dispensation could be given for the sheer *effort* to clear my head. I also considered, depending on how far I wanted to take this, that it might be time to discuss the pertinent "where do we go from here?"

question at some point before, during, or after said actual sex. It seemed doable to fit everything in but, still, I wasn't sure exactly how to play my last remaining hours in Oakland.

The TV was set to some kind of "Behind the Music" drama, and after welcoming Fiona in and getting us somewhat awkwardly situated with snacks and beverages procured from the nearby Korner Pantry, I remained seated at the edge of the bed, committed to seeing it through with the band going down in flames, pretending *not* to be supremely focused on the impossibly sexy woman on the sheets beside me. Fiona, however, appeared in no mood for pretense or restraint and, suddenly, in one swift and decidedly graceful move, had me flat on my back with her legs wrapped around my waist, my hands pinned above my head. Her expression left no doubt about what was to commence. And then it happened. Well, not *it*, but as close to *it* as we'd been so far. She stretched her body along the entire length of mine, our various parts connecting in all the ways and places one's parts do in that position, and she kissed me with as much heat as a luscious, provocative woman could embody.

For a moment I ludicrously considered resisting, but this undeniably mind-blowing activity continued unabated for long enough that I ultimately lost all interest in anything else, including what happened to the hapless band, what I did or didn't get accomplished in Oakland, who would or wouldn't approve, or why anyone had any reason to disapprove of my life choices anyway. I was a single man and this was *my* life…and I wanted this woman right here, right now.

Playfulness was pushed aside; I flipped her over and pressed myself into her with all the urgency I'd been holding back, overcome by the sensation that I couldn't get close enough, to her, her body, her touch, her smell. We were finally on the same page, eager to get past the wit and parry of the last two days, hands caressing every inch of the other as clothes got unbuttoned, unzipped, undone, and then…

BAM BAM BAM!

We both jumped up as if it were Mom. What the hell? Fiona gave me a look of such surprise I almost had to laugh. Her cheeks flushed, her eyes wide as a child's, she could not have been more appealing in that moment if she tried.

"Hold on, sweetheart," I whispered as I zipped up my jeans, leaning in for a quick kiss. Though I hated to climb from that wonderfully warm spot, I wanted to get whatever asshole was on the other side of the door taken care of tout suite so we could get back to this rapturous activity.

I got to the door, took a quick look through the peephole, then stepped back as if I'd been kicked in the groin.

"What is it?" Fiona whispered, alarmed. She'd gotten up by now and had pulled on her shirt, adjusting the bedspread as if somehow we could hide what we'd been up to.

I turned to her with all the restraint I could pull together and said, "Fiona, I want you to sit down and go to that peaceful, loving place inside you often speak of. I'll apologize for this right now, with plans to apologize again later when I call to grovel like the complete dick I am about to become."

I could see by the look of panic on her face that she had no idea what was about to happen. Nor did I. But I opened the door…to Jane.

# FIFTY-ONE

IT WOULD BE impossible to overstate the soul-cringing awkwardness that ensued from there. The amplitude of it was off the charts and seemed to stun everyone into momentary silence. After unfortunate acknowledgments were made, I stepped out to the hallway, shooting a helpless look back to Fiona before closing the door behind me, attempting next to find whatever words were possible now that I was directly faced with Jane. There was some mindless prattling, as I recall, though I did not bother to explain who Fiona was or why she was there (it seemed obvious). The shellshocked expression on Jane's face said about all that was needed on her end. It was hell in every possible way this sort of unexpected thing can be hell.

Fiona wisely made a swift departure—I have no memory of what, if anything, she might have said, only that she slipped out of the room with a pained look, and scurried off in a way I *never* want to see a girl I like scurrying from my motel room. Humiliation rolled over me like heat from an atomic bomb and to say I felt like rat shit doesn't begin to cover it.

I felt pretty ratty on Jane's behalf, as well. Despite my true infatuation for the flushed and flustered girl who just fled my room, and beyond the discomfort of tumescent interruptus, there was no denying that the devastated woman left standing in front of me was someone I loved and cared about. Hurting her yet again, as I'd obviously just done, made my heart ache right along with hers. What possible words can be said in such a moment?

Somehow we were able to utter enough to get me back inside briefly for my shirt and shoes, then get us both down to the dimly lit coffee shop next door, where we stared glumly at menus for longer than one normally would. Luckily they were those laminated kind so big you can easily hide an entire head. I wanted to stay behind mine forever, but when the waitress approached with her pad and eager expression, I had no choice but to come out and interact. Neither Jane nor I seemed willing to break the thick, glacial air between us, however.

"Um...I can come back if you guys need more time," said the young woman in the perky orange and white outfit.

Jane spoke up first. "No, it's fine. I'll have a cup of coffee."

My turn. "Um...what pies do you have? You know what, just make that coffee too." Somehow eating pie in front of Jane at this particular moment felt sacrilegious.

As the waitress trundled off, and with us bereft of our menu shields, the tension overwhelmed. There was absolutely no way to make manageable eye contact, and I got so uncomfortable I finally had to say something. "How did you get my room number?"

"I told them it was an emergency with your father."

"And how many Motel 6s did you try before you found me?"

She looked up with red eyes. "Does it really matter?"

I felt a strange mix of emotions right then. My shame moved over enough to let a little anger in. "Yes, it matters. Because, assuming it took you a while, you might have realized that maybe I didn't want to be found."

"That seems pretty clear to me now."

"And I'm not talking about Fiona. This isn't about her; this is about me and my father. And to some extent about me. But it's not about me and *you*. If this was a time I wanted to spend with you I would have told you where I was going before I left, instead of having you beat it out of Bob."

"Lucy told me."

That was a surprise. "Lucy told you?" Had my big sister finally snapped, to the point that she'd actually sabotage me for abandoning her? Somehow that didn't seem to fit.

"She just told me you were in Oakland in a Motel 6 somewhere. I don't think she knew you were hiding. I didn't either."

"I'm not hiding. I'm in plain sight, living my life, my independent life as defined by what we discussed in our last conversation. I know you were mad at me then, as I know you're mad at me now, and I'm sorry about that. But I meant what I said."

"Do you have any idea how much that hurts me?"

"Do you have any idea how much you've hurt *me*? It never seemed like that was part of the equation, how I was being treated, or how it made me feel. And I *was* hurt, Jane. You know that, don't you?"

"I wasn't trying to hurt you."

"No one ever tries to hurt anyone, I guess that's just how it is…" I felt really tired, particularly of this conversation. Because here we were again, seated across from each other, with one or the other of us either not accepting what was being said or somehow not getting the point. This had to stop. "Let me say this again and hopefully make it clearer. Something changed for me. I wasn't saying that as retaliation. I didn't mean for that to happen but it did. I'm sorry; maybe it *is* just a timing thing, like you told Bob. Certainly our timing is off, that's pretty obvious. But it doesn't change where it led us. Right here…to this exact place. This is where it led us."

She dissolved into tears.

And my most salient thought at that moment, however cruel, was: didn't we do this already? We had. Too many times. How do we get beyond this repeated scene? I didn't know. There weren't any words I could think of that would make her feel better right now. But, still…this was Jane. *Jane.* So I reached over to pat her hand. Like I do. And she pulled away like I was a viper…like she does.

"Don't patronize me, Dan; I'm not a child. I get it. You've met someone else."

"It's not about that. What happened to us happened before I came up here and before I met anyone else."

"But still…you found her."

"I didn't come up here looking for that, believe me. I happened to meet this woman and there was a connection."

"Is that supposed to make me feel better?"

"It's not supposed to *do* anything. It's just the truth."

"Have you had time yet to determine whether or not she's your soul mate?"

There was the slightest edge of sarcasm in her voice, which, in a way, was easier to deal with than her tears. "I don't think it's a good idea to get into that discussion right now."

"But I'm assuming if this girl is in your room, this girl who doesn't exactly look like Motel 6 pickup trash, then it's likely she's something else." What an odd characterization; like I'd ever have "Motel 6 pickup trash" in my room anyway. I thought about making that point, but she'd slumped in the booth. I could see sarcasm was losing ground, once again, to heartache.

The waitress approached with our coffees; set down the cream and sugar containers, all of which took long enough that everyone involved felt as awkward as three people in a coffee shop in the middle of a third breakup could possibly feel. I took the momentary distraction to consider what Jane had just asked me: about soul mates and whether Fiona was mine. Given the turning point we were irrevocably facing, I felt it deserved my honest response. When the waitress finally moved along, I shared it:

"Jane, almost everything about this sucks, we both know that. And I can't think of how to make it any less sucky. My gut says if we keep talking about it, it's only going to get worse. I actually thought we said it all the other night, but you took a day off from work and spent six hours driving up here for some reason, which implies there's more to be said. I don't want to confuse you and I don't want to be confused; I just want to feel like my life makes sense and I'm living it on my terms. So, you asked me and I want to answer you: there *is* something between Fiona and me, I can't deny it. A connection. A feeling that there's some reason we found each other. I don't know yet where it's meant to go or where I want it to go, but there is a sense that she might be my soul mate. I'm sorry. I know that hurts you." I felt as mournful as if I'd just announced a death.

Without looking up, she whispered, "Does she feel the same about you?"

That was a good question. I felt strongly enough to guess the answer. "I think so."

Jane took a reflexive breath. "Are you staying here?"

"No. I've got to get back…my dad, the job…but she'll probably come down to LA." Actually, I had no idea if Fiona would come down to Los Angeles but, considering what we were both feeling, I had confidence she would. I was certainly going to try my best to talk her into it. Though thinking about that right now, with Jane sitting across from me looking as anguished as a person can look, was surely bad form. I stopped thinking about Fiona.

Unabashed tears were now streaming down Jane's face, streaking her mascara and dripping into her coffee. She made no attempt to wipe them, as if the sheer force of her grief was unstoppable anyway. We both knew this was really it. The end. Third time's the charm, I thought grimly.

"I'm sorry, Jane." Then I was out of words.

She slowly gathered up her purse and scarf. "I'm sorry too." She started to get up, then stopped; turned and looked at me with an expression I couldn't quite interpret. "I want you to know something, Dan: I truly didn't come up here to harass you. I came because it all finally hit me and I had this urgent need to tell you. I could see I'd pushed you away for too long and I realized that all that really mattered to me was that I loved you. Everything else was just noise and old ghosts. I guess I panicked when I heard you'd left town; I was afraid you'd completely slip away from me. So I came up here to tell you what I finally understood—that I'd turned the Marci thing into something it wasn't because *I* was scared. I was terrified of making that commitment, of declaring that I was someone you could believe in for the rest of your life. I didn't know if I could love *you* good enough. And then I realized I could. I realized I could forgive you for anything and love you forever. I hoped you would feel the same way about me. And I wanted to tell you all that before it was too late."

She got up and, before I could say one word or even process the impact of what she just said, she turned and made the long walk down the aisle of the restaurant and out the door. I remained in my seat...honestly and truly devastated.

## FIFTY-TWO

I COULDN'T GO over to Fiona's afterward. It just felt wrong. Besides, I needed time to decompress. I did call, and she was as sweet and understanding as I assumed she'd be. When I reiterated some of what I'd told Jane about her, she seemed honestly touched. I'd wondered if that degree of emotional exposition might scare her off (I did leave out the actual "soul mate" part for now), so I was relieved when it didn't.

Hanging up with Fiona, I knew, after everything that had just happened, there was no way I could drive back to LA in the morning. I called Bob; I begged, I pleaded, and I think he was so blown away by Jane's incursion he took pity and agreed to change his plans to take the Saturday gig (again, the man is a god). I alerted Joaquin of the change (grumbling acquiescence), and though not sure of Lucy's blessing, we traded messages (nothing new with Jim) and she was oddly patient with me. I assured her I'd be heading back Sunday morning. That done, I let Motel 6 know I'd be staying through Saturday night and was set for one more chance with Barbara. And, yes...one more with Fiona, as well.

I called her back and she was thrilled to hear of my rescheduled weekend. We made plans to get together the next night to celebrate the day of—oh, hell, calling it the "day of" *anything* at this point was ridiculous, especially since whatever happened would be it, either way. I was at least reassured that Fiona and I would be celebrating it. Either way.

But I spent the night in turmoil, roiling between desire and regret, and, believe me, that sounded way more poetic than it felt. I couldn't sleep, restless and twitchy, and I awoke Saturday morning feeling notably out-of-sorts. It was mostly a headache, but there was also an undercurrent of tension, as if I was heading off to a last battle (which Bob would have appreciated), one with an uncertain conclusion. What *was* certain was that I was getting this task done today if I had to knock that entire house down. Which I realize just made me sound like the Big Bad Wolf, but trust me: there was nothing "fairy tale" in the way I was feeling.

I drove directly to Chantry Avenue—didn't stop for coffee, didn't stop for my morning bagel. I was determined, resolute, ultimately hungry, and glad I'd thrown the leftover protein bars in the glove box days earlier. Once on Chantry, I pulled up to the curb and sat there for a few minutes. I washed down my second protein bar with the last of my bottled water, looked in the mirror to brush off crumbs and adjust my hair, mentally setting to deploy. I got out of the car, turned to cross the street, and stopped with a start. Because, for the first time since this saga began, I was stunned to see an actual living, breathing human being in the yard beyond the wrought iron gate, a finely dressed older woman bent over a garden patch, pulling at weeds and snipping errant blossoms. And in that heart-stopping moment, I think I really *did* feel the time/space continuum shift.

There she was. Barbara (well, hopefully). The woman who changed the world, the woman who might have made everything about my life different. She stood up and I caught her in the full light of day. If a thirty-three-year-old guy could ever say a seventy-something woman was a knockout, this would be it. I could only imagine how beautiful she must have been fifty years ago. I felt for my dad.

She was tall and slim, draped in a flowing dress that rippled pleasantly every time she moved. When her face turned, the sunlight caught the lines of her cheekbones, the softness of her mouth set in a slight smile, the shoulder-length silver hair brushing softly against her pale skin. I stood in awe, thinking: "My God, that could've been my mother," and felt destiny shine down like a beam from on high.

And just as she started to turn toward me and our eyes were about to meet, the moment was cut short by the utterly incongruous screeching of a police car as it careened in my direction and slammed to a halt feet from where I stood. I practically had to leap to avoid it as it jutted in front of my car, blocking any exit I might have had. I stood there completely rattled as two policemen jumped from the car with guns drawn, and, before I knew it, I was spread-eagled on the hood while they shouted simultaneous commands so chaotically I could not understand what either of them was saying or what, exactly, was going on. It was clear I'd been mistaken for someone incredibly dangerous.

After a rather invasive pat down, I was flipped over and ordered to provide identification, which I was more than happy to do. Digging my driver's license out of my wallet, I looked up to see the cranky neighbor approaching from across the street. The triumphant look on her face was quite something to behold.

"Officers, I cannot thank you enough for responding so quickly to my call." She smiled at them so obsequiously I half expected her to pull out a plate of cookies. "It's been very scary wondering what this fellow might be up to."

"This is the man you saw earlier, ma'am?" Policeman One asked her. Happily, he'd holstered his gun by this point.

"Yes, definitely. He's been stalking the neighborhood for days, casing the Panniker's house and acting very suspicious. I've been keeping an eye out and when he came back today, I didn't want to take any chances." She looked at me like I was Charles Manson. If only she knew what a pacifist I was. And I did note the name "Panniker." Could that be Barbara's last name?

Policeman Two, after running my license and finding no felonies, offered encouragement to my noble accuser. "You did the right thing, ma'am. Members of the community are always the best judge of what's out of the ordinary in their neighborhood."

Feeling misunderstood, I was compelled to speak on my own behalf. "Listen, I know it may have looked weird to—" I glanced toward my accuser. "Excuse me, what's your name?"

"That is none of your business!" she snapped indignantly.

Policeman One turned to me. "Please don't talk to the witness, sir. Why have you been loitering in this neighborhood?"

"I wouldn't say I was loitering. I've actually been—well, as I tried to explain to this woman earlier—see, my father knew a woman who lived in this house here, and I—"

Before I could utter one more blathering word, the interrogation was interrupted. "Excuse me, gentleman, but this is an old friend of mine." Barbara (hopefully) had walked over from across the street and now stood next to me, smiling generously at her neighbor. "You can be sure he's not out to cause me any harm. But thank you, Mrs. Emerson, for being ever so vigilant. Everyone in the neighborhood is indebted to you."

The now-identified Mrs. Emerson looked none too pleased with the tone. Policeman Two frowned somewhat dubiously at Hopefully-Barbara. "You know this man?"

"Yes, I do. He's…"

I leapt for the save: "Dan McDowell, from LA. My father—"

"Yes, *Dan*, of course." She smiled, unruffled. "I understand he came by here during the week when I wasn't around, which obviously concerned my dear neighbor, but you have nothing to worry about with him." She leaned toward me and started brushing off my shirt as if she *were* my mother, which seemed to convince at least the lawmen, who appeared more than ready to wrap things up. Mrs. Emerson glared.

"All right, sorry for the inconvenience." Policeman One was directing that at me. "We have to check these things out."

I started to mumble something less than conciliatory, but Hopefully-Barbara chirped back in. "No problem, Officers. Thank you for being so responsive; makes everyone feel safer." She turned to me. "Come along, dear."

As the policemen got in their car and slowly pulled away, my kindly benefactor made a show of putting her arm through mine and leading me across the street like I was a proper houseguest…though not without a sharp look back at her sputtering neighbor. I already loved this woman.

## FIFTY-THREE

WHICH IS NOT to say I wasn't holding firm to my intent to grill the crap out of her once we'd moved past the initial niceties...though her callous act of 1965 didn't necessarily jibe with the sweet, considerate woman who was now serving me banana bread and tea. But people can change in fifty years, that we all know.

I was brimming with questions but didn't want to overshoot my approach; diplomacy had its advantages in situations such as this. As if I'd ever been in any situation such as this. I noticed she hadn't officially introduced herself. I wondered if she presumed I knew, or if...well, whatever; we'd be getting to that shortly. She was in the middle of explaining the last few days leading up to our auspicious meeting at the curb, and I wanted to just listen to her talk, see if it offered any insight into her personality. At the moment, she was apologizing for hiding behind the curtains yesterday, as I'd suspected.

"And, certainly, Dan, given this nonsense with the police, I'm all the more regretful I didn't answer the door. Particularly since that meddler from across the street seems to gain such joy from butting her nose into everyone's business. I've always despised that woman.

But, still, you *do* never know what's going to happen when a strange young man knocks! At my age, one has to be careful."

"I completely understand. I'm just wondering why you saved me today."

She smiled the lovely smile I'd noticed right from the start. "I decided you looked too nice to be dangerous."

"Yes," I said wryly. "My ability to stir fear has never been a strong suit...well, except for your neighbor."

She chuckled and finally sat down to join me, a cup of tea in hand. I thought, once again, about how much tea must get consumed in this city by the city by the Bay. I never drink the stuff in Los Angeles; now I'm starting to crave chai.

"So, Mr. Dan McDowell, tell me about your father and why you think I might know him."

I'd hoped the name "McDowell" would have jangled a bell, but it hadn't, so I launched. She listened intently as I shared details about the unpublished memoir piece, the snapshots, the gate, and the gazebo. She was particularly impressed by my detective work, which, frankly, I was as well (with kudos to my inventive and beautiful assistant!), and seemed fascinated by my commitment to finding the place. I elaborated on my father's clear devotion to the woman at the center of the story, particularly how he'd called out to her in the midst of fighting for his life. I held back the big reveal—her name—wanting to wait until the exact right moment, like one of those god-awful reality shows where they hold till after the break to make their pivotal announcement. I took a slow sip of my tea, hoping to create a void that she'd fill with...something.

Her brows knitted as if trying to make sense of this rambling, dramatic tale I'd just disclosed. "And you think I might know this woman or that I might have known your father? What did you say his name was?"

"Jim. Jim McDowell." I waited for a reaction. Nothing.

"Hmm. I can't say that brings anything to mind. And, what was the woman's name?"

She was so damn sweet I almost forgot how much I resented her. At least the *her* from fifty years ago. But we were right there now, at the climactic tipping. I took a breath, wondering if all of life would change in the next sentence. "Oh, I think you might know it...*Barbara*." There was "gotcha" all over that and, let me tell you, when her face suddenly shifted to some version of startled, I knew I had my woman.

"Barbara? The woman's name was Barbara?"

"That's right. Barbara." I folded my arms smugly, waiting to see how she would spin her response. She just frowned.

"Well, goodness. That's my sister's name. Do you think it could be her?"

Her *sister*? Oh, for fuck's sake. I'd been bouncing between falling in love with my just-discovered almost-mom and kicking almost-mom's ass, and it wasn't even her. That was a whole lot of wasted emotion. "Your *sister*'s name is Barbara?"

"Yes. I don't know if she's the woman in your story, but she was always a bit of a heartbreaker."

I was so completely thrown I had no comeback. "Okay...and so you are...who?"

"Kathryn Roland, Barbara's younger sister. Oh my, I'm sorry. I should have introduced myself earlier but somehow I thought you already knew. I can see I've disappointed you!"

"No, no, I assumed with the gate and the house, you were the..." My voice trailed off with no worthy response; I stuffed another piece of banana bread in my mouth.

"I do understand. Why wouldn't you have thought that?"

"So who are the Pannikers? Your neighbor mentioned that name."

"That's our family name. Roland is my married name."

I sat there feeling as if I'd lost my script, not sure where to take it from here. Luckily, Kathryn picked up the thread.

"This story of yours is fascinating, Dan, and certainly very touching. Another time and long ago, isn't it? I only wish Barbara could have been here to hear it."

So Barbara was no longer with us. The next disappointment. Obviously that had always been a possibility, certainly one I'd considered, but for some reason it hit me hard.

Kathryn continued, "I'm sure she would have enjoyed the trip down memory lane."

That snapped me back and I quickly regrouped. I was too far in to not at least make my case, even if by proxy. "Kathryn, with all due respect, you need to understand this wasn't necessarily something for your sister to enjoy. She *did* break my father's heart, and his entire life was affected by the way she did it."

"Heavens, what did she do?" Kathryn registered real concern. Which relieved me. She was so nice I wanted to think the very best of her.

"I don't mean to speak ill of someone who's not around to defend themselves, but she basically destroyed him, at least his view of love, his sense of faith and optimism. Which, in a way, changed his life forever. Now that he's sick and very obviously holding on to some memory of her, my hope was to find her and talk to her about it, see if there was something I could bring back to him that would restore his faith in humanity. Or love. Or something like that...I don't really know..." I was losing steam as I went. The whole endeavor suddenly sounded as idiotic as Lucy thought it was.

Kathryn, however, appeared genuinely moved by my impassioned speech. "Well, Dan, I think that's a lovely thing to do for your father—"

There was another person making the observation, Lucy be damned.

"—and I do wish I could be more helpful. But unfortunately I can't say I remember him...or anything that might have happened between them."

"I understand. It was a long time ago."

"But it's possible Barbara would. You'll have to ask her."

Wait. What? "Ask *Barbara*?"

"She might be asleep again, but it's best for her to get up now anyway. She tends to sleep so much during the day she can't sleep at night. As you can imagine, her circadian rhythms are quite disturbed."

I shook my head in confusion. "So she's *here*? In this house?" Somehow I'd gotten the impression she was…well, *not here*. It never dawned on me she just was napping in a room down the hall.

"Yes. This is actually her home, our childhood home. I moved back in with her after my husband passed a year ago, but she's lived here all her life, even after she got married. Her husband never had an easy time with money, and though they wanted their own place, they could never afford it. My father adored Barbara; they were exceptionally close. So she graciously accepted the gift of a roof over their heads, though I don't think Martin—her husband—was ever quite able to overcome the humiliation. Their marriage was a difficult one and, in some ways, I think she might have been relieved when he finally left her fifteen years ago. Goodness, I don't know why I'm telling you all this!"

"No, I appreciate it. All families have history. I've told you plenty of my own."

She gave me a wistful smile. "It's been sad for her, though. My parents died within months of each other, my mother first, then my father, and shortly after that Barbara's husband left. She lived alone here for many years, and I think that loneliness sapped her spirit in some ways. But having this house at least gave her a connection to our childhoods, which has been calming for her." And made it possible for me to find her five decades later.

I had to admit, there was the slightest twinge of vindication at hearing that her marriage to Martin, the guy she dumped my father for, was a disaster. I realized that was petty and mean, but I didn't care. It was righteous.

Kathryn looked at her watch and stood up. "Let's go see if she's awake."

My stomach lurched. "Great. Let's do it."

# FIFTY-FOUR

I RAN OUT to the car to get my envelope with the photos, having left it there in the earlier kerfuffle. Nerves were high; sweat was brewing on my forehead. This epic odyssey, with its many detours and frustrations, had finally, unequivocally, brought me smack up to my destiny, my reason for being here; for risking Lucy's good will, for taking leave from my job, my sick parents, my ex-girlfriend. It felt significant. I hoped it was.

Once back inside, I followed Kathryn down the narrow hall as she chattered instructively: "Normally we entertain in the living room, but she doesn't seem to want to come out much these days. Do you have your father's pictures?"

I had taken a couple of the photos out of the envelope, wanting to confirm what I already knew. "Are these her?"

She looked at them, her eyes misting, then handed them back. "Yes. She was quite beautiful, wasn't she?"

"She was."

"Now, Dan, I understand you've got some things you want to clarify with her, but it's important to know she's not quite the spitfire she used to be. Beyond her physical infirmities, she's in the early stages of dementia and that's taken a toll. So please be gentle with her and don't expect too much."

"Are you sure this is okay? If she's sick or something—"

"She's been weak since her hip surgery, and she's on a fair amount of medication, which makes her a bit groggy, but I want you to have this moment with her. After all your extraordinary efforts that only seems fair. And I do think a visitor with stories from her past might do her good."

I considered a reminder that I wasn't necessarily there to "do her good," but Kathryn was already knocking on the door. My insides felt like jelly. Kathryn called out: "Barbara, honey, are you up?"

There was a muffled, unintelligible response from inside.

Kathryn, however, appeared to have translated just fine. "Well, good, because I have a visitor for you."

With that, she opened the door and ushered me in. I wouldn't have expected my heart to beat this fast for a seventy-something heartbreaker with bad hips and a memory problem, but there you have it. Kathryn motioned me forward, then quietly slipped outside. I was on my own, which suddenly felt terrifying.

Across the room, seated in a wheelchair with her back toward me, was, at last, the notorious Barbara from Oakland. The sun glistened off her silvery hair. The room, much like the rest of the house, was filled with light and clever decorative flairs...clearly Kathryn was doing what she could to keep the ambiance cheerful. I waited a moment, wanting to give Barbara the first move, though none was immediately forthcoming. Then, without turning her head, her thin, scratchy voice bleated:

"Well, don't stand there all day. My neck doesn't turn so if you want to make yourself known, you'll have to walk over here."

Which I did. I walked over and turned to face the woman of my father's dreams. And...well. Though she retained a modicum of resemblance to her lovely sister, Barbara had descended further down the looks spectrum since 1965. Plain, heavy, her face drawn with the weariness of old age and ill health, her mouth drooped in what appeared to be a permanent scowl. Suffice it to say, the woman in front of me bore no resemblance to the smiling beauty in the photos of fifty years ago.

Her watery red eyes glared up at me. "Who the hell are you?"

"My name is Dan McDowell. You knew my father, Jim McDowell."

"Says who?"

"Well, there was a story he wrote about you and—"

"A story? What kind of story? Why on earth would anyone write a story about me?" She looked both annoyed and perplexed. Which, I had to admit, was understandable, given these very strange circumstances.

"I guess the two of you met, spent some time together and, according to him, actually fell in love."

"I don't know who the heck you're talking about. You say we fell in love? When was that?"

"The summer of 1965."

"Oh, for Pete's sake, you expect me to remember some fella I met in 1965? I can't remember what happened yesterday much less way back then."

I felt slightly dizzy. "Do you mind if I sit down?"

"It's a free country." She motioned to a nearby chair. "You're making my neck hurt anyway."

I pulled the chair over to where she was slouched in her wheelchair and gingerly sat. She'd turned back to the window, staring out with eyes slightly gazed and distant. Enough time passed that it seemed she'd forgotten I was there. I took the opportunity to assay the big picture. To say she was not what I expected, especially after meeting Kathryn, was an understatement. To say that the grand moment of meeting was profoundly anticlimactic was as well. I felt—

"Are you mute?"

I snapped back to attention. "No, sorry, I figured you were thinking about something and didn't want to disturb you."

"I'm old. I drift." She turned her chair slightly and gave me the once-over. "So who was this fella you're talking about?"

Grateful for the opening, I shuffled through my manila envelope and pulled out a picture, handing it to Barbara. "Jim McDowell. In case you'd forgotten, I brought some pictures. This is one of him from right around the time you met. Right after he graduated from college."

She closely examined the faded snapshot then handed it back to me. "Never saw him before."

I pulled out another. "This is one of him at Ocean Beach in San Francisco. I guess you spent a fair amount of time there together over that summer."

"We did? Which summer was that?"

Again…"1965."

"Oh, good Lord, I don't remember what happened yesterday much less way back then." And now we were repeating things. The sense that this might truly be a lost cause loomed large.

"Well, according to him you were a pretty special lady."

Nothing. She handed the picture back without a word.

"And this one…" I figured I'd try again. "This is one of him with a few of his college buddies. Maybe you remember some of these guys."

Her eyes flickered. I was sure I saw it. Then I handed her the one of my dad sitting next to her at the beach. "You might recognize this one. That's my dad sitting there next to you. That was also taken on Ocean Beach. You and he would go there, or sometimes to the library, he said, or that gazebo just down the street—" I handed her the shot of her seated inside the gazebo. "You spent a lot of time there together before he headed back to a teaching job he had in Los Angeles. The way he tells it, there was even talk of marriage and stuff."

I watched her like a hawk. She peered closely at the last two pictures, then, as if a gear clicked into place, her face lit up. "Oh, *this* fella! I do remember him!"

A rush came over me. "That's fantastic! Because he remembers you too, Barbara; in fact, he recently—"

"Kind of a goofy guy. Handsome, but real unsure of himself. Always tried to act like the big shot." She actually smirked. I felt the gut-punch. Before I could respond, she elaborated. "He wore me out with all of his rigmarole. Always such a to-do about being gallant, just a real show-off."

I was stunned. But her caustic interpretation of my father's courtesies could not slide without comment. "Or perhaps he was an authentically gallant guy who knew how to treat a woman he loved."

"Oh, he sure did!" She snickered as if her newly discovered memory was quite the comedy. "Made a federal case out of it. I figured we were out to have some fun for the summer, but he was so damn serious. Carrying on about souls and destiny and all that. Me and the girls used to laugh about him all the time!"

Why, you old bi—

"I never knew what happened to him. I think he sent a few letters, then I got married and can't say I ever thought about him again. That is, until you showed up." She turned and looked at me. "Now, why did you say you were here?"

If you've ever had that most politically incorrect urge to slap an enfeebled senior, you know what I was fending off in the dark recesses of my mind in that moment. I think I may actually have been shaking. I'm not sure what I expected, but I did not expect *this*. Knowing my dad had been lying in a coma for the last three weeks with only a glimmer or two of consciousness, and knowing he used that time to call out to this odious woman made my blood boil. Literally. I felt like my temperature had spiked beyond any measure of good health, and I just wanted to get the fuck out of there.

I grabbed the pictures from her lap, shoved them into the envelope, and didn't even try to hide the edge in my voice. "Frankly, Barbara, I didn't say why I was here. Turns out I was in the neighborhood, remembered my dad had some friends on this street, thought I'd drop by for old time's sake. He's doing exceptionally well.

He and my mom have been really happy together all these years, but he was sorry to hear you'd fallen on such hard times, asked me to make a courtesy call. I'll be sure to tell him how you're doing."

She'd already turned back to the window. "You do that. Tell my sister on your way out that I'd like my snack now."

And with that, I was dismissed.

Yeah, well…she was too.

## FIFTY-FIVE

I PRACTICALLY TRIPPED over the foyer carpet in my rush to get out of that house. I gave Kathryn the briefest of explanations and she apologized for her sister, going so far as to give me her number, insisting I call later if I wanted to talk more about it. I could tell she felt mortified by Barbara's behavior, trying to explain that dementia had changed her, that she'd once been a lovely woman, and, who knows? Maybe it was true; Kathryn seemed like an honest person.

She stood silently on the porch as I bolted to my car with little more than a terse smile and a "thanks for the banana bread." I was so consumed with rage, I knew that if I stayed one second longer I'd end up saying some truly hateful things meant for her truly hateful sister. I didn't want to inflict that on her. That Kathryn was related to the hag down the hall was her burden to bear; I wouldn't add to her tribulations.

I careened through Oakland in a state of emotional chaos. All I could think was, "How can I possibly explain this to my father without kicking the shit out of him yet again?" Considering what he was already going through—remembering the look of anguish on his face when he choked and struggled and wept just trying to say her name—made her sniggering response all the more revolting. That *this* woman, this surly, dismissive ogress, was the person he longed for, the person he reached out to in his tremulous moment on the cliff's edge...well, that was just completely fucked. I have no more poetic a way to put it.

Then it struck me: he doesn't even know I'm up here. He has no idea he said anything, no idea anyone heard what he said, and *no* idea anyone would have ever thought of going off on such a ridiculous, idiotic chase in search of this shrew. His unconsciousness saved me...saved him! I could spare him the agony of Barbara's redux rejection and would silently accept, as he had, that love isn't always kind or particularly responsive.

There was relief in the realization. And what immediately followed was the panicked thought, "What if he wakes up before I get home and someone mentions Oakland?" Someone, meaning Lucy. Which inspired a new level of urgency about getting back quickly enough to preempt the possibility. I left her a message confirming I'd be heading home tomorrow morning, adding that I "had a quick favor" to ask. The rest of the Barbara conversation could wait to be conveyed in person.

I wanted desperately to be in Fiona's arms, but she was at work until late afternoon, so I got out my camera and spent the time wisely, out on the street shooting pictures. I hit enough different neighborhoods to capture a fairly wide swath of this eclectic city. I even took a few shots of Frank the Fuck at Kenny's Gas & Mart, figuring he had a certain urban appeal that could be interesting in the right collection. In fact, while I was standing across the street snapping away, I saw him look up and catch me in the act. I've got a great shot of him giving me the finger.

By three o'clock I was on my way to Fiona's, longing for the warmth of a woman who *did* know how to respond to a man in love. After managing more traffic than I was in the mood to manage, I was disappointed to find Maris in attendance when I got there. She did, however, present me with a truly unattractive tie-dyed tee-shirt which she'd purchased as a souvenir of my newly adopted city, and after donning this sartorial wonder and hunkering over the biggest beef burrito I'd ever seen, also courtesy of the courteous Maris who was definitely *not* a vegan, I finally calmed down. What I most appreciated was her spirited participation in my debrief of the day.

"Unbelievable," Maris growled. "After all this time and all your efforts, it turns out she's a rude bitch."

"But can we call an old woman a bitch?" I honestly queried, sensing Fiona's tacit disapproval. "I mean, she categorically deserves it, no doubt about that, but isn't actually saying it out loud a little beyond the pale?"

Fiona smiled with a shake of her head. "How about we frame it that she's a lonely old woman in a lot of pain who's also dealing with dementia. Life can't be fun for her, so a little compassion might be in order, don't you think?"

Maris did not. "Fuck compassion. That lonely old bitch royally dissed his dad." She laughed; I laughed.

Fiona did not laugh. Clearly she was the kinder person. "Come on, you two! What she said was horrible, and I get why you'd feel the urge to be cruel—and maybe you do need to vent for a while to process this information, Dan—but I think there has to be a more enlightened way to look at it."

"Fuck enlightened." Maris grabbed another burrito and between exceedingly large bites, took up the debate. "Take the beetroot out of your ears, Fi, and join the real world. Not everyone deserves the benefit of your sweet little evolved self!" Then she guffawed loudly. I'd noticed guffawing was Maris's go-to version of laughter. Which I sort of loved.

"You're right, Fiona, of course you're right." I came to Fiona's defense, as I knew I should. "But, I gotta say, I'm liking this roommate of yours." I grinned at Maris, who gave me a fist bump in response.

Fiona surrendered with a grin. "All right, all right. I see I'm outnumbered. But may I never incur the wrath of you two!"

"Impossible," I said, turning and grabbing her in a slightly needy hug.

Maris, done with dinner, stood up and stretched loudly. "Okay, puppies, that's my signal…I'm off. Have fun, keep the rapture to a minimum, and, Fi, if you don't get the electric bill paid, I'm calling the fire department. I'm serious." I had noticed the candles were in full bloom again.

"Monday, I promise." Fiona giggled.

"Yeah, heard that before." Maris winked at me. "Oh, and, Dan, if you're still with us in the morning, I'm making my famous Kahlua pancakes so don't eat before I'm up."

"How could I miss that? By the way, thanks for listening, Maris. It helped. And thanks for dinner and the shirt, too; I finally feel like a local."

"You're welcome on all counts. And I really am sorry about the old bitch. Just remember not all Oakland women are so heartless!" She guffawed once more, then clumped up the stairs, flashlight in hand.

Fiona shook her head. "She can be so rough sometimes."

I laughed. "I'd say she's right up my alley."

She climbed over the furniture to get to me. Wrapping her arms and legs around me, she whispered in my ear, "I hope I'm right up your alley, too."

If only she knew how up my alley she'd been since the moment I laid eyes on her. For now I just nuzzled my nose into her sweetly scented neck and stayed there, enjoying the view.

"I'm sorry things have been so crazy while you were here, Dan. I know you have to get back to LA, but I wish we had more time, and I wish the time we had could've been more fun. I hope I'm one of the things from this week that made you feel good."

She bit my ear and I affirmed, "Oh, yes, you've make me feel very good!"

She snuggled in closer. "So did Jane go back yet?" We hadn't returned to that topic since our brief discussion of last night. It already felt like a century ago. I wondered if Fiona's curiosity was a sign of her growing sense of propriety toward me. I hoped so.

"I would imagine. I haven't talked to her since she left the coffee shop, but I presume she either drove right back down or left this morning." I shook my head. "Crazy thing, wasn't it? How are you doing on all that today?"

"I'm okay but I do feel bad. I mean, that was difficult for all of us, but especially for her. For me, it just felt awkward to know my actions were involved in hurting another woman. That's really not my way. And I'm sure she's a very nice woman; obviously she's a very nice woman if you were with her for three years."

"She was. She is. And that's really sweet of you to say. But she'll be all right; I have no doubt. She's a strong girl."

"But it can't have been fun to drive all the way up here to have what happened…happen."

"No. It can't. But, frankly, our situation hasn't been much fun for a while now. It sure wasn't fun for me when she kicked me out—or any time after that when she let me know how much she didn't want me back. So, yeah, maybe this one surprised her, but now she knows how I felt. I think when you're with someone for a long time you forget that things really *can* change, actions really do have consequences, and sometimes you don't recover from those. Sometimes change *is* the right move, and you have to let go and move on. Like when you realize you need something else in your life…you want something else."

It was now time to transition to the next chapter of this extraordinary experience we were having, but before I could frame the pitch, she was suddenly and very sensually unbuttoning her shirt. A delightful sight and one I was most anxious to enjoy, but as I watched her go slowly from button to tantalizing button, the thoughts pricking the edge of my consciousness got louder, and I was a little unnerved by where they were inexorably leading me—to the big leap. I reached out and stopped her mid-unbutton. She looked up with justifiable surprise.

"You want me to stop?"

"Not really, no. But I do need to talk about something first." There was a pause as I decided how far I wanted to take this. "Today was really a pretty major day for me."

She pulled her shirt closed and reached up to gently caress my cheek. "I know, Dan."

"It was major for a lot of reasons."

"I can't imagine how strange it must have been to deal with both Jane and Barbara within one twenty-four-hour period. "

"Yes, strange is a small but accurate word. But it's even more than that."

She cocked her head in that incredibly charming way she had. "What else is it?"

"Fiona, we met not even a week ago, which is hard to believe—"

"For me, too! I feel like we've known each other forever."

"And that's it. That's how I feel too, like I've known you my whole life. And that's what I want to talk to you about."

"Tell me," she said ever so sweetly.

"You just do something to me. I'm someone around you I don't think I am with anyone else. Like I know who I am and what I'm doing."

"That's how you should always feel."

"I know, but it's not a state I'm particularly familiar with, so there's that whole quivering doubt thing. Like, I want to be sure I've got it right."

She leaned in and curled into my arms. "I think you've got it right, Danny. You know how much I want you, don't you?"

"Yes, and I want you too, but that's the question."

She pulled away and looked at me, perplexed. "What's the question?"

And with perfect timing, my phone jangled; I'd turned it on to leave the message for Lucy earlier and had clearly forgotten to mute it again. "It's Lucy." Fiona got up. "No, don't go, it's okay; I'll call her back later," I insisted.

"No, you should take it, Dan. It might be important." She smiled and went into the kitchen.

So I answered. "Hey, Luce."

"Your phone is on."

"Yeah. Hell froze."

"I believe it. I got your message. You sounded weird."

"Just checking in. How's Dad?"

"He actually opened his eyes at one point today, looked at Mom and smiled. Of course, she then burst into tears and he went right back out."

"Probably scared the crap out of him. But, wow, that's progress, right?"

"Seems like it. So what's the favor you wanted to ask?"

"It's no big deal, but if he wakes up before I get there, don't mention that I came up to Oakland, okay? I'll explain why when I see you."

"Believe me, I have *no* intention of getting into all that."

"Cool. So, how's Mom doing?"

"Better. Except now she's into her Tony Orlando and Dawn phase. She's been singing 'Tie a Yellow Ribbon' since last night. Actually had some of the nurses tie yellow tape around Dad's IV pole. It's gettin' crazy around here!"

I had to laugh, picturing some badgered nurse running around doing Esther's bidding. "She's one for the books, that's for sure."

"Jane's here."

She must have driven back last night. I wondered how much she'd told Lucy about her field trip. "Really? Why is she there? You do know we're officially over, right?"

"Yes, but she's still a nice person who cares about our parents and I still need some help."

Suddenly another thought struck me. "How is it, by the way, that Jane's been allowed in the ICU? I thought they were pretty strict about only letting family in."

There was the slightest pause on Lucy's end. "Okay, don't go all ballistic, but we told them she was your wife."

I almost felt my head explode. "Are you fucking kidding me? You told them the woman who kicked me out of my house, who I just officially broke up with, is *my wife*? That is so completely and utterly fucked up and invasive and inappropriate I don't even know what to say."

"I know, it really is, but here's the thing: you took off, I needed help, she wanted to help, and that was the only way we could get her in here. You picked your poison, brother."

There may have been logic to that, but it was all too messed up to process at the moment. "Fine, whatever."

"Look, I know it's weird, but with Mom and Dad both needing medical attention, and me having to get to the restaurant every day, it was necessary."

"I get it. Fine." I did. And I knew I should be grateful.

"She's also been taking care of their bills and things, which needed to be done over these last few days."

And now I also felt usurped, having expected Jane to slip quietly off the stage of my life. "I'll take all that over when I get back tomorrow."

"So you're definitely back tomorrow?"

"For what it's worth, my work here is done."

"Is it?" Her curiosity was clear.

"Yes. It is."

"Anything I should know?"

"Lots. Believe me."

"Can you give me a hint?"

"I'll share all the details when I get there, but Lucy, thanks, really, for all of it. Beyond the mind-blowing boundary invasion of the Jane thing, I really appreciate your taking care of everybody. And for not making me feel like too much of a shit."

"Well, a little bit of a shit."

"Yes, a little bit of a shit, sometimes more than a little, but not *too* much. Seriously, thanks for all that."

"Why, are you dying or something?"

"No. I just wanted to let you know I appreciated it. It's been a weird few days, that's all."

"You sound defeated yet somehow more mature. How does that work?"

I had to laugh. "The mystical powers of Oakland."

"By the way, I'm back in Dad's room; you want to talk to anyone here?" I could hear the implication in her tone.

"Nope. Give Mom a hug for me and say hi to Jane; tell her I appreciate her helping out."

"Tell her yourself."

"No, Lucy. This is not the time. And stop trying so hard. I'll talk to you tomorrow."

"Okay, bro. You better show up."

"I will. Goodnight!"

Fiona peeked out from the kitchen as I snapped my phone shut. I was immediately cheered. "It's okay. We're done."

She came in and climbed into my lap like a kitten. I circled her with my arms, appreciating her warmth and softness, but it couldn't be denied the mood had shifted. Or that her shirt was once again buttoned up.

"Is everything okay with everyone there?" she asked.

"Yeah. Sounds like my dad might be coming out of it."

"Oh, Dan, that's wonderful. You must feel so relieved!" She kissed me and, oddly, I pulled away once again.

"Fiona, before we get to that—and, trust me, I really *do* want to get to that—I'd like to finish what we started a few minutes ago, okay?"

She smiled. "Okay, Mr. Serious. Carry on."

I took a requisite deep breath then began. "See, I just spent the day finding out that the woman my father believes was his one true love, his soul mate, is just some bitchy old broad who thought he was an idiot with a crush. Now, I gotta tell you, that's caused me to think a little more carefully about anything I might presume from here on out."

"Meaning what?"

"Meaning, I don't want to jump into this with you only to find out later you think I'm a loser who takes pictures of eight-year-olds."

She sat up and looked at me, startled. "Dan, I would never think that!"

"What *do* you think?"

"About what, exactly?"

"About everything we're flirting with here, literally and figuratively."

She gave me a seductive smile that sent a sharp jolt to my lower pelvic region. "I think it's all wonderful, literally, figuratively, and in every other way you want to imagine. I think you're sexy and smart, incredibly compassionate, and I'd love to stop talking and take your clothes off so I could lick you from head to toe."

My head said, *Dammit, listen to the lady!* My head with the brain said, "That sounds like an excellent plan, Fiona, but if you could bear with me for just a sec longer, I'd like to clarify where we both see this thing going. I mean, beyond the amazing, very memorable one-night stand it will surely end up being."

She giggled and leaned in, put her arms around my neck. "Well, beyond that, I think if you lived here we would have an awesome time together. But for right now, I want to enjoy the time we do have, even if it is just this one night."

"Or, how about this? We enjoy this one night, then you come with me to Los Angeles tomorrow morning, come to Toluca Lake. I want us to spend time together when I'm not in crazy mode, time we can get to know each other beyond family crises and old girlfriends and all that. And since I've got to get back, I'm hoping I can talk you into taking some time off to see what it might be like in my world." Which was incredibly presumptuous, considering she had both a job and a business to manage, but we were onto something, we both knew it, and the leap had to be made.

She was thrown, however; I could tell by the way she stopped purring. "Um...okay...I could probably do that for a few days. I'd have to figure out my schedule and everything, and I don't think I could actually leave tomorrow morning, but it might be fun hanging out in Los Angeles for a bit. I haven't been down there in a long time."

It was a good start, but she didn't quite seem to grasp the magnitude of my point. Of course, how could she? More specificity was in order. "What I'm really fishing for here, Fiona, is solid ground. A sense that there's logic to basically changing our whole lives to be together."

Fiona laughed. "Dan, we don't have to change our whole lives to be together! Why would you even think that? I would never ask that of you. We can make this easy. I'll spend a few days in LA with you as soon as I can get down there, then the next time you'll come back up here for a bit, and in between we'll have lots of long, hot Skype sex. How does that sound?" She was purring again.

"Like way too much freeway driving and I'm lousy with phones, really, even Skype. Even for sex." Which I meant. Though I'd never actually had Skype sex.

She frowned again. "Then what *do* you want? I'm not sure I understand."

I sat back, pondering if I really wanted to go any further with this. Then I thought of my father and Barbara and decided there was nothing to lose. "What I wanted last night was to make love to you like I hadn't to anyone in my entire life. What I wanted this morning was to tell you I think you're my soul mate. And what I want right now is all of that *plus* I want you to come back with me. I mean, if not tomorrow, eventually—actually *move* to LA or Toluca Lake or wherever you'd like...with me. I realize it may seem nuts to talk about something like that so quickly after just meeting, but we're both feeling this otherworldly connection to each other and that's not something to walk away from, not in my experience."

"Not in mine either, Dan. I'm excited to explore this with you and I think it will be great fun to spend more time together."

"Well...good."

She looked at me, her brow slightly furrowed. "But there's something else, isn't there?"

See, she already knew me so well. "I feel silly even bringing this up..."

"What?" She smiled gently, as if coaxing a child.

"Okay, I'll just say it. I guess I'm a little stuck on this soul mate thing. Inane, I know. It's not even something I've put much stock in throughout my life. But I made the point that I think you're my soul mate and...well, to be completely honest, I kind of want to hear it back."

In my hypervigilant state, her pause was unmistakable. "You want to hear me *say* you're my soul mate?"

When she put it like that, I had to admit it sounded stupid. "I'm not trying to be ridiculous, Fiona, but I would like to know if we're looking at this through the same filter."

She cocked her head...and not in that cute way. "The same *filter*?" Yeah, that did sound weird.

"Maybe I'm not using the right words and I apologize for that. But my urgency on this is only because of the time factor. I have to head home tomorrow, there's no getting around that, and before I go, and before we take this any further tonight, I want to be sure we're honestly in synch with each other." Yep, I'd become the girl. The girl who didn't want to get down to it until she knew it "meant something."

"I understand, Dan. I don't know that we really need to define things quite that way, but if it would make you feel better to hear me say it, then...yes. I think you *are* a soul mate for me."

The nuance was inescapable. "*A* soul mate. Non-specific. Like, there could be another soul mate out there for you at any time?"

"That's a slight exaggeration." The tiniest frown line appeared between her eyebrows, one I'd not seen any time prior.

"But possible?"

"Oh, Dan, I don't know...come on." She looked a little beleaguered, but I was compelled.

"But didn't you say that a soul mate was someone you were meant to be with and it was just a matter of finding each other? Or did I get that wrong?"

"No! I do believe that. I was meant to be with the man I was with before you, as I'm meant to be with you now."

"And will, most likely, be meant to be with whoever's next, say, next month, or maybe next year?" I knew I was being an ass, but the strain of despair was now upon me. I was waiting for her to snap and throw me out into the foggy Oakland night, but, instead, she grabbed my face in her hands and kissed me—hard, passionate, and maybe even slightly, though erotically, annoyed. I was duly impressed, incredibly turned on, and profoundly hopeful that what she would say and/or do next would solve everything.

"Dan, listen to me." Her eyes bore into mine with a directness that was uncharacteristic for her dreamy self. She knew this was serious. "I adore you. I do. We've just met and yet I adore you. And, no, I can't predict if or when I'll need to be with someone else down the line, but *right now* I need to be with you. You are the only one I want to be with. You are as much of a soul mate to me right now as I am to you. It feels good and right and I'm excited to see where this goes *right now*, in this moment of our lives that we're sharing together. What happens in the future is not important; what matters is this moment. And we don't have to know how long this moment will last; it will last as long as it feels good and right to us both. And that's enough for me."

I noticed she said "right now" so very many times. Clearly she felt the point needed emphasis. Yet she was still staring into my eyes, still with her beautiful mouth in a soft smile of deep, sensual need. No denying she still really wanted me. *Right now*. What more could a guy want?

More. A guy could want more.

Maybe it was all the weeks leading up to this night. Maybe it was being thirty-three. Maybe it was the heartache of Jane, my father, even bitchy old Barbara. Maybe it was "reading between the lines" of Fiona's declaration. But I couldn't deny the cumulative impact and the revelation it inspired. "Strangely enough, Fiona, and I can't believe I'm going to say this, I don't think it's enough for me."

She gave me a half smile, not sure if I was kidding. I wished I was but I wasn't. Certainly I'd enjoy being the "right now" guy *right now*. But I knew I couldn't spend tonight making love to her, feeling the things I was feeling while she was feeling her version of the same, then leave in the morning to drive back to my life, my family, my sense of self, with no commitment about what this might be beyond...*right now*. I'd been unequivocally changed by these last two months. Dammit to hell.

I looked at her and just felt sad, like I was losing something before I even got to have it. I leaned forward and hugged her gently, kissed her forehead, then got up and started gathering my things.

"Dan. Come on, what are you doing?" Fiona remained on the couch, a look of consternation on her face. "I don't understand."

I stopped for a moment. "I'm...not sure I do either. I'm going to have to think about it. But I've got an early start in the morning so I should head out. Tell Maris I'm sorry I'll miss the pancakes. And thank you, Fiona, for everything. You saved me this week....and you inspired me. Those are two things I've never said to anyone and I'm so grateful. You are an amazing woman, and I really, truly appreciated all your help." I went back to the couch, leaned down and hugged her closely, then turned and walked out of that charming, whimsical, candlelit place.

As I headed to the car in a daze, I thought: "What I am doing is walking away from hot, noncommittal sex for the sake of a higher principle. I am speechless. I am...an adult."

# FIFTY-SIX

OVER THE NEXT many hours—extending through the long sleepless night and overlapping into the steely morning, as I packed my things, paid my bill, loaded up the car and took off south—I ran through about as many thoughts as I could process without my brain exploding. Even then it was touch and go. One minute I was browbeating myself for pushing the soul mate thing too hard, the next I was stunned by her nebulous idea of a relationship. One minute I felt sick about walking away from the opportunity of something as exquisite as making love to Fiona, the next I clutched my grudging sense of pride at not being led around by my dick. Then thinking about my dick got me back to severe regret, and these thoughts spun around for hours. It was a fascinating mental exercise in the confusion of contradiction:

1. God, she was beautiful.
2. I think I may have experienced a parallel universe of surreal madness.
3. Did I actually ask her to move to Los Angeles with

me after just four days? Did I? DID I?!
4. What would I have done if she'd said yes? Call the realtor? I barely know her; we'd have to rent first.
5. But then again, we'd probably be horrible roommates. I like electricity. And meat. Even gluten.
6. Clearly there is something about McDowell men and Oakland women.
7. Is it possible I have a personality disorder?
8. Let's be fair; I'm taking something from that godforsaken place, right? A better sense of myself, a clearer understanding of what I need, a new appreciation for my father's pain, a tie-dyed tee-shirt.
9. God, she was beautiful. Did I already say that?
10. I should turn around. Why couldn't I drive back there right now? Enjoy the time with her for as long as it lasts? Be with that gorgeous, wonderful woman and shut the fuck up about soul mates?
11. Really? I'd head back north? I'm ready to pile up frequent driver miles to pant after Gorgeous Miss Freedom Queen until my time is up and she's ready for the Soul Mate Behind the Curtain?
12. I sound like Bob with the titles. Bob, My Browbeating Roommate, The Voice of My Neuroses.
13. I've got a job; they want me to be a partner. My father may be dying. How the fuck can I even think about heading back north?
14. She wasn't just beautiful, she was kind and sweet and helpful. A truly wonderful person. Why the fuck am I leaving?
15. The ten-year age difference is too great, clearly. She's got ten years to get where I've gotten. Then I'll be forty-three. Dear God. *That* old.
16. Life is short though, right? Sometimes, against all

logic, you gotta grab what you want.
17. Bay area sirens, every one of them! Women, rendering us blithering idiots of misguided love.
18. I want Fiona. I want her. I want her to want me more than just *right now*...
19. I clearly don't know what I want. I am in a state of perpetual confusion.
20. But, God, she was beautiful...

Somewhere around #16, or maybe it was #17, I actually swerved across three lanes and pulled off onto the freeway ramp. I parked on the shoulder and sat there, heart pounding, confusion-sweat pouring down my forehead. It felt akin to a panic attack but was just *me* trying to figure out *me* before I got farther south than I might want to go.

But as life would have it, my inner dialogue was rudely interrupted by a CHP motorcycle officer who pulled behind me, lights on and a quick burst of his siren. If nothing else, I was developing a close and personal relationship with local law enforcement.

I dutifully opened my window and handed him my license and registration. He leaned in a bit, I presume to check the olfactory options, but I was clean. Crazy, but clean.

"Having a little trouble here today, Mr. McDowell?"

A *little*? "No, Officer; thanks. I thought my engine might be overheating but it must have been freeway exhaust. Everything seems fine now."

"If you're okay to move along, you should do that. This isn't a safe place to stop. If you need service, there's a Shell station up ahead."

"Thank you, I think I'll take my chances and move along." How metaphorical.

He roared off and I quickly got moving along, as promised, pulling back onto the freeway south. But it wasn't long before the confusion litany started rattling again:

1. Why am I mad at Fiona? She's probably clearer about what she wants than I'll ever be.
2. She's a beautiful twenty-three-year-old woman, so much of life yet to experience. Why wouldn't she want to be in the moment with no other commitments?
3. And maybe she's right. Maybe I just need to relax and quit trying to define everything.
4. Oh, who am I kidding? I'm all about definition. I like knowing what things mean. I was that kid who hated piñatas because nobody could tell me what was inside.

And that was as far as I got. I was utterly wiped out. I turned on the radio and found my blues station. It was time to go home.

# FIFTY-SEVEN

IT WAS ABOUT three in the afternoon when I finally made it to the hospital and, being Sunday, the parking lot was full. Which meant I spent the next twenty minutes driving around the neighborhood until I found a spot that didn't require a permit sticker or wasn't impacted by roadwork. I was surprised to notice I didn't get as annoyed by this activity as I usually do. I'd either become a calmer person by virtue of my concluded vision quest or my senses had just been deadened.

I'd called Bob along the way, and he was delighted by the direction I was headed, ready for me to be home after a week of wrangling with Joaquin and Zoey. He had a list of questions, which was expected but far too exhausting to ponder. I assured him I'd be at the house later to fill him in; he promised he'd have a hot meal and some good booze ready. I was at least comforted by my plans for the evening.

As I trudged up the steps of the hospital, it seemed like I'd never been away. On one hand. On the other, I felt as if I'd been gone a year and been through a war that had changed me forever. Post Traumatic Vision Quest Syndrome. PTVQS. Too many letters, that one.

I knew I'd be faced with Lucy within moments and that realization sparked some thought. Bob told me he'd talked to her pretty much every day and each time he called she was at the hospital. I'd felt a rush of brotherly love when he told me that. She was quite something. Crabby, creative, wonderful Lucy.

She was also the first person I saw when I hit the ICU floor. Standing at the doors leading in, cellphone in hand, she started shaking her head as I approached, a look on her face that said something like, "I've been calling you for hours, and you're driving me fucking nuts." Though she would have used more swear words. Instead, she startled me by throwing her arms around me in a big, unexpected hug. "He's awake!"

As we maneuvered quickly down the hall to his room, I noticed how she smiled and greeted the various nurses and doctors in passing—even some of the other waiting families. She'd clearly figured out the lay of the land while I'd been gone and seemed to have taken to it like a diplomat.

"So…is he all right? I mean, does he have all his faculties?" I was afraid to ask but knew it would be best to get that covered before we got there.

"It turns out the stroke was on the right side of his brain, which, in his case, means his speech wasn't as affected as it could've been. It is a bit slurred and sometimes the wrong words come out, but he's all there and most of what he says is understandable. He and I actually had a pretty long talk early this morning, at least long for the circumstances, which I'll tell you about in a minute. Dr. Kamen says he does have some motor damage that'll require physical therapy, his left side is a lot weaker than his right, but his cognitive skills, his thinking, his memory, all seem to be basically intact from what they can tell so far. They'll be moving him out of ICU later today, and there'll be ongoing tests over the next few days, but overall he dodged a bullet, I think."

She was beaming. I could almost believe the sheer force of her will had somehow conjured his recovery. "Wow, Luce, the old man's really back."

We were at the door of his room, but, surprisingly, Lucy stopped me. "Listen, Dan, before you go in, there are a few things you need to know."

My stomach dropped. "What?" After my last few days, I was up for no big surprises.

"Calm down. It's just a couple of things. First of all, Jane's in there, and I don't think she knew you were coming home today."

This recurring theme was starting to feel manipulated. "You're not going to get us back together with this stuff, you know that, right?"

"Okay, prodigal son, before you start giving me a lecture, she came in before me this morning and by the time I arrived she was involved in some bookkeeping stuff with Mom, so what was I going to say at that point? I figured if you got here before I could tell her, we'd all act like grown-ups and figure it out from there."

"Fine. But let's be clear: the situation with Jane and me has nothing to do with *all* of you. We're the ones who'll figure it out from here, her and me. None of that will involve any of you."

"She's been helping out a lot, that's all."

"And I appreciate that as much as the rest of you, but considering we're no longer together, it also feels a little stalkery. Like, what's the statute of limitations on hanging around your ex's family after a major break-up?"

"Stalkery? You haven't even *been* here, so what are you talking about?"

"I get that I haven't been here. I'm just saying that at some point she needs to move on, so we can *both* move on. That's how these things work. I mean, to be blunt, this isn't her family." Lucy looked at me like I had no soul. I didn't even wait for her retort. "I know, that sounded creepy even to me." I wanted to sit down somewhere and cry.

Lucy noticed and took pity. "I understand, Dan, I do." I could tell she meant it.

"Good. And you and I can talk it over at some point but—"

"She's been incredible with Mom and that's the only reason I kept calling her—"

"You already said that. And I know you're jabbering about this because you feel guilty about outing my Oakland trip to her."

She looked almost relieved to have that on the table. "I know and I'm so sorry! I had no idea she'd go up there, honestly. Was it horrible?"

"Completely."

"Look, I don't know what happened with you guys—"

"See, you're still talking about it! And this is why I'd rather she wasn't around right now. I'm here to see Dad; I want this to be about him, about Mom, even about you. I don't want to talk about what happened with Jane and me. End of story." *End of story.* That sounded like Jim. Apparently, and particularly considering Oakland, he and I were destined to be similar kinds of idiots.

"Okay, I won't ask. And believe me, I'm not taking sides or lobbying or anything. End of story." We both smiled...our homage to Pops. I turned toward the door to Jim's room and, strangely, Lucy stopped me again. "Real quick, there's something else I need to tell you—"

Before Lucy could continue, we both heard a squeal from inside the room, luckily a happy one. My mom had seen me through the door window and her eyes widened like a kid seeing Santa. Jane glanced over as well; I mentally winced but she just smiled and went back to whatever it was she was doing.

Esther burst into the hallway with a flurry of sound and motion, throwing herself in my arms. "Oh, Danny, your father's back, he's really back! Can you believe it?"

Her eyes radiated joy, and I was struck by how vibrant, even pretty, she appeared in that moment. Maybe I was developing a certain appreciation for kindly older women. Or maybe she'd always looked that way and I just hadn't noticed. Whatever it was, I hugged her as tightly as I could and it was with a genuine urge for closeness. "Mom, I knew if anyone could pull him out of it, you could."

Lucy leaned in to interrupt. "Mom, let me have one more quick minute with Dan before—"

But Esther was so focused on me she didn't even acknowledge Lucy. "Your Dad's catheter is getting changed in a minute, so Jane said I should take you downstairs to the cafeteria with me. I haven't eaten since this morning and, besides, I want to introduce you to all my boys."

I shot Lucy a "what else did you want to tell me?" look, but she just held up her hands in surrender. Which made me wonder what news was worthy of such a gesture. We'd get to that later, I presumed.

Esther put her arm through mine, chattering nonstop as she walked with me down the hall. "My goodness, what a day this has been! Your father waking up early this morning and then you coming home...I feel like the ice cream truck just pulled into my driveway!"

How bizarre that she'd make an ice cream truck reference! It, of course, got me to thinking about Tomas and his much-missed toffee bars, but also made me wonder if I'd inherited my confection obsession from Esther. Which would be kind of sweet. Certainly better than some of what I'd inherited from my dad.

"I'm glad, Mom. I know it's been a tough few weeks; you deserve to feel a little giddy for a change."

"I have to agree. It has been a little bit of hell on earth. But Lucy has been my champion. And everyone here is so nice. All the boys in the cafeteria couldn't be more helpful; I want to adopt every one of them. And Jane? Goodness, that girl knows how to get things done. I can see why you fell for her—"

Oh, God, here we go. "Mom, you do know that Jane and I aren't—"

Esther threw me a steely look. "Daniel, I know you and Jane are not together anymore. Which is really too bad. But that doesn't change the fact that we all love her and she is a good person. What happens after that, well, I don't know. That's your business."

"Yes, it is, Mom," I replied as gently as I could. "How's your arm, by the way?" Figured a spider bite might trump further discussion of my failed almost-marriage. It worked.

"Goodness, that was a terrible chain of events, wasn't it? They said I was twenty minutes from death's door. And I am completely mystified as to how I even got bitten. Wouldn't you think you'd feel something like that? But no little secluded spider is going to keep Esther McDowell down!"

I grinned, not bothering to mention that the spider was less "secluded" than "reclusive," especially since she'd triumphed over the little fucker. I was mostly glad we were laughing about it rather than fitting her for a prosthetic arm.

But she prattled on, and this is when the world started spinning in a different direction: "Oh, by the way, did Lucy tell you we finally figured out what your father was trying to say to us every time he woke up and kept making those weird sounds no one could understand?" My mouth suddenly went dry; I *so* did not want to go down that particular road with her right now, especially not in this blissfully cheerful moment.

"No, Mom, she didn't mention it, but—"

"It was one of the first things he said when he woke up this morning, too. Guess what it was?"

"I don't want to guess, I—"

"'Call the barber.' Can you believe it? *'Call the barber'*!"

**[Intentional blank space]**

The gap inserted above represents a silent psychic lurch… because something needs to stand in for the explosive skip in my brain function that occurred right after those three words came out of my mother's mouth.

*CALL THE BARBER!?*

From there I only grasped bits and pieces of her continuing

chatter, my mind too frozen in the churning, shattering reality of what she'd just said, but I think the rest went something like this:

"It turns out he had a barber appointment the day he collapsed, which I didn't know, and he being the considerate man he is, didn't want to leave the poor fellow high and dry. So every time he'd start to wake up, all confused about time and where he was and what was happening, he'd think it was the day of his appointment and would try to get one of us to call the barber. Even when he first woke up today, he thought he still had that appointment. It's so amazing to me how the mind works! So here we all were, going crazy trying to figure out what that 'caaa baa baa' stuff was, and he was just worried about letting Mortie Shankman know he wouldn't be making it into the shop! Isn't that the sweetest thing?"

No, not really. *Earthshaking* would be far more accurate.

Esther, however, laughed with real verve, delighted to have finally solved that particular mystery. By now we were in the cafeteria line and, as she got her food, chirping like a little bird with all her "adopted sons" skittering around her (young Hispanic kitchen staff who seemed genuinely delighted by her unabashed affections), I was lost in the eddy of cold, hard revelation. There was an odd sensation of the plates in my skull popping and shifting into some corrected, adjusted position, as if I'd been operating with misaligned frontal or occipital bones, only, in this case, it was the bones of a powerful delusion now dispelled. Painfully, excruciatingly dispelled.

The barber. *That's* the person he was angsting over; *that's* whose name he was calling out. Mortie Shankman, the short, balding putz with the shearing tools, not Barbara, the She-Devil of Oakland. How could I have gotten it so wrong? I mean, all of it, everything? If I didn't have such disdain for that crotchety old hag I'd spent days tracking down, I'd be mortified that I even approached her. In fact, I *was* mortified, despite her not deserving my shame.

While Mom ate her late lunch of enchiladas and cole slaw, joined by a busboy named Julio who she'd invited to the table, I was spared her attentions long enough to collect myself as best I could, pondering this new set of facts in an earnest attempt to reframe my world. It was not easy. At the moment, it was all but impossible. I'd built an entire theory—one with an accompanying vision quest, for God's sake—based on what was a complete misinterpretation. Who *does* that…who does that who isn't insane?

The only good thing—and it was a pretty big good thing—is there was now *nothing* to tell or not tell my father about Barbara. Not a thing. Ever. There was nothing to angst over, worry about, or suffer along with him. Because *there'd never been any suffering in the first place!* At least not about Barbara from Oakland. The only one in this family who'd suffered on her behalf in the last forty-nine years was *me*! And maybe, a little, my mother. But Jim McDowell could be spared the knowledge that his dream girl became—or perhaps, always was—a bitch, because she wasn't even his dream girl!

My stomach hurt, and it wasn't from the half an enchilada I forced myself to stuff down while Esther chatted up the very polite Julio.

When we got back, Jane had mercifully left and Jim was asleep. Esther slipped into the room to sit by his side, while Lucy, who clearly noticed the shellshocked look on my face, came out and gave me the gentlest, most loving hug she could, whispering in my ear, "'Call the barber,' huh? I wanted to tell you…I'm so sorry. I thought about calling you this morning after he woke up and we got this shocking dose of reality, but after everything you went through, I wanted to tell you in person. Sorry Mom beat me to it. That must have knocked the wind out of you. But Mortie says he can reschedule any time." She tickled me in an effort to lighten my gloom, but I stopped her.

"Don't, please. I'm not ready to smile or laugh or put anything into perspective quite yet; I'm too busy wallowing in humiliation."

She gave me a sympathetic smile. "You meant well. That counts for something."

"No…not really. Maybe. I doubt it."

"But listen, there's one more critical issue I need to tell you, related to all this stuff."

"I can't even imagine what's left."

"I just want you to be prepared, because I—"

And once again, as if choreographed, Esther popped her head out of the door before Lucy could conclude her provocative preamble. "He's awake! He wants to see you both."

"Mom, let me finish with Dan for a sec."

Esther then responded with something we rarely experienced from her: true anger. "Listen to me, daughter, your father has been out for a very long time, and he wants to see both his children now, and we're not going to make him wait even one second to do that, do you hear me?" She actually stamped her foot. I half expected her to grab Lucy by the ear and drag her into the room.

Lucy could only shoot me a wide-eyed look and another shrug before our mother swung open the door and ushered us inside. Once there, however, all thoughts were appropriately focused on Jim. The rush of emotion I felt when he turned his head and winked at me was powerful. It felt like the entire world had changed since he'd last done that.

There was lots of hugging and crying, Lucy holding one of his hands, Esther the other, everyone smiling at the altar of familial relief and gratitude. At one point I took pause to take it all in and was again struck by the misguidedness of my thinking…about so many things. It was as if a pall had been lifted from my eyes, and everything and everyone appeared somehow altered, different, as if I was seeing my family in a whole new light, particularly my mom and dad.

Had they always looked at each other the way they were now, in this moment, with a warmth and love I don't remember them sharing much or maybe just hadn't seen? Had I been too conditioned to see *only* their edges, the parts that stuck out and rubbed raw, the annoyances and resentments, without any awareness or observation of what bonded them and kept them close to each other? How could I have been so childish and myopic?

And Luce…well, what can I say; she's humbled me.

## HYSTERICAL LOVE

How do I fit in here now? What's my role? I feel like such a fool. And life feels so very, very mystifying.

# FIFTY-EIGHT

ABOUT AN HOUR later I was sitting alone with Jim, who had drifted off after the exhausting session with all of us, followed by an equally exhausting series of poking and prodding by various doctors who all seemed quite pleased with his progress, each mentioning that they'd be moving him out of ICU and into a "step down unit" within the hour. I figured I'd wait around until that process began.

Esther had finally hit the wall, so Lucy got her bundled up and out the door with a promise we'd talk later. I knew we'd have to discuss, in much greater detail, the stunning revelation shared by Esther over hospital enchiladas. I also needed to know what that "one more critical issue" was she'd been so determined to share with me.

After everyone finally vacated the room, I sat at my dad's bedside, still feeling distanced and dazed, trying to reattach in some way, to reconnect; to feel like I was once again part of the circle that was my family. I figured I'd get there after a few days home. Amazing how a week away, immersed in more than one delusion, can change the shape of one's worldview.

An intercom announcement blared loudly out in the hallway (why do they do that in hospitals?), which startled Jim awake. He turned to me, looking momentarily like he wasn't sure where he was or who I might be, then rasped, "Water…" I grabbed the straw-cup at his bed table and helped him get it to his mouth. He took a good, long draw then settled back onto the pillow. As I set the cup down, he fumbled with the sheets until his right arm was free and, with some difficulty, reached out and took my hand. He cleared his throat and said haltingly, "Guess you could…beat me now."

His voice was garbled, his eyes teary, and I'm not sure I ever felt more like crying than I did in that moment. "Nah," I tossed back. "Give you a few months and you'll be kicking my ass again."

He forced a lopsided smile then closed his eyes. Just getting those six words out had wearied him. After a couple of minutes he slowly pulled his hand from mine and tucked it back under the sheet. I think that was the longest I'd had physical contact with my dad since I was a kid.

We sat together in silence for long enough that I thought he'd said all he had to say. Nope. He turned and looked at me with what I was sure was a glint in his eye.

"So…Oakland?"

And there you have it. *That*, no doubt, was the other warning Lucy had hoped to convey. The man had been awake for less than twenty-four hours, had to struggle for every movement and syllable, yet somehow, and inexplicably, Lucy felt he needed to be informed of this choice bit of family news in spite of my insistence that he not. Real anger sent a flush over me, anger mixed with deep embarrassment. I certainly did not want to discuss this with him right now—or *ever*—but he seemed intent on continuing.

"Yeah?"

"Yes. I was. So Lucy told you?"

"Mentioned it."

I seriously wanted to throttle her.

"Have fun?"

Just my luck he seemed to be finding his vocal strength. I gave him a quick look, wondering if, maybe, hopefully, he didn't actually know *why* I'd gone up there. But no…there it was. The wicked Jim McDowell wink, which was, as always, more of a jab, a dig. If he could've slapped my back or poked me in the ribs, I'm sure he would have.

"Did I have fun? No, not as much as you'd think."

"Oakland…can be that way."

A look was exchanged. Oh, *he* knew.

"So you read an old story of mine."

Wow. Lucy had made a complete sweep. Exposed the entire plot. Drove me, herself, even our mother, right off the edge of the cliff. Unbelievable.

"I did."

"You know it was for the garbage?"

"That's what I heard, Dad." I didn't bother to mention it was now tucked in the camera bag in my trunk.

"There was another one."

"Another what?"

"Story. About your mom. Know about that one?"

"No, I didn't." Did Lucy?

"I kept that one. It was about her smile…how it lightened my load. Might surprise you."

That would surprise me: knowing he felt that way, that he wrote about my mother that way. But then it was *all* so surprising. "Does Mom know about that story?"

"No."

"Why not?"

"She never found it."

He was tired and seemed ready to stop talking, but I had a sense we might never broach this topic again; I had to get as much out of him as I could.

"But why wouldn't you have just shared it with her? Maybe if you had, the whole Barbara thing wouldn't have made her feel like she was second best."

He gave me a look that was as edgy as he could manage in his current state. "Your mother was *never* second best; get that...stupid idea out of your head!" Now *that* sounded like the father I knew. "Didn't know she dragged it out of the garbage. How could I know what she felt?"

"That's a good point, Dad. But, still, why didn't you share the one about her anyway? Seems like the sort of thing a guy would do for his wife."

"Figured she'd find it after I died...it'd make her happy then. Wasn't our way to be romantic."

"I noticed."

"Still a smart ass, even with your old man down and out."

"I'm just saying I know you and Mom aren't romantic with each other. But either way, I'm sure she would have appreciated it."

"Time went on...I forgot about it."

He motioned for more water and as I helped him with the cup, it struck me how ambushed he must have felt upon reentry: finding out about all this subterfuge, past and present, at the moment he was crawling back from the brink. And here I always figured he was the craziest one in the family. Lucy was now edging into position. Then, of course, there was me.

"Well, Dad, I'm sorry all this came out right at this particular point, when you could have used a little more peace and quiet. You probably think we're all a bunch of idiots."

He gave me a sharp look. "I'd never think your mother was an idiot. You kids, that's something else. Don't pay one damn bit of attention to what I'm really saying...conscious or unconscious." He gave me a sly grin.

Yep, he'd been spared nothing. I'm pretty sure I blushed.

"Dad, I...see, I read the story, and then I honestly thought you were calling out her name and—"

"Listen to me now." He cleared his throat again, like he had something important to say. And he did, in a voice almost as strong as normal. "I threw that story away because it didn't mean anything to me. Barbara didn't mean anything to me. Everyone gets their heart broken when they're a kid... that's all she was, a point in history. I wrote the story not long after it happened, so, sure, it was emotional. And, frankly, pretty crappy. But I got it out of my system and basically forgot about her after that."

I felt a strange mix of emotions: vicarious relief for him that there really wasn't a long-lost, angst-inducing ghost who'd impacted his entire life; mortification for me for...well, I don't think I need to spell it out. Let's just say, *everything*.

"I understand, Dad. And I'm sorry we all got into your business while you were out of it."

He managed a fatigued smile. "If I felt better I'd be kicking some ass right now, you and your sister! Your mom and I will talk...but I know her heart was in the right place." He leaned back on the pillow. "I will show her the other story."

"That'd be good, for her sake."

"For *your* sake...your mother knows. Not sure you do."

"Knows what? What don't I know?"

He closed his eyes again, exhaustion rolling over him like a wave. "Your mother is my life, son. Since the day we met, till the day I die. She knows that. She knows what love is."

"And you think I don't?"

"Do you?" His eyes opened again.

Good God, he'd probably been brought up to speed on the Jane situation, too. Didn't anyone in this family have *any* sense of discretion? But who am I kidding? Certainly after the fiasco that was Oakland—and thank God no one had (yet) heard about Fiona—even I have to admit his question is a valid one.

"No, Dad. I don't think I do know about love. I thought I did, but I don't."

He leaned back again. "It'll come to you. I gotta sleep." It seemed like he drifted off before the words were even out of his mouth.

I got up, squirmed out from behind the wires and machines, and made my way to the door. Just as I reached for the handle, in a voice so quiet I could barely hear him, he said, "Thank you, Danny. I know why you went. I appreciate the thought."

I didn't turn back. "No problem, Dad. See you tomorrow."

I walked out the door and couldn't stop myself: I ran down the hall, tears finally rolling down my face.

# FIFTY-NINE

THERE IS NO way to describe the next hour without sounding like a complete emotional lunatic pussy. But it happened and it involved me sitting in my car on the darkened street of some neighborhood I didn't know and crying like such a freaking baby it was ridiculous. It was the kind of crying where your nose runs and you're choking on it and you want it to stop but the sobs are like vomit, and they keep coming and coming, and you need to get them out or you'll explode or die or crack up. I ran out of whatever Kleenex I had in the car and still I cried. I cried until I'd wiped my nose on my jacket sleeve so many times it was soaked with snot and still I cried.

I cried for my dad, surely, for his pain and his weirdness and his honor and his love. I cried for my mother, my ditzy mother, whose heart was so good it could hold everything needed for a man who loved her but didn't share his story with her, and two children who were fools but still smart enough to always adore her. I cried for Lucy, the smartest, bravest, most loyal, accepting friend I would ever have. I cried for Jane, who broke my heart, whose heart I broke, who loved my family but didn't know how to love me. I cried for Fiona, who was kind and beautiful and deserved someone who only needed as much as she could give. I even cried for Kathryn, who saved me from jail, gave me banana bread, and listened to my story without judgment. Barbara, I didn't cry for.

I cried for myself. For being so caught up in who was right or wrong for me, in what my life was supposed to entail or not, in what kind of man I wanted to be or not be. I cried for hurting people, for being hurt, for being an asshole who'd leave my sister alone to care for two elderly parents struggling with life and death issues for the first time in their lives. I cried for making Bob and Zoey—even Joaquin—cover for my life while I was out chasing delusions. I cried for myself. *Myself.* For being thirty-three and still afraid. Afraid to commit—to a woman, a career, to an understanding that I could be everything I was without losing who I might still be. That I could take beautiful pictures *and* pictures of fourth graders shooting the moon. That I could make mistakes and fight and scream and be angry and still feel love like there was no tomorrow.

And finally, after my jacket resembled a dog's grooming towel, and my head throbbed like a jackhammer, and my stomach rumbled with queasy hunger, and I just wanted to sleep until there was a new day that wasn't *this* day, I stopped crying.

Then I drove to Bob's house.

# SIXTY

AND WHEN I got there, I was greeted by a sight that can only be described as stunning beneficence: Tomas's ice cream truck was parked in its usual spot, lights on as he conducted evening commerce with the working families who'd just gotten home or the earlier ones who'd already finished dinner.

I cannot fully express the jolt of pure, simple joy inspired by this happenstance. I don't know when he'd returned, but how could I *not* see something profound in his being there on this particular night? It was a sign, of what, exactly, I couldn't say, but it had something to do with things being more right with the world than they'd been prior...or something like that. I walked over, likely surprising him with the enthusiasm of my greeting, and grabbed as many toffee bars as I could carry, a simple act that shifted the plates just another little notch.

Bob and I talked for hours, reminding me of our all-nighters back in college. When I'd walked in looking like a red-eyed waif who'd been hit by a truck but was still clutching his ice cream bars, the man took pity and got me a clean shirt, a hot towel, and a shot of bourbon. Over a much-needed and deeply appreciated meal of homemade chicken curry and naan bread (seriously, the guy is insane), I unloaded the whole tale while he transitioned through the spectrum of corresponding emotions: mirth, discomfort, hard laughter, and true, empathetic misery. He made a comment about me "fitting an entire reality series into a five-day time slot" and I had to agree; it was sensational, outlandish, and would, no doubt, have been a hit.

He was particularly fascinated with the Fiona portion of the narrative. "I cannot get over that you actually asked her to move down here with you. You don't even have your own place at the moment; how did you figure that'd work if she said yes?"

"Believe me, bro, there was no 'figuring.' I don't think my thought processes got much beyond 'I think you might be my soul mate.' It was like I was high or something. Seriously out of my mind. When I try to pull it apart, try to analyze it, it's all a blur. Which is very strange."

"Hysterical Love."

"What?"

"A case of Hysterical Love…in the clinical sense."

I felt like he'd jabbed me with a needle. "Is that a real thing?"

"Just think about it."

So I did. Interesting. Can't say I would have thought of it myself, but something about the diagnosis struck a nerve. I mean, she was obviously extraordinary but I really couldn't come up with an explanation for my utterly manic response to her. "Hysterical Love. Huh. You might be onto something."

"Put the pieces together, Dano, and it ain't that hard to figure. You were over a month into Jane's cruel and unusual banishment, which would tend to throw even the sanest guy off his game. Your dad took a dive that looked like it could be the end of things. Your boss waved a partnership in your face. And then you thought you were getting commands from Jim's unconscious to go find his long-lost love. I mean, come on; who wouldn't get hysterical somewhere in that cyclone of crazy?"

"You think so? I can just write it off to all that?" I so wanted an explanation that didn't make me look like a complete mouth-foaming fucktard.

"Yeah, I do think so. Then once you got to Oakland, you're out of your comfort zone, especially having to get all Sherlock Holmes and everything, and then, cue the angel choir, there she is: the gorgeous, magical Fiona. Convenient, particularly after your whole reason for going—the abominable Barbara—turned out to be a clusterfuck. That your new sherpa also happened to find you appealing was the tipping point that triggered the syndrome. Hysterical Love. Who, honestly, could resist that set-up?"

"I don't know…a *sane* person? It relieves me a bit to know you've given my disturbance a name, but I keep thinking, like you, what would've happened if she'd said yes? Would I have snapped out of it before we hit the Grapevine and looked over at her wondering, 'Who is this fine lady and why is she in my car?' Or would I have been sold on the decision and ready to leap into a new life with a woman I barely know, regardless of the ramifications? Either one seems fucking nuts."

"Because they both are. But here's the beauty of it: neither of those things happened. Somehow, even amidst fantasy and duress, some part of your true self crept through and guided you to the light. You didn't leap, not even for one of those fabulous 'right now' fuck fests, as any hot-blooded man with a pulse would have. You're to be commended; you pulled back just in time to realize some things about yourself you never realized before. I'd say that's sort of genius. You may also be a test case for Sudden Epiphany Syndrome."

I had to laugh. I'd always appreciated Bob's unique, and usually accurate, perspective. If he hadn't cut it as a photographer he'd have made a great therapist. We leapt from that topic to the more mundane happenings of the week, including life at Joaquin's. Apparently all went well, if a little frantic. Joaquin was the fussy sort Bob couldn't typically abide, but he appreciated the man's business acumen and so tolerated the hissy fitting. He relayed Joaquin's parting words, which had been, "please remind Daniel of our conversation of last week," which, of course, I hadn't forgotten. How could I? I wasn't ready to decide what I wanted to do about all that, but I knew it was too good a deal to dismiss out of hand. I also knew that no matter what I did end up deciding, I had to find a way to incorporate my creative Muse back into my life. She'd been gone too long and after hanging with her in Oakland, I wanted to keep her around. How that might work, I wasn't sure, but that would have to wait for another day to get sorted out. Right now all I could think about was a hot shower and bed, in that order.

Bob was headed out to the clubs, so we said good night, though not before taking a moment to toast my dad's progress, something that could not be minimized to two sons of fathers. We had talked often about ours over the years, what they meant to us, particularly as men, and why, even with difficult fathers, that tether is always there. I felt more grateful than I had in a long time that mine still was…the man and the tether.

Later, lying in bed with the lights off and B.B. explaining why he sings the blues, I made note that it was only nine-thirty but felt like the middle of the night. Time had taken some odd turns for me recently. I wondered how long it would be before I synched up again. Emotional jet lag.

I'd been mulling for a half hour (I think it was a half hour) but came to the conclusion I was weary of the activity. There'd been *lots* of mulling in the many hours since leaving Fiona's house last night (was that *only* last night?), and I felt as though I'd thought it all to death. Wisdom told me I needed to give it some breathing room before I attempted analysis again.

But I had a sense of having lost my insides. Like nothing was in there anymore. I was emptied out, drained, waiting to be filled up again by…something. Something else, something new, some bracing new thought, purpose, idea, ambition. I had no idea what.

One thing I *did* know was that I had a couple of phone calls to make, starting with Kathryn. And while it might have been a little late, I had a feeling I wouldn't be able to sleep without lightening that particular burden.

She answered on the first ring, assuring me she was up reading. The sweetness of her voice reminded me of how regrettable it was that this really nice woman had been unwittingly swept into my witless "vision quest." Or, rather, my witless "*lack* of vision quest." I quickly got to the meat of my call, apologizing for my rude and hasty exit of the day before (again, that was only *a day ago?*). She said she understood and apologized again for Barbara, admitting she had no idea why, beyond what pain and the onset of dementia might have wrought, her sister had been so particularly mean-spirited. I bought that. I thanked her for her help, we said goodbye, and I hung up knowing we'd never talk again. Which seemed right...especially since there'd never been a valid reason to talk in the first place.

Fiona. There was true anguish over that one. I hadn't yet worked out how to explain it all to her, if she even needed or wanted an explanation...if I even had one to give her. I didn't. At least not yet. Though I had the feeling she didn't or wouldn't need one; that she'd likely shaken off the week as a fleeting encounter that popped into her life for some "learning experience." She'd probably already moved on with a smile and an eagerness about what was next for her. She was fine...it was me who remained thrown by the experience.

When I thought about her in *this* moment, back here in the sharp-edged reality of my world, away from candles and tea and twinkle lights and pungent herbs and bad pie and slightly insulting presumptions about my work and inspiring self-help books I'd probably never read...well, away from all that, I just thought of her as a sweet, gorgeous woman who was kind and helpful and utterly guileless and, without a doubt, of another tribe. My soul mate? If I truly, honestly believed in the theory, I'd have to say...no. I don't think so. But who knows? No. Probably not. I don't know.

But I will call her. She, like Kathryn, did not deserve my unexplained, unexpected, fumbling retreat. I'll call her tomorrow. Or maybe the next day. I need time to create a little distance before I do, time to get past the Pavlovian gut lurch that hits me when I think of her staggering beauty and its warm availability. I need to regroup and regain some semblance of the saner, more grounded man I am versus the frothing idiot who paced the boards of her candlelit living room. I need to be *me* the next time I talk to her...not that other guy.

And once again I thought, "it's only been *a freakin' day*?" Maybe I did break the time/space continuum.

## SIXTY-ONE

THE PHONE RANG, waking me from a sleep I didn't realize had commenced. It was eleven pm. I answered because it was Lucy. I felt like I was going to be picking up whenever Lucy called for the rest of my life.

"I just got home from work and wanted to check in on you. Are you breathing yet?"

"I was sleeping. Having awful nightmares about Mortie Shankman, the barber, about Dad knowing I went to Oakland, about my *going* to Oakland, you know, all of it, everything that's been revealed."

"Jesus...I deserve that," she laughed with a touch of chagrin. "I honestly tried to warn you but there didn't seem to be an opening in the chaos of the day."

"I appreciate the effort, sis, and there wasn't much you could do about the Mortie Shankman reveal, but why the hell did you tell Dad about Oakland after I specifically asked you not to? Honestly, I don't get that. It made me look like a fucking idiot. And the stuff with Mom and the story and the garbage and all? I mean, come on. You burned the whole house down!"

"Okay, okay, stop, I know, I'm an asshole; I get it. But honestly, it wasn't like I planned to do any of that. You had to be there. It was such a weird situation when he woke up and wanted to talk. It was the middle of the night, I was half-asleep, and it was all so very strange. Of course, in the light of day, under normal circumstances, there's not a chance in hell I'd have told him *any* of that. These were not normal circumstances."

"How so?"

"I don't know exactly; it was a very unusual night, one of those profound spiritual experiences you have with a person who's almost died and then come back to life." She paused, as if waiting for a response.

"You're going to have to give me a little more than that."

"Actually, I was running it over in my head again right before I called. It does take some analysis and I wanted to be able to explain it right to you. I don't want you to be mad at me."

Me, mad at Lucy. Lucy, who'd stayed put handling the crisis of our family's life while I ran around like an imbecile in the thrall of Hysterical Love. "Lucy, come on, I can hardly be mad at you. I just don't get why you told him, that's all."

"I understand, it's hard to explain. It's not like profound spiritual experiences are a normal thing with me, especially not with Dad!"

"I would have to agree with that."

"Here's what happened: I'd decided to spend the night at the hospital, give Mom a break. Jane took her home around ten o'clock, and I was exhausted so I turned off the lights in Dad's room, lay down on the cot, and drifted off. A few hours later, I think it was about one in the morning, I wake up to hear this weird mumbling noise, so I sit up and realize it's Dad. He's awake…and sobbing."

Hard to picture my dad sobbing, even now. Even after seeing his eyes tear up. Even after the softening-of-skin that seems to have occurred with him in the wake of near-death. "Sobbing?"

"Yeah, it was so weird, Dad crying. I got up, went over and sat in the chair by his bed and took his hand in mine, kept saying I was there and he was all right. He was still disoriented, but it wasn't like before; he wasn't thrashing around or trying to say anything. His eyes were open; I could see he was in there, clearly aware and, I'd guess, pretty devastated about what was happening to him."

"Why, did he say something about that?"

"No, but I sensed it was really overwhelming to suddenly realize he was in a hospital bed having a hard time moving his limbs or forming his words. Which freaked me out, because I'd been scared all along that he might lose his ability to speak. Weren't you?"

"Hell, yes! That's been one of my biggest fears. Not hearing Jim McDowell's same old voice…that would be so strange, wouldn't it?"

"Truly. But after a few minutes it was like he figured it out and started making more sense. And you know the very first thing he said?"

"What?"

"'Where's Danny?'"

I felt the now-familiar tsunami of tears threaten to roll in again but held it back, wanting to keep the attention on the story rather than my newly acquired emotional wellspring. Thankfully, Lucy kept going.

"I didn't know what to say, so I said the first thing I thought of, that you had to go out of town. Then he wondered why you would go out of town when he was in the hospital, which was a fair question. It was so odd, Dan—the room was dark, it was the middle of the night, there were no sounds around, and I felt like Dad and I were in this little pod of otherworldliness, just him and me, and, in that pod, I wanted to tell him the truth. I don't know if you can understand that, but I didn't want him to be hurt thinking you'd left town while he was sick, and I also didn't want to concoct some bullshit story about why you were where you were. And, to be honest, I wanted him to know how passionately you felt about your mission. Somehow I thought that would make him feel, I don't know…loved. And I felt like he needed that right then, do you know what I mean?"

I actually found what she said quite moving, particularly since she'd given me such hell about my field trip the entire time I was there. Her greater understanding of my initial impulse was appreciated, even at this late date. "I can understand what you mean."

"We were both inches away from each other, whispering for some reason, and it was a very emotionally intimate moment. We weren't doing our usual dance; we weren't cranky Jim McDowell and his quirky daughter, Lucy. We were just two people connecting to each other over some pretty serious stuff and there were no barriers in between. Does that sound bizarre?"

"No. Well, yeah, it does. But I get it. I felt some of that with him today, too."

"Anyway, I decided to drop the charade, just let it go, and explain the whole damn thing to him: Mom finding the file years ago, why she thought it was worth saving, how she felt after reading the Barbara story, me keeping it, you reading it, and how it struck you when you thought he was calling out her name."

I shook my head, once again trying to picture how all of that must have struck him in the moment of his return to consciousness. "Wow. He must have felt like he was caught in a hurricane, with all that information spinning around. Did he have a field day with the last bit, me going up to find Barbara?"

"I think you'd be surprised." She stopped. I waited for a second, thinking she was…thinking. Then I heard her sniff.

"Lucy, are you crying?" My heart felt such a tug. Lucy, indomitable Lucy, getting emotional.

She *was* crying. "When I told him you thought he was calling out for Barbara, and that's what made you feel so intent about going up to find her, to get her to explain why she'd hurt him so badly, he started to cry again, just softly, crying and squeezing my hand until it hurt. We were both crying. It was unbelievable, Dan."

And now I was crying again too. Lots of crying going on in this family these days. "Aw, Luce..."

"He just said, 'that boy of mine has a heart of gold.' That's all he said. Then he told me he loved me, said he was glad to be alive, and that he wanted to go home."

A heart of gold. My dad thought I had a heart of gold. That would hold me for a very, very long time.

I could feel my insides start to fill up again.

# SIXTY-TWO

WE TALKED ABOUT many more things after that: Barbara, Mortie the barber, the visit from Jane, even Jim's story about Esther, which was as much of a shock to Lucy as it had been to me. I considered telling her about Fiona but decided to wait on that one. The hour was late and we were both tired; we'd need a new day to launch into that full and colorful saga. It was also clear we'd have to revisit, likely many more times, each of the chapters already discussed, the details too rich to cover completely in this weary moment. We bid each other "good night" in the kind of loving tones we'd probably never again use with each other, though I think we both appreciated the warmth on this particular, very remarkable, night.

I walked out to the kitchen and grabbed the last of the toffee bars from the freezer, ready to declare this unfathomably long day officially over. I sat in my moonlit room thoroughly enjoying my well-deserved treat and, like an old habit, found myself looking out the window toward the house across the way. Since my B.B. playlist had expired, and in the silence of the deepening night, with the windows open and no noise to distract, I could hear the strains of Aretha's "Ain't No Way For Me To Love You" wafting from that house. Jane's house. I wondered if it was a message or just a random song shuffle.

I finished my bar, got up, pulled on a jacket, and walked outside to the front yard. I didn't know why. I didn't know what I expected. I stood there staring at the house where I used to live and pondered the woman inside. What was I thinking about her now, after this week that had lasted a year? After these last couple of months that seemed to have started eons ago?

I didn't know. The empty sensation I'd been feeling, the one ever so slightly adjusted after the call from Lucy, was also about a deficit: a deficit of anger, of sadness, a shifting away of resentments and defensiveness. All of which left me with an emotional blank slate. Like a newly birthed baby just out of the womb staring around wondering what part of this world belonged to him.

And Jane? We'd essentially ended our relationship more times than some people fall in love. I'd pushed my thoughts of her, my feelings for her, aside like so much old news, reacting to her reacting to me, and now I couldn't remember what got us so turned around, so far away from who we were to each other, how we felt, and what we wanted. While I was embroiled in my Hysterical Love affair, Jane simply didn't register for me; she was nowhere in sight. Well, she *was*; she came around trying to save us, save me from myself, but I couldn't see her in that setting, couldn't connect to her there. She didn't belong in that chapter, so I thought she didn't belong in any part of my continuing journey. Maybe it just meant she didn't hold a place in *that* part, the delusion I'd built upon some serious misinterpretations and miscalculations.

What *did* I feel for her now, in this post Hysteria moment? I couldn't say. It was too soon, too fresh, and my feelings were in abeyance. I felt incapable of making significant decisions on any topic, much less this one. A lot of life was going to have to go by and get sorted out before I could know that. But what I didn't feel was anger. That was gone.

I'm not sure how long I stood out there pondering Jane and my blank slate, but suddenly, as if she could feel the electrical impulses of my ruminating mind, her front door opened and she stepped out onto the porch. The outside light wasn't on, but I could see her face clearly in the moonlight. She looked thin and tired, like someone who'd been through something difficult and wearying. I felt a stab of appreciation for what she'd given my family these past weeks: her time, her help, her simple devotion to a group of people she loved despite the chaos with one of its members. In the midnight glow, which was so striking I had one of those "I wish I had my camera" moments, she looked so undefended and open, as if her own psyche had been wiped clean too. Had it?

"Dan."

"Jane."

"You're standing in the lawn."

"Yes, it seems I am."

"It's midnight."

"I know."

"Are you okay?"

"That might take a while."

"Are you back?"

"I'm back."

"For good?"

"Back for good."

"Alone?"

"Completely alone. Nothing happened. Nothing's going to happen. I got it wrong."

"She said no?"

"I said no."

"Oh." Her expression was inscrutable, but I thought I noticed her face visibly soften.

"Thanks for being so good to my family, Jane. Lucy said she couldn't have done it without you."

"I love your family."

"They love you too."

We both stood there, not having moved an inch either way. She looked inside, then back at me. "Would you like a piece of pie?"

That surprised me. And, yet…didn't. I nodded and simply replied, "I would."

She gave me a sad smile. Sad, but sweet. Sad, but forgiving. Like we both knew what the invitation meant and didn't mean. What it symbolized, but couldn't define; what we had yet to figure out. She walked back into the house, the door left open.

I remained still for a moment. Thinking. Weighing. Questioning. Then I walked slowly across the lawn, each step carrying the measure of some meaning. Mostly, the simplicity of gratitude and reconnection. Beyond that…a blank slate.

Because this isn't a Hollywood ending where everything gets neatly tied up. It can't be. No sunsets, no riding off. I truly have no idea what's going to happen with Jane and me. I don't know if we're ultimately meant to be together or if we'll discover we really aren't each other's best bets. I don't know if there's something we can rebuild or if we've changed too much or moved too far apart to honestly come back. In fact, to bring this story full circle, I remain flummoxed by relationships—certainly this one—as I do about so many things. Obviously about what happened, likely about where we all go from here, and definitely about the whole soul mate thing. But maybe less about love in general. Less about why we do this. That seems clearer to me than it's ever been. We do this because love is the reason for…everything.

As I walked up the steps and into that house, that kitchen, and sat at a table set with a perfect piece of apple pie baked and served by a tired woman I'd once loved and wanted to marry, I flashed on my dad's theory that love is only about playing the hand you're dealt. I suspect that may have changed even for him in these last few weeks. Or maybe not. He's still Jim, and one stroke is not about to reset his entire personality. But I realized I had my own altered analysis about it all.

It's not about a theory, soul mate or otherwise. There is no theory. Life is what we make it, and it's best lived openhearted and attentive to what comes. Maybe that's something I learned from Fiona. Or even Zoey. I don't know yet; there are kinks to work out. What I *do* know, as I look at Jane pouring coffee and wiping a hand across her weary eyes, is that in that tiny moment, the one about the pie, I felt a kind of tenderness for her I'd never felt before.

That seems worth pursuing.

# THE END

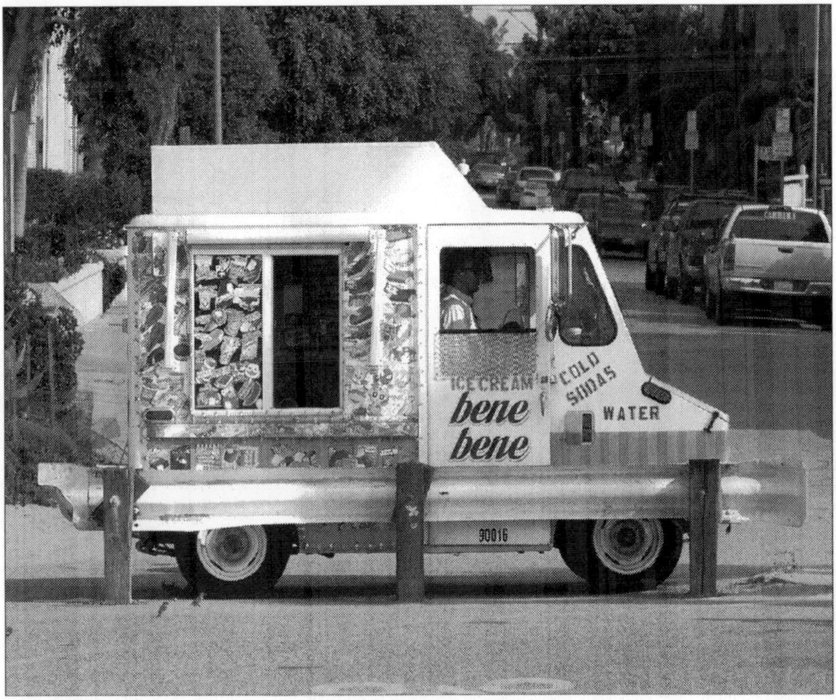
ICE CREAM
bene
bene
COLD
SODAS
WATER
90016

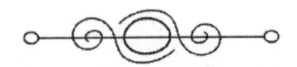

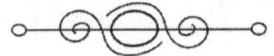

# READING GROUP/BOOK CLUB GUIDE

The themes, questions, and talking points that follow are intended to enrich your group's discussions about *Hysterical Love*, Lorraine Devon Wilke's irreverent and insightful exploration of love, relationships, and how we define and discover the ones that are right—or not right—for us.

**The story of *Hysterical Love*:**
Dan McDowell is thirty-three, gainfully employed as a portrait photographer, and marrying Jane Bennett in July. He's thrilled to be taking this seminal step with the woman he loves, doesn't mind the leap into adult life that will inevitably follow, and is certain he's finally gotten the mystery of love all figured out. Until Jane discovers he slept with a former girlfriend weeks after they'd started dating. His argument: it was once...maybe twice, it was three years ago; it was overlap. Hers: the party's over.

So it's next door to best friend Bob's, where Dan is offered solace and a room, for what, he assures his gracious host, won't be long. It's long. Dan's sister, Lucy, convinced of the "soul mate theory," suggests that Jane simply might *not* be his... soul mate, that is, and the ramifications of that send him spinning. With Jane immersed in her own interpretation of events, and his plans shattering to pieces all around him, Dan is further shaken when Jim, his oak-tree of a father, the loud, opinionated, ass-kicking force that has overshadowed his entire life, is unexpectedly downed by a stroke.

While his slightly daffy, always endearing mother, Esther, takes cheerfully to the nursing activities with Lucy's help, Dan is left to ponder the meaning of life and love, a quest profoundly altered when his sister shares with him a story their father wrote earlier in life.

Reading the thoughts and words of a man he loves but doesn't understand proves a revelation, particularly when he discovers his father harbors an unrequited love in the form of a beautiful woman named Barbara, met and lost decades earlier. Dan is transfixed by this mystery, certain this woman was his father's soul mate and that life would have been far different had they gotten together. When he hears his father utter the name "Barbara" in a moment of disorientation, a light bulb goes off. Convinced that righting this long-ago wrong would set the world straight, and against the better judgment of pretty much everyone he knows, Dan sets out on a mission fraught with detours and semi-hilarious peril in search of the mysterious woman from the past.

Clues lead him to Oakland, California, where along the way he meets the lovely Fiona, herbalist and flower child, and life changes once again. Fiona assists in his quest while quietly and erotically shaking up his world. When, against all odds, Dan finds the elusive Barbara, the ultimate discovery of who she is and how she truly fit into his father's life leaves him staggered, as does the reality of what he stirs up with Fiona. He returns home to discover another set of truths about his family that shakes him to his core but ultimately forces him to face who he is, what he wants, and who he might truly be able to love.

Mixing humor and drama in a narrative told from the first-person point of view of its male protagonist, *Hysterical Love* explores themes of family, commitment, creativity, facing adulthood, and digging deep to understand the beating heart of true love.

**Suggested Questions for Discussion:**
1. Is Jane just being overwrought about Dan's past situation with his ex-girlfriend, or does she have a valid point? Is sexual

"overlap" at the beginning of a relationship more forgivable than cheating that happens further in? And if that overlap does happen right at the beginning, is there logic in not telling the other party based on the rationale that it would be more hurtful than helpful? Is Jane's continuing rejection of Dan, lasting into weeks and months, overkill, or does she have a point about it portending future betrayals?

2. The theory of "soul mates" has been around a long time and has inspired many a relationship. Do you believe the concept still resonates in modern-day society? Does the notion of love being guided by "Divine Intervention," Fate, or a predetermined "plan" seem a logical approach when choosing a partner or assessing the validity of a love affair? Does Lucy's rationale that it's better to be alone than settle for someone who's potentially not your soul mate seem an authentically good reason for solitude? Or does embracing the idea that only one person is really right for you create the very real potential of rejecting valid relationships?

3. Do you admire Dan's decision to regularly spend time with his father for the sake of familial obligation, despite the fact that he hates the activity involved (tennis) and resents the recurring competitive dynamic with his father, or do you perceive him as a passive or malleable son? Are adult children obligated to sublimate their own wishes to placate a demanding parent, or is it acceptable to define your own boundaries and stick to them, regardless of how that parent may react?

4. If you read a love/heartbreak story written by your parent decades after it was written, and without the benefit of contemporary conversation with them about it, would it affect your feelings about their current relationship, particularly if their partner was also your parent? Is it inherently difficult for children, even adult children, to view their parents as sexual, romantic beings, and accept their very human need for love, companionship and intimacy?

5. Can you ever imagine a time when you would be compelled to

track down a long-ago love interest from your parent's past in hopes of clarifying ancient confusions and heartache that you still perceive in the present? Does Dan's decision to go to Oakland to find Barbara, the woman from his father's past, come off as crazy, self-indulgent, or protective?

6. When Dan meets Fiona in Oakland, her beauty overcomes him. He candidly expresses how almost incomprehensible it is to him that beauty alone should have such an impact on an intelligent, evolved person. Yet we live in a culture in which beauty is deeply valued, to the point that women—and men—undergo potentially dangerous cosmetic surgeries, get ensnared by eating disorders, and women, in particular, feel pressured to meet standards of beauty that are generally impossible to reach. Given that, how did you respond to Dan's infatuated reaction to Fiona? Does it seem understandable, or does it make him seem shallow and superficial? What are your thoughts about modern culture's obsession with youth and beauty? Have you ever been with a partner who was extraordinarily attractive, and how did it impact the balance of your relationship? Does her beauty affect Fiona's likeability?

7. Fiona's view of relationships is almost a throwback to the "love the one you're with" concepts of the sexual revolution. In modern culture, however, there is a contingent that believes monogamy is unnatural and open relationships are more conducive to happiness. Does that seem realistic or workable, or is human nature more apt to expect monogamy as a standard? If you fell in reciprocated love but the other party wasn't interested in making a commitment of exclusivity, would that be a deal-breaker? Do you believe serial monogamy is more realistic than "till death do us part"?

8. A sibling relationship plays a central role in this story; does the push and pull between Dan and Lucy resonate as a common reality between adult siblings? Do you think siblings are more or less judgmental of each other? Is it realistic to expect that siblings

who were not close or compatible as children could become closer as they get older?

9. Dan struggles with finding the balance between expressing his inherent creativity in more artistic ways and using it more commercially to make a living. Does pursuing a creative career seem foolish in light of how difficult it is for most artists to make a living from their art? Do you think society admires a poor artist more than a well-paid artistic sell-out? Would you be accepting of a partner who struggled financially because he or she chose to pursue their art?

10. Dan discovers that his entire mission to find Barbara was based on a misinterpretation of what his father said while going in and out of consciousness. Have you ever based an action, a belief, a decision on something that later turned out to be false or wrong? How did that impact the consequences of those beliefs or actions taken?

11. There is a good deal of discussion in the book on the topic of death: its unexpected nature at times, the pondering of it as a child, the idea of it being an inherent part of life. And yet it remains something we avoid thinking too much about. How does the specter of death impact the way we deal with aging parents? Are we wise to reconcile this inevitability so that we're better poised to deal with it in our own circle of family and friend?

# ABOUT THE AUTHOR

**Lorraine Devon Wilke**—writer, photographer, singer and songwriter—started early as a creative hyphenate. First, there was music and theater, next came rock & roll, then a leap into film when a feature she co-wrote (*To Cross the Rubicon*) was produced by a Seattle film company, opening doors in a variety of creative directions.

In the years following, she wrote for and performed on theater stages, developed her photography skills, and accrued a library of well-received feature screenplays; *The Theory of Almost Everything* was a top finalist in the 2012 Final Draft Big Break Screenwriting Contest and, most recently, *A Minor Rebellion* was a 2014 quarter-finalist in that same competition. She kept her hand in music throughout—songwriting, recording, performing—leading to the fruition of the longtime goal of recording an original album (*Somewhere On the Way*). Accomplished in collaboration with songwriting/producing partner, Rick M. Hirsch, the album garnered stellar reviews and can be found at CDBaby and iTunes. She continues with music whenever she can (which, she maintains, is never, *ever*, enough!); a collection of her recorded material is available at SoundCloud.

Devon Wilke's current life is split between Playa del Rey and Ferndale, California, and is shared with her husband, Pete Wilke, an entertainment and securities attorney, her son, engineer and web designer Dillon Wilke, and stepdaughter, educational administrator Jennie Wilke Willens and family. She curates and manages both her fine art photography site and personal blog, is a regular contributor at *The Huffington Post*, and writes a monthly column for the award-winning northern California newspaper, *The Ferndale Enterprise*.

Both her debut novel, *After The Sucker Punch*, and her short story, "She Tumbled Down," were 2014 publishing successes she hopes you'll enjoy, and she invites you to access her essays and journalistic pieces @ Contently.com. You can follow her journey with this book and her other books at her publishing website, AfterTheSuckerPunch.com. Check back often for links, updates and information.

**Contact**: info@lorrainedevonwilke.com
**Information/details**: www.lorrainedevonwilke.com
**Online connections/links**: See Page 309

## "THANK YOU" TO MY READERS

Thank you for purchasing this paperback of *Hysterical Love*.

It is, in some ways, a bookend to my debut novel, ***After The Sucker Punch***. Though very different stories told from very different points of view, both involve narratives of adult children reading the written words of a father and being propelled onto a journey of a personal and/or transformative nature as a result. I hope you found the adventures (and misadventures!) of *Hysterical Love* both entertaining and thought provoking, and if you haven't yet picked up a copy of ***After the Sucker Punch***, I hope you will...and enjoy it!

Certainly for independent authors like myself the involvement and support of readers in getting the word out about books they like is essential. In that spirit, and if you're so inclined, I invite you to leave a short review of *Hysterical Love* at the page where you made your purchase. Positive feedback goes a long way toward advancing the cause of independent publishing and I thank you in advance for your contribution!

I always love hearing from readers, so feel free to get in touch via **info@lorrainedevonwilke.com** or through any of my online connections listed in the pages ahead.

## ACKNOWLEDGEMENTS

Writing a book, however solitary an endeavor, ultimately involves at least *something* akin to a village. Those people who climb onboard at one point or another to participate not only in the fulfillment of the final product, but the launch, sharing, promotion, and enjoyment of the work. I've been fortunate to have an amazing group of villagers, so, while this may seem a longer acknowledgement page than most, it's quite well deserved!

 I must first acknowledge my husband, Pete Wilke, who not only sees the dreams that propel my life, but does everything in his power to "build the house," so to speak, in which they can flourish. There is no one who more unconditionally loves and supports me, and there is simply no way to imagine any of this without him. To my son, Dillon Wilke, whose professional role is to create and keep my web presence beautiful and functional, but whose role as my life's greatest gift makes his contribution to everything I do both essential and beloved. And to my dearest stepdaughter, Jennie Wilke Willens and her precious family, who complete our circle in all the ways that most matter in life.

 Next, I have to acknowledge my brother, Tom Amandes, who has been unflagging in his support of me and my work, whether producing/editing my book trailer, shooting stills at readings, or just being my general sounding board and all-around support system. On this particular book, he got in the trenches with me as my main editor, spending countless hours, days, weeks, reading, rereading, analyzing, defining, and sharing his imaginative, creative, and utterly essential perspective to help mold this into the best book it could possibly be. I am so very grateful, brother.

The book cover, to my mind, is one of the most important elements of any book—not only from the standpoint of artistic professionalism and creative marketing, but as the initial visual and artistic statement of that book. Many of us, to borrow from an old cliché, *do* judge a book by its cover which, for me, meant I had to get the very best to design mine. And I did: Grace Amandes, who also created the beautiful cover for **After the Sucker Punch**, brought her skills and clever imagination to the creation of the colorful and eye-catching cover of **Hysterical Love**. She is a true talent (who also happens to be my sister!).

Every story starts somewhere, and for this one I have to thank my brother, Vince Amandes, who shared a tale with me many years ago that became the spark for **Hysterical Love**. To my sister, Eileen Amandes McNally, my consultant on all things Oakland and herbal; to my other sibs, who always circle the wagons with and around me as part of our fierce and wonderful family of origin: Peg, Mary, John, Paul, Gerry, and Louise Amandes; to all my extended family of nieces, nephews, and in-laws, particularly Nancy Everhard Amandes, Ben Amandes, and Meg Broz, for time and efforts spent in getting the **ATSP** book trailer done; to my mother, Virginia Amandes, whose love of the arts is unparalleled, and to my father, Philip Amandes, who inspired my passion for words, one of my most cherished gifts.

One learns, particularly as an independent writer, how important marketing and promotion are to the launch and lifespan of a book. I'm delighted, this go-around, to have the assistance of JKSCommunications, the publicity firm that has worked with tremendous warmth and enthusiasm to launch this book: Founder, Julie Schoerke; Managing Director, Marissa Curnutte; Chelsea Apple, Angelle Barbazon, and Mike Matesich. I want to additionally thank Vicky Sarris Blanas, my creative cousin, whose "book cover cookies"—made by her and her husband, Larry Blanas, of Lawrence Deans Bake Shop—triggered the fortuitous introduction with Julie and the gang at JKSCommunications, as well as made a lot of people happy at book readings and in specially mailed book packages!

I have some new people to acknowledge, as well as an enduring list of those who are, and remain, staunchly in my corner and who never seem to grow weary of sharing my posts, spreading the word, reading my articles, writing reviews, joining conversations, sending me information, Tweeting and retweeting, buying books, voting in contests, trying to get paperbacks into their local bookstores, coming to readings, sending me jam (thank you, David Duplessis!), enjoying my work, and just showing up when and where they can. There is truly no limit to my gratitude for all of you:

To Lisa Schultz, founder of The Whole 9 and The Peace Project headquartered in Culver City, CA, who invited my participation in The Peace Project's 2014 Traveling Art Exhibit, as well as gave me the opportunity to stage my very first book reading and signing at her beautiful gallery.

To Mark Barry of Green Wizard Publishing, brilliant UK author, book blogger, and friend, who has gone above and beyond to beautifully write about and share my work; to Brenda Perlin, one of the most generous and thoughtful members of the indie writing community; to Geraldine Clouston and Stephanie Moore Hopkins of indieBRAG for their very active support of indie authors; to Laurence O'Bryan of BooksGoSocial, K.S. Brooks at Indies Unlimited, Alan Healey at Indie Author News, and the gang at Master Koda, for all their invaluable support of indie writers and their books; to those who asked me to participate in author interviews: Sonya Kemp, Fiona Mcvie, Vinny at The Awesome Gang, and Stephanie Moore Hopkins at LayeredPages.com; to my wonderful editing readers: Susan Morgenstern, Joyce DiVito Jackson, and Pamela May; and to my hawkeyed copyeditor, Laurie Boris.

To the women of the Valencia Hills Book Club, Minda Burr, Catherine Curry-Williams, (and the supportive woman of Wine,

Women & Chocolate); Tina Romanus, Patricia Royce, Nancy Capers, Susie Singer Carter, Barb Tyler, Don Priess, Glenn Rueger, Dan Danner, Gail Myers Jaffe (won't forget that tiara anytime soon!); Lauri Johnson, Nancy Eaton, Jill Weintraub Klausen, Mary Ann Bernal, Heather McLarty, Troy Evans, Jan Sousa, John Matson, Junior Burke, Eileen Butler, Arnie Saks, Jason Brett, Lauren Streicher, Fran Briggs, Tracy Trivas, Kathy Shuker, Shirley Lipner, Marina Terzopoulos, Steve Dereby, David Duplessis, Arnie Saks, Dawn Kaufman, Mags Proctor, Jim Kennedy, Carolyn Sutton, John Cardella, Jake Drake, Steve Brackenbury, Nancy Andres, Wendy Treptow Johnson, Debra Sanders, Lane Aldridge, Van Fox, Maureen Haldeman, Rikki Kapes, and Caroline Titus.

I also want to acknowledge Skylight Books in Los Angeles for their very welcoming support of indie writers.

And, lastly, to all my readers—even those whose names I don't know—whose purchase and enjoyment of my work makes it all worthwhile.

Deepest thanks to every one of you…more as we go!

# LORRAINE DEVON WILKE'S OTHER BOOKS

*After The Sucker Punch: a novel* *(available in e-book and paperback):*

They buried her father at noon, at five she found his journals, and in the time it took to read one and a half pages her world turned upside down... he thought she was a failure.

Every child, no matter what age, wants to know their father loves them, and Tessa Curzio—thirty-six, emerging writer, ex-rocker, lapsed Catholic, defected Scientologist, and fourth in a family of eight complicated people—is no exception. But just when she thought her twitchy life was finally coming together—solid relationship, creative job, a view of the ocean—the one-two punch of her father's death and posthumous indictment proves an existential knockout.

She tries to "just let it go," as her sister suggests, but life viewed through the filter of his damning words is suddenly skewed, shaking the foundation of everything from her solid relationship and winning job to the truth of her family, even her sense of self. From there, friendships strain, bad behavior ensues, new men entreat, and family drama spikes, all leading to her little-known aunt, a nun and counselor, who lovingly strong-arms Tessa onto a journey of discovery and reinvention. It's a trip that's not always pretty—or particularly wise—but somewhere in all the twists and turns unexpected truths are found.

*After the Sucker Punch* takes an irreverent look at father/daughter relationships through the unique prism of Tessa's saga and its exploration of family, faith, cults, creativity, new love and old, and the struggle to define oneself against the inexplicable perceptions of a deceased parent. Told with both sass and sensibility, it's a story wrapped in contemporary culture but with a very classic heart.

*"A realistic and profound journey of realization and forgiveness…a solid novel that admirably explores the fragile, fraught relationship between parent and child."*
—**Publishers Weekly/BookLife**

*"With bare-bone honesty and fiery dialogue, Wilke explores the loaded relationship between parents and their adult-children, examining the brave and lonely journey of self-discovery, reinvention, and healing…raw and brave—a great read."*
—**Tracy Trivas, author of The Wish Stealers (Simon & Schuster)**

*"A keenly executed character study. The novel is tightly structured and holds its complex elements with a sure and skillful grip. The dialogue pops…a thoroughly engaging and enjoyable read."*
—**Junior Burke, author of Something Gorgeous (farfalla press/McMillan & Parrish)**

*"A great, sweeping, beautifully written, page turning read, gripping from page one. A family saga with ambition and class. Meant to be read in bed; absorbed, over time, savoured by lamplight."*
—**Mark Barry, author of Carla and The Night Porter (Green Wizard Publishing)**

*2014 indieB.R.A.G. Medallion® Honoree*

*2014 Best of Summer Reading List Selection—Fran Briggs, publicist*

*She Tumbled Down: a short story* (available in e-book):

New Year's Eve. It's late, well past the midnight hour. A woman looking for respite from noise, champagne, and tensions with her boyfriend steps out to clear her head. She calls out that she'll be back shortly and heads down the quiet neighborhood street…and never comes back.

A man who's had too much to drink, driving too fast a car, roars by on that same darkened street and, in a flash of motion and impact, is stunned to see the face of a startled woman smash into his windshield. When the car stops he shakes in silence, waiting for…something. But when no one approaches, no cars go by and no inquiring lights flick on, fear and panic take over and he makes the unfathomable decision to drive away…and never look back.

"She Tumbled Down" follows the ripple effects of this tragic hit-and-run attempting to answer that unanswerable question, "Who could do such a thing?" From that first fateful moment through the months and years that follow, the narrative weaves through the lives of seemingly disparate characters, threading the initial event into another story, a love story, that ultimately links to the tragedy in unexpected ways.

*"There is lightness and there is dark. The story travels around to both sides. As a reader I wanted, hoping to know everything would turn out okay but guessing it would not. I was left to guess as I read at a feverish pace."*

*"Rarely, if ever, have I read a short story that was so incredibly good that after finishing it, after drinking a cup of tea and reflecting on it, I sat down and read it all over again. But that's what I did with this one, and now three days later I find*

*myself STILL thinking about it; still talking about it to every bookaholic I know. It's a story that begs for discussion, so provocative is the subject matter and story line."*

*"I was engaged right from the outset, and this was one story I couldn't put down. I liked how the author played with time, and covered a very sensitive subject that ended up being satisfying in its conclusion. Secrets have a way of tumbling out, and the results are not often predictable, as Lorraine Devon Wilke shows in this gripping drama."*

Connect Online With
# LORRAINE DEVON WILKE

Website:
www.lorrainedevonwilke.com

Rock+Paper+Music Blog:
www.rockpapermusic.com

Adventures In Independent Publishing Blog:
http://www.AfterTheSuckerPunch.com

Goodreads:
https://www.goodreads.com/user/show/30949096-lorraine-devon-wilke

Twitter:
https://twitter.com/LorraineDWilke

Facebook Page:
https://www.facebook.com/lorrainedevonwilke

Facebook Writer's Fan Page:
https://www.facebook.com/lorrainedevonwilke.fans

Instagram
https://instagram.com/lorrainedevonwilke/

LORRAINE DEVON WILKE

Google +
https://plus.google.com/+LorraineDevonWilke/posts

Photography website:
http://lorraine-devon-wilke.artistwebsites.com

SoundCloud Music Page:
www.soundcloud.com/lorraine-devon-wilke

CDBaby:
www.cdbaby.com/cd/wilke

iTunes:
https://itunes.apple.com/artist/lorraine-devon-wilke/id119681867

*The Huffington Post* column:
http://www.huffingtonpost.com/lorraine-devon-wilke/

Article Archive:
https://lorrainedevonwilke.contently.com

Email contact @ info@lorrainedevonwilke.com

Made in the USA
Lexington, KY
24 May 2015